Sometimes

Never

By

Cheryl **McIntyre**

Cover by Charles Mullen

Cover model Charles Mullen

This book is dedicated to my editor and sister, Dawn.

For telling me to write now and worry later.

1
Mason

When people talk about what initially attracts them to someone, that first glimpse that makes them turn around and take a second glance, they usually say something sweet. Like pretty eyes or a nice smile. For me, it's her toes. Shiny, bright pink, polished toes dangling from the passenger side window of a car. Her milky white feet bounce up and down as she sways her legs to the beat of music I'm unable to hear. And I really wish I could hear it. To know what sound flows through her ears and makes her move like this.

My eyes trail up her legs, over her knees, and follow the path down her thighs. I don't think I've ever seen skin so smooth and pale. My gaze sticks on her faded Beatles tee shirt for several seconds before I finally find her face. Her eyes are closed, long dark lashes resting on her cheeks. Her lips are shiny and I catch myself wondering what they taste like.

Tearing my eyes away from her mouth, I flick them up to her hair, pooled around her like spilt silk.

Shades of pink, purple, blue, and green peek through the otherwise dark strands. She has ear buds in, the cord stretching to the iPod clutched in her hands above her head as she lies across the bench seat. I can see the red vinyl through the gages in her earlobes. Everything about her is different. Singular. Special.

She is the most beautiful girl I have ever seen.

I don't use the word beautiful often. It's an overly used word that has begun to lose its importance. But it fits here. Every one of my senses recognize this girl as just that. Beautiful.

I force myself to keep walking toward the school, but I allow a quick look back as I step out of the parking lot. Her feet are gone. The car windows closed.

I'm about to turn back around when I spot her walking next to a girl that fits into what I refer to as "the mass produced" category. Tall, tan, blonde hair, name brand clothes that half of the girls at this school probably own as well. She looks like the perky cheerleader type—popular and well liked for her status. I'm not trying to stereotype. I'm just good at reading people. It throws me off to see these two completely opposite girls walking together. Their heads are turned toward each other, engaged in conversation.

I wonder for a second what they're discussing. What topic could be mutually gratifying to such different girls? It bothers me that I really want to know. *Why am I even thinking about this?*

Then the one girl, the blonde, stops abruptly, her attention sliding to a big guy in a letterman jacket. Probably a football player. Probably her boyfriend.

Blondie shakes her head and glares at the jockstrap as if the sight of him makes her sick. He laughs and takes a step in her direction. And something very much unexpected happens. The other girl, the beautiful one, puts herself in between them. All of a hundred pounds and she's what stands in the way of this guy getting to the blonde.

The jockstrap laughs again, but there's no humor to it this time. He's pissed. His face is red and his eyes narrow. And now I'm not thinking about anything. I just start heading in their direction. I'm about twenty feet away when the asshole puts his hand up and actually shoves the girl backwards. *What the fuck?* But she doesn't fall. She was braced for it, which I find extremely interesting.

I'm ten feet away now and I have absolutely no plan. All I know is I am not about to just stand by and let this dickhead intimidate someone smaller just because he thinks he can.

"Don't touch me again," the girl says. "And stay away from Annie." My eyes flick to Blondie. She must be Annie.

Jock-boy smirks, his lips turning up in this smug, assholey way that makes me want to punch him right in the face. He extends his meaty fingers and brushes them over the girl's cheek. I cringe and I'm not sure why the idea of his sweaty fingers on her skin bothers me, but it does. A lot. Her eyes, which I can now see are blue, slit into a murderous glare. Obviously it bothers her too. I open my mouth to say something, to tell this guy to go fuck himself, but before anything comes out, the girl swings her leg up and kicks him right in the balls.

Priceless. I throw my fist over my mouth to hold in the laughter threatening to explode. Jock-boy grunts, his face somehow manages to turn an even brighter red, and grabs himself as he falls forward. The girl doesn't miss a beat. As soon as he's down, she swings her leg again, kicking him in the chin. The snap of his teeth slamming together makes me cringe. But the girl swings again, thrusting her foot into his stomach. Air rushes out of his mouth sending a spray of saliva and blood across the blacktop.

"I said not to touch me again," the girl says in an unnervingly calm voice. She picks up her foot and I know she's going to kick him again. I should let her. I should stand back and enjoy the show. But I don't. I step up behind her, wrap my arms around her waist, and swing her so she is facing the other direction. I can feel her shaking with adrenaline or rage, so I let her go quickly. But in the two seconds she was against my body, I caught the scent of her shampoo, something fruity that will drive me crazy until I can identify it. I also decide I like the way her back felt pressed to my chest.

She looks up at me, her mouth opening in shock. "I don't think he'll touch you again," I say, and I can't help the smile that forms. I don't know this girl, but I feel some unwarranted sense of pride as I gaze at her.

And she does something else that surprises me. The anger leaves her face and her lips turn up in a way that has my brain stumbling all over itself. For a second, I feel like a complete idiot because I've lost all ability to speak. The words *tongue tied* finally make sense and all I can do is stare at her mouth. "Thanks," she says.

The blonde—Annie?—grabs her hand and pulls her away before I have a chance to respond. What was she thanking me for? For what I said? For pulling her off that guy? For staring at her like she's my favorite flavor of ice cream?

They make it about five feet before an older man in a suit, probably the principal, takes her by her upper arm and drags her off in the direction of the school. She doesn't fight him, but after several steps she turns her head and looks back at jock-boy as his friends help him stand. There's blood dripping from his mouth and he seems to be having trouble straightening up. The girl's lips form into a radiant smile.

"Fucking bitch," jock-boy spits. And she winks. *She freaking winks at him.*

I realize I'm grinning like some psycho. Because what just happened, the entire situation, as crazy and violent as it was, was so frigging hot.

I think, for the first time in my life, I'm in love.

2

Hope

So here I am sitting across from Mr. Andrews, listening to him drone on and on about school policy and blah, blah, blah, bleck. Really what I hear is this: "Christian Dumbshit Dunkin is a star athlete while you are a loser, freak with psychotic tendencies. So therefore, even though he put his hands on you first, I will do nothing about it. Oh, and you're suspended for the rest of the week."

The events of last night play through my head as Andrews' voice fades into a blurry hum.

ASL flashed on the computer screen. Age, sex, and location. I sat back and thought, *Who do I want to be today?* I never tell the truth. Seventeen, female, living in a house with seven other kids in Ohio. Like a fucked up, twenty-first century version of *The Brady Bunch.*

Usually when the first question has to do with your age and sex, it's a horny, middle aged man looking to cyber. When I'm in a mood, like I was last night—sick of the world and all its bullshit—I like to put on my

Fergus persona. Fergus is a fifteen year old boy, recently discovering his gay sexuality. Misunderstood by his parents, and too afraid to come out to his friends, he's lonely and looking for anyone to understand. I based him on my old neighbor, just changing the name to that of a cat I had when I was ten. The cat ran away. I'm pretty sure the neighbor did too.

I was instantly disconnected. "Asshole," I muttered.

"What?" Guy glanced at me, putting his own online chat on hold.

"Nothing. Just some douche bag homophobe."

"He didn't want to talk to Fergus? What the hell?" He shook his head, his blonde hair tumbling into his eyes.

"I hate people," I said as I hit enter. "Next."

"I don't know why you're always on here when you don't really ever want to talk to people."

I ignored Guy, partly because I love him, so his sarcasm never bothers me. In fact, I often appreciate it. But mostly because I just didn't feel like another "Hope Hates the World" speech. Guy actually is gay. I think he's a little addicted to sex. Or he's a typical teenage boy. He truly loves the online sites, especially the live video chats, and not for the conversation. I've seen Guy's nether regions more times than I'd like to admit. I think that's why I love him; he's messed up, just like me. Also, I feel bad for him having a name like Guy. It was like his parents didn't even try. Or like, I don't know, they set him up. As if they were expecting a manly football player and got a sensitive homosexual son instead. Like my name being Hope. It was a guarantee I was going to have the bleakest, blackest of souls. I'm not even about to get into my last name.

ASL lit the screen again. I sighed and typed, forty, male, Texas. Instantly got disconnected. I didn't even get to tell them about my stance on the death penalty—which being a proud Texan man, I was for, of course.

The door swung open so fast, it hit the wall. Annie ran past, her hands over her face. "Hey, there may be ten of us, but this is still not a barn, Annie! Close the damn door," Guy yelled. He used his foot and kicked the door. It closed halfway and he shrugged.

"Dylan, close the door," I said to Guy's brother as sweetly as I'm capable of speaking.

"Close it yourself," he said in a high pitched, squeaky voice. He was jumping up and down, bursting with hysterical giggles as he killed a zombie on the Xbox.

“Just do it, Pickles!” I shouted, no longer trying to be nice about it. Dylan paused his game and shot me the death stare.

“My name is not Pickles!”

“Wait, when did we start calling him Pickles?” Guy looked at me, confused.

“Ever since I heard Jenny call him Dill,” I explained. And proving to be deserving of my love, Guy needed no further explanation. He chuckled and pushed Dylan’s head. “I thought I smelled something. I have a sudden craving for a sub sandwich with turkey, and lettuce, and tomato.”

“With extra Pickles,” I added and we both rolled with laughter. Not Dylan though. He just glared at us as he slammed the door.

“You guys are jerks.”

We laughed harder.

“Screw you! I’m telling Dad.”

Guy stopped laughing, which just made me start crying, I was laughing so hard. “Don’t be a nark, you little rat! If I get in trouble one more time, Jenny said I’d be grounded this weekend.”

Dylan shrugged and took off running. Guy jumped up so fast his chair fell over, thudding loudly on the hard wood floor. He lunged across the table and snatched the back of Dylan's collar.

"Stop, you're choking me!" Dylan screamed. "Dad! Jenny!"

Guy slid his hand over Dylan's mouth. "Shut up. I'm not choking you, but I swear to God, if you don't shut the hell up I will choke the life out of you. And I'll tell Dad you said 'screw.'"

I shook my head and hit enter on the computer again. Like I said, we're the damn Brady Bunch.

ASL again. "Fucking horny losers!"

"Hope! Watch the language," Jenny scolded me as she came into the kitchen. "What is going on? Why were you screaming?"

Guy nudged Dylan. "Nothing," he grumbled.

"Hey, Annie's home. She seemed upset," I said to get the attention off Guy. He grinned at me over Jenny's shoulder.

"What do you mean? Upset how?" Jenny chewed her lip as she stared at me. Annie is Jenny's oldest biological daughter from her first marriage. And her precious little angel.

I shrugged then. "She busted in and ran up to our room."

"Hope, honey, will you go check on her? She's more likely to talk to you than me."

I closed my laptop and tucked it under my arm shooting Guy the "you owe me so big" look. "Yeah, I'll try."

Jenny tapped her fingers on her chin. "Thank you, sweetheart. You're a life saver."

"Mmm. What flavor?" Guy whispered as I pushed past him.

I flipped my pony tail in his face. "Cherry, of course."

"Oh, uh-huh. You know that's right, Cuz," he called after me.

Up in our room, I sat outside the bathroom door. I could hear the shower running and I could hear Annie crying. She had been out on a first date with Christian, the asshole. She was so excited about it. I have no idea why. He's such a dick. So, I sat there in front of the door, listening to her cry, and I had such a strong feeling that this dumb jock did something to her. Probably forced her into something she wasn't ready for. Possibly raped her. Part of me was so sad for her. I wanted to go into the shower and hug her, letting her know she wasn't alone. Another part of me was so mad, I wanted to go get Guy, go to this dude's house so I could cut off his favorite appendage, and shove it down his throat. But then there was this big other part of me—part of me that is truly scary—that just didn't give a shit enough to do anything.

So I stood up. Looked at the pretty, flowery neatness on Annie's side of the room, and then to the purple mess of my side. I decided, *Screw it.* She's always judging me. Always looking down on me. She was the one who thought she was such hot shit for going out with this dude. So, she got exactly what she deserved. I turned and walked away, leaving her crying in the shower, alone.

What does that make me? I don't know. I don't even know if I care. All I know is, I wanted to cut so badly my hands were shaking, but that wench was hogging our bathroom. I quietly made my way to Guy's room and snuck into his bathroom. I locked the door and checked it three times to make sure nobody could walk in on me. I opened his medicine cabinet and took out his razor. I checked the door one more time then dropped my pants around my ankles and sat on the closed toilet seat. Spreading my legs wide, I looked for my old scars. I only cut over the old ones, no longer making new. It doesn't really count that way.

After I readied a wad of toilet paper in one hand, I ran the razor slowly across the raised pink skin. It didn't hurt in the way I like, so I cut over it again, deeper. A thick line of red appeared on my inner thigh and it was the best feeling in the world. As it started to glide down my leg, I wiped it away quickly and moved to the next scar. I automatically went deeper, moaning with pain and pleasure. There were no band aids in Guy's bathroom, so I pushed the toilet paper against my leg and pulled up my pants. I put the razor blade in my pocket and went back to my room to get the band aids I keep stashed in my underwear drawer.

I am seriously messed up.

Though I may have felt better, I could hear Annie still crying once I was back in my room, and it all rushed back. So I used my next coping skill. I acted like a bitch. I slammed my fist against the bathroom door and I yelled, "Hurry the hell up. You aren't the only person in the world."

"Shut up, Hope. I hate you. I fucking hate you so much."

"I hate you too, you selfish slut."

I know she isn't a slut. Not even close. I also know it is the last thing I should have said to her. But I did. I didn't feel bad for her after she told me she hated me.

And now, all I can think is...*so much for not giving a shit.* As soon as I saw Christian today, my body went cold with anger. I wanted to hurt him for hurting Annie. When he touched me with the same disgusting hands that violated her, I just lost it. I kicked him and didn't stop until some dude pulled me off.

I could speak up. I could tell Mr. Andrews right now that Christian, being the douche bag jock he is, in all probability, raped my foster cousin. But I don't. One, it's not my place to tell Annie's secrets. Two, I don't think he'd believe me. And three, I just don't even care about a suspension. A week at home, alone, sounds great to me. So I continue to sit here, glaring at the coffee stain on my principal's yellow tie. It's an ugly yellow. The stain reminds me of those ink blots. It looks like a turtle. I wonder what that means about my mental state.

He hands me a pink sheet of paper.

"Make sure your parents sign that before you return Monday," he says sternly.

I rip the paper out of his hand and look him in the eyes. "My mom's dead and I don't have a dad."

His cheeks turn a satisfying shade of pink before he tries to backpedal. “Right, excuse me. I’m sorry. Have your foster parents sign that please.” We stare at each other for several seconds. He looks away first, dropping his eyes to his desk. “You can go home now,” he says as he tries to appear busy.

I slam the door on my way out.

“What happened?” Annie asks. She hands me my backpack and hurries to keep up with me. “Hey, slow down and talk to me.”

“You have long legs, keep up,” I say annoyed. “I got suspended for a week.”

She grabs my arm, stopping me in the middle of the hall. “I’m sorry, Hope.”

I shrug weakly. “Yeah, whatever. It’s not your fault.”

“You were standing up for me. It is my fault. I’ll take your punishment at home.”

I sigh and look up at her. “I think you’ve been punished enough,” I say quietly. She flinches and I look away. “You don’t need to tell me what happened. Just tell me this, was I right to do what I did?”

She's quiet for so long, I don't think she's going to answer. I finally look back at her and there are tears in her eyes. She nods her head once.

I nod back. "I'll, um, see you at home."

"Okay." I can feel her watching me as I start to walk away. "Hey, Hope?" I stop, but don't bother to turn around. I can't stand to see the look on her face again. "Thank you," she whispers. Her feet squeak on the linoleum as she walks away and I let out a long breath.

There is something you should know about me. I am not a sociable person. I like to spend most of my time alone or with Guy and the band. I absolutely, positively live and breathe music. I do not believe in falling in love. Except when it comes to a song, or a band, or an instrument. I write lyrics every day on everything. Mostly in notebooks or on myself, but I like to leave a line or two in strange places. Carved into a tree, scribbled on a bathroom stall, on the side of a building… Maybe it will mean something to someone. You never know.

I'm addicted to my blog. I ship whoever the hell I want. Gay, straight, animal, inanimate object—I don't care. My one true pair is chalk and eraser. I also like any variation of the two. Pencil and eraser, ink pen and white-out, enter and back space keys. Something that can amend the mistakes of the other. I don't know—I just like it.

I have a tattoo that I got from some guy at a party last year. At the time, I didn't think anything of it. I mean, he was giving them to everyone and his work was nice, so I got a black bird on my shoulder. It didn't occur to me until weeks later how unsafe it was. Sometimes I wonder if I may have caught something from the unsanitary needle. It scares me too much to think about, so I try to ignore it.

Cigarettes are gross, so I have never, and will never smoke them. I do, however, smoke pot occasionally. My biggest vice is alcohol. I'm not an alcoholic or anything. I just like to drink when I'm out with friends or before a show. It helps me open up and not be the crazy, shy girl. Oh, and I'm cheap too, so I have never bought my own stash. I just mooch off my friends.

My mom is dead, and I hate her. I mean, I loved her, but even as a kid, I knew it was only because I was supposed to. She was a bi-polar, alcoholic, drug addicted, whore. Half the time, I didn't know where she was or when she'd be back. Sometimes, I spent days alone, living off Ramen noodles and dry cereal. I never knew my dad and the losers that came in and out of Mom's life did not even come close to counting. The ones that stuck around long enough to know I existed were only there because I did. Fucking creeps. Well, except Jenny's brother, Donnie. He was pretty cool. When he told my mom he'd marry her if she cleaned up, she actually started going to meetings. Donnie even said he wanted to adopt me. I probably would have believed him if it wasn't for the fact that he was dating my mom. I mean, there had to be something wrong with anyone that wanted to be with her for any length of time, sober or not. Anyway, it obviously didn't work out. Mom and Donnie were killed in a car accident two years ago. There was alcohol in both of their systems. The irony is not lost on me.

I hate attention. Most people think the exact opposite is true because of the band, and the fact that I have gages in my ears, and my hair is dyed a multitude of colors. Honestly, I just wanted to change my appearance. I can't really explain it. It's like, when you have men looking at you like they've looked at your mom most of your life, you just don't want to look like that same person anymore. At least, that's the best way I can explain it. Jenny is always trying to play dress up with me, like she wants an Annie duplicate. I can't stand it. But Guy makes it a little easier. He gets it. He gets me.

I was fifteen when my mom died and had just lost the only life I had ever known. And there was Guy in his too small, black suit. He stuck out from everyone else in the sea of black at the funeral. It wasn't his shaggy blond hair that stuck up in every wrong direction or his super cute baby face. It was the bright pink tie he wore. When I saw him, I laughed. I laughed at my mom's funeral. While everyone else stared at me like I was a sick, twisted, freak, Guy looked at me and smiled while he straightened his ridiculous tie. He looked at me like he knew what was inside of me. Like he saw the tears I didn't cry. Like he saw the scars hidden on my legs. He understood.

During the wake, I stayed outside hiding in the tree house Alec had built for the other kids. Guy brought out a bunch of food and we ate and talked until everyone left. That night, he snuck downstairs to the couch where I slept before I had a room. We talked half the night. Like, really talked. He asked me questions that I had never been asked before. Guy wanted to know me. When I admitted I had never kissed anyone, he leaned over me. With the tips of warm fingers, he brushed my hair off my shoulder. Then he put his hands on each side of my face, positioning my head up toward his. He kissed me. Softly at first, then he slipped his tongue in between my lips and found mine. He tasted like cinnamon toothpaste and it burnt my mouth. He slid his fingers down my neck, across my shoulders, and as he made his way down my arms, I pulled away.

"Interesting," he sighed as his eyes appraised me.

"You're my cousin," I said to him and wiped my mouth.

He smiled and shook his head. "No I'm not. Jenny is my step mom, not my real mom. You aren't even related to her, technically. Besides, foster parents aren't real parents anyway."

We stared at each other for the longest minute before he finally smiled again and asked, "Did you like it?"

"Like what?"

"The kiss."

"Yes," I said quietly. Because I really did. I could still feel it everywhere in my body and it scared the shit out of me.

"It wasn't bad," he said wonderingly. "I usually just kiss guys."

"Wait. What? Really?"

He smirked and nodded. "Yeah. Do you have a problem with that?"

I shook my head. "No. But why would you kiss me if you're into dudes?"

"I don't know. Maybe we should do it again so I can figure it out."

We did do it again. A few times actually. I don't know what he ended up figuring out, but by the time I hung out with Guy and his friends, it was clear I had nothing to be scared of. He definitely was attracted to men. I put a stop to the kissing, which he had no qualms about. He's been my best friend ever since.

3

Mason

Mom sets a plate in front of me with three grilled cheese and tomato sandwiches. *Hell yeah*. "How was your first day?" she asks.

My mind instantly flips to the girl from this morning. I found out her name in second period when everyone was talking about "the incident". Hope Love. What kind of name is that? It's as if karma is straight up screwing with me. *Hope Love.*

"I think I'm in love," I say. And then I laugh because I hear some kind of pun in my statement. I play around with the words in my head. *I Hope I can get in Love. I'd Love to have some Hope.*

"Mason, don't play with me," Mom says, but I hear that little sliver of hope in her voice. *Ha, I'd Love a little sliver of Hope*. I could do this all day.

"Mom, I promise you, I am not playing. This girl is amazing."

Mom glares at me, trying to get me to admit something. What, I don't have a clue because I'm not lying. "What's she like?"

"She's fucking gorgeous."

"Don't say fuck."

"You say fuck," I say.

"Well I'm an adult."

"Mom, last time I checked, eighteen was the legal age of adulthood."

"Mason Xavier Patel, you are still in high school, and as long as you live under my roof, you will not say the word fuck."

"We rent."

"Shut up. Now tell me about this girl. What's her name?"

I grin at her. "Hope Love."

"Mason, I told you not to play with me. I am too old and too tired for your shit."

"Mom, don't say shit." I duck my head as she swings at me. "All right, calm down. I swear her name's Hope Love. Is that not the best name you've ever heard? And she's freaking beautiful, and *tough*. I watched her kick a football player's ass today."

"That's it. I'm done trying to talk to you," she huffs. "I don't know why you get my hopes up."

Ha, Hope can get me up. Literally, can do this all day.

"I'm being one hundred percent honest. I had to pull her off this stupid dickhead. I think she may have killed him if I hadn't stopped her."

"Don't say dickhead." She crosses her arms, but asks, "Well, why was she beating him up? What'd he do?"

"I'm not sure how it started, but he pushed her and she didn't do anything, just told him not to touch her and this di—asshole—straight up touches her face."

"Asshole isn't okay either." She clucks her tongue. "So she just beat him up?"

I nod. "Beat his freaking ass." She rolls her eyes, giving up on my cursing, and I take a bite of my sandwich. It's so good I moan. "I think she got kicked out though. That's what people were saying."

"That's it? You didn't talk to her?"

"Didn't get a chance," I say with my mouth full.

"Then how can you say you're in love? You don't even know her."

I finish the last bite and scoop up the next sandwich. "I know enough. She's got this skin..." I trail off and shake my head as I recall my first glimpse of her in the car. “She’s beautiful, Mom. Don’t you believe in love at first sight?” I know Dad did.

“Hmph,” Mom scoffs. “Mason, you find most women beautiful.”

“No, most women find me beautiful. I can’t help that.” I chuckle and take another bite. “I just find something to appreciate in women.”

“We both know damn well what you appreciate about women.”

“Mom, come on. I have always been careful and respectful.”

“What kind of example are you setting for Kellin?” She glares at me again. I’ve heard this before. She’s overreacting as usual. Kel has no idea what I do when I’m not here. I’m not stupid. It’s not like I’m going to tell him about my sexual exploits. And I have never brought anyone into my mother’s home.

“Where is Kel?” I ask to change the subject.

“He’s next door. His dinner’s in the microwave. Makes sure he eats and takes a bath.”

“And does his homework, and brushes his teeth, and gets to bed on time. I know.”

Mom kisses my forehead. "I love you, Mace. I don't know what I'd do without you."

"Love you too, Mom. Have a good night." I watch her leave and finish my dinner before starting on my homework.

I'm getting ready to throw my calculus book when Kellin gets home. "Where's Mom?"

"Work," I say as I start the microwave. "Grilled cheese tonight. Then homework and bath. If you're quick enough I'll play some *Call of Duty* with you before bed."

"Sweet." He opens his math book while he eats and starts multitasking.

****

The following day I search the parking lot for Hope's car. I'm not surprised it isn't there. Disappointed, but not surprised. I park, but stay in the car. I want to finish this song and chill before I have to go in there and deal with the fake smiles and leering eyes of girls I have absolutely no interest in. Don't get me wrong, I love women. I can usually find some redeeming quality in any female. But right now, I'm only interested in one girl. A girl I found out yesterday isn't well liked by most of the other girls at this school. This obviously just intrigues me more.

The lot has cleared out, so I decide it's time to get my ass inside. The halls are packed, so I know I'm not late. I stop at my locker and am instantly attacked by two of the mass produced.

"Hi *Mason*," one breathes. She says my name like it's a secret. I put my head in my locker so I can roll my eyes. She may not have a redeeming quality.

"So, how are you liking it here?" the other one asks.

I toss a few books inside and glance back at these girls. They're both smiling so big, I half expect their lips to split in the middles. "It's all right, I guess."

"You can sit with us at lunch if you want," one of them says. She bounces up and down. My eyes are drawn to her chest and I toss one more book as I stifle a laugh. Guess I found her saving feature.

I slam my locker and turn to face them. I smile at each of them, focusing my attention on these girls one at a time. I can't help it. It's like it's embedded into my DNA to be flirty. I'm just naturally superior at it. "Uh, yeah. I'll see. I've got to go. I'll talk to you ladies later." I flash one more smile before I turn and head for class. I have no intentions of sitting with them. Hell, by the time I slide into my desk for first period, I've already forgotten their faces.

At lunch time, the girls are back at my locker, waiting for me. At least, I think they're the same girls. Either way, I duck into the bathroom and give it a solid five minutes checking my facebook from my phone before I decide they've lost interest. I head back down the hallway and my feet slide as I try to stop mid-motion. I was wrong. One girl is still there, leaning against my locker like she has every right to be there. The bell rang at least a minute ago. *What the hell?* I'm not in the mood for this drama. I turn down another hallway instead.

There are two guys standing near an empty classroom. I go toward them. I figure I can hide out in there for a few minutes until my groupie finally gives up, but as I get closer, I notice one of the guys look up and nudge his friend. He nods at a kid coming down the hall in the opposite direction. His eyes are cast down, blonde hair in his face as he stares at his shoes, minding his own business.

The other guys push off the wall and follow close behind him. "What's up faggot?"

I freeze as his words hit me. This kid's pale face blotches pink and his eyes narrow in anger, but he keeps walking like he's used to being treated like shit in the hallway.

"Hey, we're talking to you, homo."

The kid doesn't react and it's obvious they aren't going to let up. He looks like he can handle his own, but I have this problem—I'm allergic to homophobic asses. I step into their personal space. "What the *fuck* did you just say?" And now I realize I'm dealing with the same jockstrap dickhead that messed with Hope yesterday.

"What, are you a little faggot too?" he says.

And this is where I lose it. Why can't he stop using that word? I drop my backpack and take hold of the bastard's collar. I have him against the lockers before I know what I'm doing. But hey, I've already gone this far, so, what the hell? His friend stands there like a moron, not sure what to do. "I better never hear that word out of your mouth again, you bigot asshole," I yell right in his face.

"Get the fuck off me," he spits. I shove him sideways and scoop up my pack. Then I turn my back on him so he knows I'm not afraid of him. I'm nearly daring him to come at me.

I round the corner, my hands shaking. I want to go back and punch that guy in the face.

"That. Was. Awesome."

I glance sideways and realize the blonde kid followed me. He smiles and I can't help but grin back at him. "He fucking deserved it."

He nods, not taking his eyes off me. "Yeah, he did. For a lot of reasons." We're standing outside of the cafeteria now and I am even more not in the mood to deal with crazy chicks.

"You in this lunch period?" I ask.

"Yeah. You want to sit at my table?"

"If that's cool."

He smiles again. "You just saved my ass and *pwned* Christian Dunkin. You, my friend, just earned head of table."

I don't have a clue what he's talking about. I'm just glad I don't have to sit with the femme fatales. "Sweet. Let's eat."

While in line to buy lunch, I learn that my new found buddy's name is Guy. *No shit*. He's gay and often tormented because of it. He's in a band. And he loves chili cheese fries.

"Just so we're clear, you don't happen to play for my team, do you?" he asks as I pick up a plate of fries.

I look at him sideways and smile. "No, man. I bat straight."

He nods, not affected in the least. "Didn't think so, but I had to ask. Don't worry, I won't judge you. A lot of my friends are straight." I laugh. I like Guy. He's funny and a smartass. I think we'll get along pretty well.

****

After school, Guy is sitting on the hood of my car. Well, it's not my car. Mom bartends nights and sleeps days. I get the car for school in exchange for dropping and picking Kellin up.

"What's up?" I say as I unlock my door.

"I need a ride," Guy says.

"Get in. I have to pick my brother up first, though."

"You've got a brother?" Guy asks a little too excitedly.

I stare at him over the roof. "He's twelve," I say flatly.

"Oh. I've got a sister that's thirteen. You guys should come over."

I slide into the car and start it. "Yeah, all right."

4

Hope

Today has been a good day. I didn't wake up until eleven. Didn't get out of bed until noon. Took a super long shower, using up all the hot water without anyone complaining. Ate a bowl of cereal and didn't have to worry about the twins begging me to share. Laid on the couch and channel surfed until two. Now I'm lying in bed using up the last hour of silence to write some lyrics.

The hour flies by. I hear the front door slam and eye the clock. *Shit.* Where did the time go? Feet shuffle up the stairs and there's banging on my door. "Get your fine ass out here. We've got company," Guy yells.

"Your lame ass friends don't count as company," I say as I jerk my door open. Then I realize he isn't talking about our band. There's a kid beside him and behind the kid is the dude from school that stopped me from murdering Christian Dipshit Dunkin. I definitely remember those green eyes and that black hair that falls across his forehead. It's flipped up at the ends, looking windblown and adorable. I hadn't realized how tall he was. I have to lift my chin to look up at him. He towers over Guy, who is pretty damn tall himself. Wow. This dude is kind of beautiful.

Guy smirks at my awkward faux pas. “These are my friends,” he says pointing to the kid. “Kellin.” He thrusts his thumb over his shoulder. “And Mason Patel.”

“It’s you,” I say.

One brow quirks up in this extremely attractive way and Mason smiles. “I get that a lot.” With just one look he has me squirming, but it’s the way his eyes hold me. Like he’s soaking me up nice and slow, and enjoying every single second of it.

My hair is in a sloppy bun on the top of my head and I’m wearing an old *Quiet Riot* tee shirt, left behind by one of my mom’s “boyfriends.” I tug the hem trying to cover my thighs.

Mason’s eyes rake over me and he grins. “Do you feel the noise?” he asks. I immediately laugh at his joke, but Guy and Kellin both get this strained, confused look.

“Hold on. I’ll be out in a minute,” I say as I slam my door. I slip on some jean shorts and shuffle through my drawer for a better fitting shirt, settling on my little white *Italian Stallion* tee. The shirt is so old and worn it may as well be made of wheat, and I got it when I was thirteen, so it’s a little snug, but I love it. Gotta represent.

“You’re related to her?” I hear Mason say through the door. Then he laughs loudly. He has a great laugh. “Your name is Guy Love?” He barks out a laugh, louder this time. “Ironic, isn’t it?”

I start laughing too as I slide the shirt over my head. I like the easy way he teases Guy about his sexuality. He isn’t afraid to broach the subject. I mentally give him ten cool points and then I realize he knows my name. I am not one of those girls, the kind that get all flirty and giggly over every cute boy that walks by. But my stomach instantly fills with butterflies on speed and I feel giddy and nervous at the same time.

“Ha. Ha. Ha,” Guy says. “We foster her. My last name’s Handlin, dick wad.”

“Like that’s better.” Mason is still laughing when I open my door. All three boys look at me and I remember my hair. I pull the band from it, letting it spill across my shoulders. Mason’s lips part in this way that causes my heart to flutter. “Uh… What are we doing?”

Guy looks at his bare wrist. “We have a couple hours before Dad and Jenny get home. You wanna bounce?”

I glance at Kellin. “You cool, little man?”

He straightens his stance and nods. “I’m cool.”

I give him the test I give everybody. I stare at him for several seconds, then say, “What’s your favorite band?”

“Green Day,” he says without hesitation.

“Do you play an instrument?”

“My brother’s teaching me to play guitar,” he offers.

I feel Mason’s eyes on me, but I don’t look away from Kellin. “You any good?”

He shrugs and his cheeks turn pink. “Not like Mason.”

“Not yet,” Mason adds and ruffles the kid’s hair. Kellin tries to fight a smile, but fails, and now I’m smiling.

“Okay, you’re cool.” Guy twirls his finger, telling me to hurry up, and then crosses his arms over his chest. I finally turn my attention to Mason and repeat my interrogation. “What’s your favorite band?”

He smirks at me, his eyes full of amusement. “Is this a test?”

“Yes.”

His smile spreads wider and I notice a dimple in his right cheek. “I don’t have one favorite band.”

His answer catches me off guard. Nobody ever says that. Guy laughs and slaps Mason's shoulder. "Great. We can go now."

"Did I pass?" Mason asks.

"Oh, yeah," Guy says. He looks at me and wiggles his eyebrows. "You definitely passed."

I turn and proceed down the stairs so they can't see the ridiculous flush heating my pale skin. Cheese and rice. I think I just found my kindred spirit. Or my male alter ego. The Jekyll to my Hyde.

Outside, I head straight for Neko, my car, named after Neko Case, a red haired Indie singer. It's a cherry red 1967 Chevy Bel Air. The car is the only possession my mom left behind that's worth anything. Of course, at the time it was a heap of junk, but Alec and Guy helped me restore her to her former glory. I used my bare hands to put her back together and make her beautiful. I love her.

Dylan runs out of the house and eyes Mason and Kellin suspiciously before stopping in front of me. "Where you going?"

"Store," I say at the same time Guy says, "Library." I make a face at him and sigh.

"You're not supposed to go anywhere. Jenny said you're grounded for getting superended."

I snort. "Damn, Hope," Guy sings. "You got superended? I think we need to drop the p in your name 'cause you is a hoe."

"I got *suspended*, Pickles. I'm just running to the *library*," I mentally roll my eyes, "and then to the store to pick up candy." I bend toward him. "If you promise not to tell, I'll bring you back a Reese's."

Dylan puckers his lips while he thinks it over. "And a Snickers. King size."

I shake his hand. "You drive a hard bargain."

"And," he adds as I open my door. I turn around and glare at him. "You can't call me Pickles anymore."

Damn. The kid is good. I feel strangely close to him all of a sudden. "All right. Deal. Now get back inside with Misty." I watch him run to the door before I slide into my seat. Guy climbs in the back with Kellin and I can't decide if he's up to something or just being polite to the new dude. I look at him in the rearview mirror. "We need another name for that little shit," I announce.

Mason plops down beside me and openly admires his surroundings. "This is a nice ass car." I watch as he glides his palms across the seat slowly and I shiver. This dude is freaking hot and the way he touches my car is just…oh my Buddha…freaking sexy.

I force myself to stop staring at his hands and look up to see him watching me. The dimple's out again as he smiles down at me. I clear my throat and crank the engine. "Thanks."

"What about Relish?" Guy yells over the music and rumbling engine. I turn down the volume on the radio and plug my iPod into the speaker.

"Wait, what about relish?"

Guy rolls his eyes. "For Dylan. Dill Relish."

I scrunch my nose. "It's not as good as Pickles. Keep thinking." I toss my iPod over the seat to Guy. "Find some tunes."

Mason turns to me and I notice he doesn't have his seat belt on. It probably stems from the fact that my mom and would-have-been stepdad died in a car accident, but I have a rule. It's really quite simple: "You don't buckle up then get the fuck out."

Nothing seems to rattle this dude. He somehow manages to look happy that I just cussed at him as he reaches over and pulls the belt across his chest. "So, where are we going?" he asks.

"Hope has a terrible addiction," Guy explains. "We have to stop by The Dealer's so she can get her fix."

I see Mason look back at his brother from the corner of my eye and I laugh. "It's cool," I say. "I'm not taking you and your brother to a crack house or anything." I chance a glance in his direction. He's staring at me, waiting patiently for my explanation. "I have a candy problem," I admit. "It started off small. One, maybe two pieces a week. The next thing I know, I'm waking up on top of candy wrappers wondering where all my money went to."

Mason laughs. I even get a chuckle from Kellin in the back. Guy grunts. "You think she's joking, but that's a true story. The girl has serious issues. If she doesn't get her sugar rush, things get ugly."

"Things get ugly even when I've had my candy," I mutter.

With a defeated sigh, Guy throws my iPod onto the front seat between me and Mason. "That's bullshit, Hope. You don't have any *Maybe It's a Catastrophe* on there."

"What's *Maybe It's a Catastrophe*?" Mason asks as he scrolls through my music. "I've never heard of them."

Guy huffs. "Yes you have. That's our band. We told you all about it at lunch."

"You didn't tell me the name. It's kinda cool."

Guy sits forward, his hands resting on each side of Mason's head. "Hope named us. She also writes all our lyrics and plays drums."

Mason is staring at me again. I can feel it. Like his eyes are burning my skin, scorching me with their intensity. Guy's phone goes off, playing the Star Wars theme song and I know it's somebody from the band.

"Yel-low?"

I keep trying to catch Guy's eye in the rearview mirror, but he's staring down at his knees, playing with a loose thread hanging from the unintentional hole there.

"We're almost to The Dealer. Meet us there. Later."

"What's up?" I ask.

"Chase and Park are meeting us at the store," Guy says. "Park's pissed."

I ignore that. "So, Kellin," I say changing the subject. "I have, like, every Green Day album on that nifty little device in your brother's hand. Maybe you could talk him into putting one of them on while he inspects my collection."

"Do it, Mace. Put on Dookie," Kellin tells him. I shoot him a smile in the mirror and he grins back. He's a little cutie. In a couple years, he's going to be upsetting girls' tummies just like his big brother.

A Beatles song comes on and when I look over at Mason, he shrugs. "I don't like to be told what to do."

I roll my eyes. "You're such a rebel." I'm rewarded with another one of his laughs. It's one of those big, deep, whole body laughs. *Damn it.* He's a *happy* person. On a normal day, with anybody else, this would annoy the shit out of me. I hate cheerful people. The kind of people that never let anything get to them. I bet he never frowns. How could he? He's too busy laughing at everything.

I pull into a parking space and don't wait for the others. I need some high fructose corn syrup and red dye number 40, right now.

Guy takes my hand and intertwines our fingers. "Penny for your thoughts," he whispers.

I hand him Dylan's two candy bars and then pick up some Twizzlers. "I can't decide between Skittles or Nerds."

Guy releases my hand to snatch up a Hershey bar. "That's not what I meant."

"Definitely Skittles," Mason says.

I pick up a box of Nerds and bat my lashes at him. "I don't like being told what to do either."

He grabs the big bag of Skittles and that smile is back. "Why not be a real rebel and get both." He dangles it in front of me and I pluck it from his fingers. I put both candies back and go with Star Bursts. "Touché."

I fight my own smile and turn to Guy. I don't like the way he's looking at me. Like he knows I'm into Mason and it's about to spill out of his big mouth. "So, how did you two meet?" I ask, grasping for something to distract him.

"Oh my God, Hope," Guy begins excitedly. "It was awesome. Christian and Adam were giving me shit again and Mason here came along and jacked Christian up."

"You beat someone up?" Kellin asks. He's looking up at Mason with big eyes full of awe.

Mason shakes his head and picks up the bag of Skittles again. "I didn't beat him up. I just pushed him a little." He glances at his brother and sighs. "It's not okay to put your hands on someone, but the guy was being a homophobe, and that's not okay either. Don't tell Mom. She'll freak out."

Kellin nods slowly. "You should've beaten him up."

I tend to agree and I award him another ten cool points.

"Hope! What the fuck?" I turn around to see Park coming straight for me. "You don't tell me you get kicked out for fighting with Christian Dunkin and then you ignore my calls. What's up with you?" He stops in front of me and kisses my forehead. "You know I worry about you."

He pulls me into a hug and I return it, burying my face into his warm chest. He smells like cigarette smoke and Axe body spray. As if a little cologne is going to cover the stench. I pull away from him quickly and cross my arms. "I worry about you too." I thrust my hand out, palm up. "Give them to me."

Park rolls his big brown eyes, but to his credit, he doesn't even try to play dumb. He reaches into his pocket and pulls out a pack of Marlboros. I wiggle my fingers and he drops the pack into my hand. He leans in to give me a kiss on the lips and I turn my head. "You stink."

"Baby, I'm chewing gum and they're milds."

"Ugh. Shut up, Park. I'm completely disgusted with you right now."

Chase comes down the aisle, hands shoved in pockets. "I told you she'd smell it on you," he says smugly.

"You should have taken them from him," I say.

Chase throws his hands up in defense. "I didn't feel like getting my ass kicked. Sorry."

Park places his hands on my hips. "Hey, we all have our vices," he murmurs and I look up at him, shooting him a menacing glare. He better not go there. Not in front of everybody. Park's known about my cutting for awhile now. It's kind of hard to get that close with a guy and him not notice, but I don't think cutting is comparable to smoking. My vice, as he likes to put it, isn't going to give me cancer and kill me.

"I'm just saying, I'm trying," he continues, noticing the look I'm giving him. "Nobody's perfect." He leans in to kiss me again and this time I let him because he's right. I'm far from perfect and he puts up with all my shit.

5

Mason

I can't remember ever being jealous of another guy before. But as I stand here watching Park, with his hands on Hope's waist, kissing her, I kind of want to put my fist through his face. Here I was thinking I had the best luck ever. I stick up for Guy, who ends up living in the same house as Hope Love. I'm invited into their little group with open arms. And Hope winds up being even cooler than I thought was possible. I mean, her iPod could be the mirror image of my own, and I have a freakishly unusual collaboration of music. She writes lyrics and plays the drums. And her sense of humor matches my smartass, sarcastic, slightly offensive jokes.

When her bedroom door opened and I saw her standing there looking sexy as hell in a Quiet Riot tee shirt, I thought I hit the freaking lottery. Twice I had stumbled upon this girl. That's fate, right?

Wrong.

Unless fate is a cruel, twisted bastard.

Park finally takes his hands off of her and notices me standing here awkwardly as I die slowly inside. He nods. "Hey, man. What's up?"

I nod back. "Not much."

Chase waves two fingers through the air in greeting and I nod to him too. I'm ready to go. I know I shouldn't be so pissed off that Park is dating her. He seems like a decent person and I have no claim to Hope, but I can't shake it.

I have two options here. One, I can take my brother and walk away. Avoid these people like the plague. Or two, I can suck it up and act like a man. I can stop being an obsessed asshole and just be a friend. Of course, there is always option number three. I can bide my time and wait for Hope and Park to break up before I swoop in for the win. I'm really liking option three. I just hope it doesn't crush me first.

I buy Hope the Skittles. I don't know why I do it, but I do. We get in her car and Park and Chase follow us back to her house. As everybody piles on the couch and floor in the living room like this is their own home, I figure this is an everyday occurrence. This is the house where everyone gathers.

I sit on the floor and lean back against the part of the couch where Hope's sitting with legs crossed, bag of candy in her lap. Guy turns on the XBOX and starts handing out controllers. Park takes one so I opt not to. I hand mine to Kellin instead and he moves closer to the big screen TV.

I rip open the bag of Skittles and take a handful before I hold it over my head for Hope. She takes it, slipping a handful of Starbursts into my hand. I tilt my head back and grin at her upside down. She smiles back. She has a nice smile. It's real.

It occurs to me that I keep comparing her to other girls. But she's not like any girl I've ever met before. I contemplate this while I eat my candy and pretend to watch the guys play Halo.

"You aren't eating the yellow ones," Hope says.

I turn around so I can see her face to face. "I'm saving them for last. They're the best ones."

She stares at me blankly and I'm trying to get a read on what's going on inside her head. "Everyone knows the pink are the best," she finally says. "And you eat them first so nobody else can steal them." She reaches toward me and plucks a yellow Starburst from my hand, her lips curving as she pops it into her mouth. I'm frozen, watching her hands, her lips, her jaw as she chews on my piece of candy. "Yellow are second best, by the way."

I finally pull myself together and thrust my hand into her lap, grab the bag and start searching for the first pink square I can find before she takes it back. I find one triumphantly and toss the rest back to her. Holding her gaze, I tear it open and place it slowly on my tongue. Then flash her what I trust is the smile that makes smart girls go a little dumb.

Hope raises an eyebrow and licks her lips. She bites into a Twizzler and as my eyes are once again glued to her mouth, I pick up on the fact that my game just got turned around on me. "Do you want some?"

I jump and try to play it off like I'm stretching. "What?"

She holds out the package. "I asked you if you would like some," she says through a sinful smirk.

Yep. She definitely turned the tables. I nod and we stare at each other as I put my fingers into the bag. "I would *love* some," I say.

The room explodes as Guy and Kellin cheer and Chase and Park mourn their loss with frustrated groans. Hope sits back and takes another bite from her Twizzler.

Who knew a bag full of cheap candy could be so freaking hot? I turn back around and press my neck against Hope's knee like I don't notice it's there. She doesn't move, which I spend some time speculating. I also wonder what her lips taste like right now. I'm sure they're super sweet and probably a little sticky. I moan quietly in my throat and decide to focus on the game. I don't know who's who, but I figure it out as Kellin yells and a red team member goes down.

Dylan comes in the room and squishes himself between Hope and Guy on the couch. I nod at him. "What's up Dill Weed?"

He gives me a dirty look and I just chuckle as I finish off my last bite of candy. Hope hits my shoulder hard. "YES!" she squeals. "Dill Weed, that's it. You are fucking awesome, Mason Patel."

****

I didn't want to leave. If I could, I would still be at Hope's house right now. But Mom needed to go to work, so here I am, staring at my ceiling and thinking about Hope instead. I'm fairly certain one person shouldn't consume this much of my thoughts. It's probably unhealthy.

"Hey, Mace?" Kellin says as he pushes my door open.

"What's up?"

He sits on the end of my bed, rolling a baseball between his hands. "Can we go there again? Back to Guy and Hope's?"

"You like it there?"

"Yes. I had fun. And Misty is nice."

Ah-ha. There it is. "Nice, huh? She's pretty too."

Kellin's face glows red and I cover my laugh with a cough. "She's all right," he admits.

I know he likes her. He gave up video games to go outside and play basketball with her and Dylan. I punch him lightly in the arm. "My little brother the player."

He moves with my fist and smiles. "Whatever." He tosses me the ball and we start a game of catch. "You like her."

It isn't a question and he doesn't say who, but I nod. "Yeah, I like her. But she's got a boyfriend."

Kellin rolls the ball over his palm. "Park's not her boyfriend," he says. He waits for my reaction. I don't say anything, just sit up and wait for him to tell me what he knows.

"Misty said Hope doesn't like labels, and commitments "freak" her out." Kellin throws up finger quotes and I laugh.

"Well, what are they then?"

Kellin gives me a dubious stare. "How the hell am I supposed to know?"

"Hey, watch your mouth. Mom hears you cuss, she'll kick my a—butt."

"Whatever. You cuss all the time," he points out. And it's true, but he's just a kid. It sounds wrong coming out of his mouth. Ah, hell. Mom was right. I need to watch my mouth. At least around little ears.

"Isn't it past your bed time?"

He throws the ball to me and ducks out the door. "Night, Mace."

"Night, *Little Man*."

6

Hope

Not only am I awake, but I'm actually jealous when everybody goes to school. Because I can't go see Mason. I wonder if we have any classes together. I should have asked him. I should have given him my cell phone number. Along with email address, blog, Facebook and Twitter accounts. I have a very serious problem.

So instead of addressing it, I shuffle out to the couch for some mind numbing T.V. I eat the rest of my candy for breakfast while I watch about five hundred judge shows. Then I finally force myself to get up and take a shower.

My phone vibrates across the nightstand as I'm getting dressed, and yes, I dive across my bed in a hurry to see who the text is from. Even though I know it can't be Mason, I'm still disappointed when Guy's name shows up.

Guy: GUESS WHO'S BEEN ASKING ABOUT U?

I bite my lip and smile. I know exactly who he's talking about. This is the kind of thing that freaks me out. Big time. When a dude shows interest in me, I usually run. It took me a year to hook up with Park. The only reason I didn't scare him off is because he's as demented as I am. Also he's in the band and best friends with Guy, so we were pretty much stuck with each other. Even with Park I refuse to make it official. Not that either of us are seeing anybody else. I suppose we're kinda, sorta like a couple, just without any labels, but it makes me feel better to have boundaries, and Park plays along.

For some reason, I'm not freaking out right now. I'm excited. I text back.

Me: UM, WHO?

Guy must have been waiting for me because his response is immediate.

Guy: MASON <3 PATEL! YUM!

I drop to my bed and sigh. If he's asking about me then he must be interested. Not that I hadn't suspected that yesterday, but I wasn't sure if he just had one of those personalities. All flirt, all the time. He likes me enough to want more info and now I'm wondering what he's been asking and what people have been telling.

Me: WHAT'S HE WANT TO KNOW?

Guy: ASL. JK. UR RELATIONSHIP STATUS, AMONGST OTHER THINGS.

Me: WHAT DID U SAY?

Guy: THAT U SUFFER FROM PHILIPHOBIA.

I roll my eyes. I am not afraid of love. Mostly. Me: U SUCK.

Guy: JK. I TOLD HIM 2 ASK U.

Me: WHY???

Guy: GTG. TTYL.

Of course. I knew Guy was up to something yesterday. *I knew it!* What's really weird is I'm still not freaking out. Something about Mason feels right. I like him. A lot. I've never met anyone like him. The only person I've ever felt this comfortable with is Guy.

I feel jittery like I drank one too many cups of coffee. I have too much time on my hands. So I do something very out of character for me. I clean my room. I mean I really clean my room. In the closet and under the bed. It's one of those cleanings where I find all sorts of cool things I forgot I had, which consists of two notebooks full of partial lyrics and old poems. I could probably put several new songs together with these. Also I found a tin of those tiny little squishy animals I used to collect from the quarter machines. I totally forgot I had them. Taking them out one at a time, I try to remember their names as I inspect each one.

I find about twenty jelly bracelets and slide them on my wrist. When I come across a plastic cup with who knows what growing at the bottom of it, I decide I'm done. After tossing the cup in the trash, I wash the dust off my fingers and glance at the clock. My stomach lodges itself in my throat. Guy should be home in a few minutes, hopefully accompanied by Mason.

I'm just heading down to the living room when I hear the front door open. My feet hesitate for a moment.

"…so I explained that just because she's a bitch, that doesn't mean she has to go around flaunting it," Guy is saying. The door closes with a click.

"What did she say?" Mason laughs.

I let out the breath I was holding and continue down the stairs.

"She told me to fuck off, which I believe validated my point."

I hop off the bottom step. "Fighting with Annie again?"

Guy sighs dramatically. "She started it."

"She usually does, but you need to be nice to her right now," I say and glance at Mason. He's wearing a tee shirt that hugs his torso in a truly amazing way and is a shade darker than his eyes. Guy is so right. *Yum.*

"Yeah, I know." Guy claps his hands together and looks between me and Mason. "So, what are we doing today?"

I look at Kellin and smile. "Hey, Little Man. You wanna wait outside for Misty and Dylan with me?"

Kellin shoots a quick look at Mason. "Come on, Kel. Let's go wait on your girl," he says grinning.

Kellin glares at him, but follows me out the door. I sit down on the porch and Mason sits on the steps in front of me, leaning back on his elbows. He tilts his head and grins at me. "Hey."

"Hey."

He pulls a box of Nerds from his pocket and places it in my hand. "For you."

Guy throws himself down beside me, bumping me with his shoulder. "Is that the equivalent of bringing you flowers, Hope?"

I rip the box open and shake some of the grape candy into my hand, ignoring Guy. "Thanks Mason." I use the tip of my tongue to grab the small pieces.

Clearing his throat, twice, Mason says, "You're welcome."

The bus pulls up in front of the house and Kellin jumps off the porch. Guy leans into me. "I can't tell if you're clueless or an evil genius," he whispers conspiratorially.

"What color is my tongue?" I ask and stick it out at him.

"It's purple, bitch." He laughs and shakes his head. "I'm going with evil genius."

"Who's an evil genius?" Mason asks.

Guy raises his eyebrows and smirks at me. "Hope."

"Oh, really? Why's that?" Mason inquires. He's got that grin plastered on his face that shows off the dimple. Cheese and rice, he's cute.

"I think she's some form of succubus."

"My virginity's still intact, Guy," I say as I stand up and brush the dirt from my butt. "Yours, on the other hand, has been gone for so long I think I've seen it on the side of a milk carton." I wink at him and head to the door. "Besides, if anybody has the power to steal a man's virtue, it is definitely you."

"You may have a point there," he yells over his shoulder.

Dylan runs past me, dropping his book bag and going to the kitchen. "How was school?" I ask him.

He shrugs. "Fine."

I try again. "What'd you do today?"

Another shrug. "I don't remember."

Okay. "Well, what'd you learn?"

"I don't know. Stuff."

Yeah, I'm done. That's my quota of caring for the day. "You want a snack?"

"Yes. I'm starving. I was at the end of the line at lunch because I took too long on my science test, so I didn't get to eat all my food. And it was pizza day."

I pour him a glass of milk and set out the package of Oreos. Pulling one apart, I lick the cream from the middle and throw the cookie parts in the trash. Misty and Kellin join Dylan at the table and I pour them milk as well.

"Do your homework while you eat," I remind them and am surprised when Kellin pulls a book from his bag and gets busy with the other kids.

Guy and Mason come in next and both steal an Oreo. I watch Mason pull his cookie apart and scrape off the icing center. He flicks it into the trash can before popping the dry cookie in his mouth.

My mouth nearly falls open. Dear Buddha. It's as if we were made for each other. Mason Patel is my counterpart. He is the eraser to my chalk. The milk to my cereal. The chocolate to my peanut butter. We were made for each other in cookie heaven. Guy chokes on his bite as he witnesses Mason's cookie habits and my embarrassingly obvious reaction. I hit him on the back, possibly with too much force.

When he can breathe again, Guy stares at Mason intensely. "This is very interesting," he says.

Mason's eyebrows lift in question. "What?"

Guy picks up another cookie and begins pacing back and forth like he's a lawyer addressing a jury. "Did you know that Hope here only likes the creamy center of the Oreo?" Before Mason can respond, Guy continues. "And I was just saying that I think it's interesting you appear to only like the crunchy outside." He's waving around the Oreo in his hand like it's a piece of evidence. Mason's eyes dart to me for a moment before returning to Guy. "It's almost as if…you complement one another. Or balance, if you will." He runs his finger over his lip and I swear I think I'm dying of humiliation. Can he please stop speaking my thoughts aloud?

"No, no. I've given this some thought," Guy goes on, now holding up his finger. "It's more than cookies. I mean, Hope is moody and, I'm sorry," he says glancing at me. "But let's just put it out there. Bitchy. And you,

Mason, you're all sunshiny and…nice." He takes a seat and eats the stupid cookie looking all too proud of himself.

I can't even look at Mason right now. I cannot believe Guy is doing this to me. I'll show him bitchy.

"You have a lot of similarities, though, too, I noticed," Guy goes on. Oh, I wish he would shut his evil, evil mouth. "Like the whole music thing you were talking about earlier." He gestures at Mason and I finally look at him.

"What music thing?" I realize Mason is smiling. *Why is he smiling?*

"Your iPod is nearly identical to mine. I think you have more songs on yours, but the wide range in artists is pretty much the same."

They're ganging up on me.

He pulls a dark blue iPod out of his back pocket and hands it to me. What, now he has evidence too? I scroll through his artists and he isn't lying. His music tastes are as unusual as mine. From rock to rap to folk to heavy metal to pop. I know I'm grinning as my thumb trails down the screen. This is scary. Awesomely scary.

I look up at him. "What are your feelings about Ramen noodles?"

"Hate them."

So do I. When I lived with my mom, I ate them nearly every meal because they were pretty much the only things she could afford.

"Super Mario Brothers or Crazy Taxi?"

Mason turns a chair around and straddles it. "Both."

Damn. Me too. Okay. Now I'm starting to freak out.

7

Mason

I like this game. Hope isn't giving her opinion, but I can tell by the expression on her face I'm giving the right answers. I'm not sure if she's trying to see how opposite we are or how similar. If I had to guess, I'd say the latter.

Everyone is watching us go back and forth. She doesn't seem to care. Neither do I.

"Oh, I got one," Kellin says. "It's not a question, just something else that's the same." I nod my head at him and wait. "You both beat that mean guy up."

"Yes!" Guy exclaims. "You're both bad asses."

I laugh and gaze at Hope. "My turn," I say. "Pizza?"

She shakes her head. "That's too easy. Everybody likes pizza."

"Toppings," I clarify.

"Saliva," Misty grunts disgustedly and Hope and Guy laugh.

"Hope likes to spit on pizza," Guy explains. I turn to her for verification.

"It's not that I *like* to do it." She makes a face that has me grinning at her. "It's a necessity of living in a house of ten people."

Guy nods in agreement. "It doesn't stop me, but no one else touches her pizza." Hell, it wouldn't stop me either.

Misty grunts. "Nobody touches it because she orders it with pineapple instead of pepperoni."

"I just pick it off," Guy says, shrugging.

"I'm scared," Kellin says with big eyes.

I know what he means. I'm a little anxious myself, but I pretend like my heart isn't racing. "What? It's good," I say defensively.

"Nu-huh," Guy explodes. "You do not eat pineapple on your pizza!"

"Yes he does!" Kellin says excitedly.

Hope drags a chair away from the table and sinks into it. She has this look on her face that I can't read. And I really wish I could. Is she freaking out inside like I am? Does she want to go somewhere and talk to me alone like I'm dying to do with her?

I clear my throat. “Books or Movies?”

“Movies.”

I actually like both pretty evenly, but she didn’t shed light on anything, so I choose not to either. “Okay. Horror or romance?”

Hope snorts, which may not be flattering on most girls, but it’s cute when she does it. “Horror.”

The front door opens and we all look up. Park comes in, striding directly toward Hope and my good mood is gone. And not just gone, but knocked down and stomped into pieces. I sit up and take the last Oreo. I pull it apart and hand Hope the side with cream. “I got one more,” I say. And I know I might be pushing it, but jealousy doesn’t sit well with me.

Park puts his arm around Hope’s shoulders, hugging her to his waist. Everyone is looking at me. Guy’s mildly amused expression took off with my mood. He now appears to be bordering somewhere along the lines of worried and guilty.

“How do you feel about committed relationships?” I lock my eyes on Hope’s, daring her to answer me honestly.

And like she's done several times before, Hope surprises me.

"I lived with a mother who couldn't make an obligation to her own child, let alone to a boyfriend. I had a hard enough time deciding what candy to choose at the store yesterday. I can't even commit to a hair color. I suck at relationships and I don't do commitments."

Hope says this casually, as if it doesn't bother her, but how can it not? I don't know a lot about how Hope ended up in foster care. All Guy told me was her mom and his uncle died in a drunk driving accident. He didn't say anything about her life before or where her dad is. She just made it pretty clear she didn't have a great childhood. And now I feel like a total dick.

The only positive aspect, she just confirmed Park isn't her boyfriend.

Guy pushes his chair back and stands. "Where's Chase? I thought we were supposed to practice?" he asks Park.

"I don't know," he says. "I'm not his mother." He winces and kisses Hope's temple before releasing her. I release a breath I didn't know I was holding.

Sitting at the table, Park looks into the empty cookie package. *Yeah, that's right, fucker. I took the last cookie*. "If we're not practicing let's go do something. I don't feel like sitting around all day."

"I'm grounded, Park, and I was already blackmailed once." Hope glowers at Dylan who smiles back proudly. "But you guys go ahead."

I'm surprised when Park stands up and pulls a set of keys from his pocket. He says something quietly in Hope's ear and kisses her cheek before glancing at Guy. "Let's go get something to eat," he says.

"You coming?" Guy asks me when I remain seated.

I can't believe Park's ditching Hope like this. If she was my girl, I'd spend every possible moment I could with her. Of course, she's not his girl either. She's not anybody's girl. Not yet anyway. But I'm the one staying, while Park's the one going. "No, man," I say, glancing at Kellin talking to Misty, and then at Hope. "I think I'll stay here."

****

"No way," Hope insists. "As remakes go, *Friday the 13th* is clearly superior to *Halloween*."

The kids are now outside, so we're the only ones left at the table. "All right," I agree. "But the original *Halloween* trumps all other horror movies."

"Except *Night of the Living Dead*, of course. It's a classic. Followed closely behind by *Nightmare on Elm Street*. Again, the original."

I crinkle my eyebrows. "Obviously. I can't believe they remade that movie without Robert Englund."

"Right? I know," Hope exclaims. She smacks my arm and shakes her head. "I mean everybody else they cast in that movie was perfect, but they replace Robert Englund who *is* Freddy Krueger. It just didn't work, but I will admit I've watched it several times."

I chuckle at her ashamed appearance. "Me, too. Every time it comes on HBO."

"So, who do you have first period?" she asks.

"Mr. Langford for Calculus."

She bites her lip and nods. "What about second period?"

I have to think about it, my schedule's still new to me. "Um, Mrs. Harper?"

Hope sighs and looks at her hands. “Okay. How about third?”

“Mrs. Bates. Why?”

“I’m trying to see if we have any classes together,” she says quietly and tucks a strand of hair behind her ear. God, I want to touch her so bad. I wonder what her hair feels like. Is it soft? It looks soft. Thick, too. I keep watching her. Does she want to have classes with me? Probably if she’s asking.

Why am I such an idiot around her? Questioning everything. Forgetting how to speak like a human being. Tripping over all my thoughts. How is it that my confidence soars when I talk to any other girl, but I feel like a bumbling fool when I talk to Hope? How does she have so much power? Either I get caught up in our conversation and start saying whatever pops in my brain without filtering, or I sit here staring at her, overthinking. I’m a mess.

“I have Mr. Roberts fourth period,” I finally say.

She looks at me quickly, smiling. “So do I and I know you have lunch with us fifth period. What do you have sixth?”

"Gym with Mr. Varner. Seventh I have art with Mrs. Guevara."

"Oh, yes. I have art too." She smiles at me again and I start gazing at her mouth. Again. "I go to music eighth."

"You play the drums in the school band?"

Hope traces the grain in the wood of the table with her index finger. Her nails are painted with some kind of glittery clear polish. The light keeps hitting them, causing a sparkle effect. "No. I play the cello."

Hmm. "That's awesome. Do you play any other instruments?"

She shrugs her shoulders. "The piano some, but I'm not very good yet. The cello's newer too, just since I moved here. I'm better on drums. I started when I was eight, playing on a drum pad since my mom couldn't afford a set. But that's all."

That's all. As if it's no big deal. I feel inferior. "If you ever want to learn how to play the guitar, I could teach you. I bet you'd pick it up right away since you're used to a stringed instrument."

"I've played a little with Guy. It's so weird though. I'm used to using a bow. With the cello, how you hold yourself, the cello, the bow, it all affects the sound. With a guitar, you could lie on the ground and pick at the strings and still get the desired notes. I haven't been able to get the hang of it."

I study her for several seconds. "It's the control," I say aloud even though I don't mean to. I just figured something big out about Hope.

"What do you mean?" she asks.

I hesitate, deciding if I should just shut up or go with it. This has been nice, me and her talking. I don't want to screw it up, but I kind of want to know if I'm right. "You like the things you have control over."

After a few heartbeats that pound against my rib cage, she nods slowly. "That's frighteningly accurate," she whispers.

This is why Hope doesn't do relationships. Because she can't control the other person's commitment, most likely afraid they'll leave her like her mom did. It's also probably why she likes the drums. She controls the pace of the entire band with the beat of her drum sticks.

Now that I found this piece of the Hope puzzle, I'm yearning to put the rest together.

8

Hope

We're both quiet so long I'm starting to worry I said something wrong. Maybe I shouldn't have owned up to his control theory. I don't know what it is about him that has me saying so much. I've known him for two days and he probably knows as much about me as Guy does.

Mason clears his throat like he's about to say something when Alec clomps through the door with Addie and the twins. Archer is crying uncontrollably, so I get up and take him from Alec. "It's okay baby boy," I soothe. "It can't be all that bad being two." He hiccups in my arms and digs his fingers into my hair. I have no clue why he does this, but since he became a master of his motor skills, he's liked holding onto my locks. I rub his back. "There. That better?"

He nods at me and I kiss him before setting his feet on the floor. Alec puts Amy down and sighs. "Thanks Hope. Jenny's not home yet?"

I shake my head as Addie puts her foot on my shin wanting her shoes taken off. I bend down and start untying them. "No, not yet."

Addie sticks her other foot out and I begin on that one. She looks at Mason for a moment then turns her head back to me. "Who is he?" she asks in her quiet five year old voice.

"That's Mason," I say. I glance over at him. "This is Addie. My foster mom's daughter from her second marriage." I nod my head at the twins. "That's Archer and Amy. Jenny's kids from her current marriage. And that's Alec, Jenny's current husband."

Alec gives me a look. It's similar to Dylan's death stare and just as unintimidating. He looks at Mason and offers a smile. "That would make me the dad," he says. "It's nice to meet you."

"You too," Mason says standing up. He leans across the table and shakes Alec's hand. Alec's thrown off a bit by the gesture. We don't typically have such polite friends.

Mason turns to me and I can tell he's getting ready to leave. I don't want him to, but can't think of a reason for him to stay without looking stalkerish. "I should probably go. My mom will need the car for work."

"Okay," I say trying not to look disappointed.

"Walk with me outside?"

"Um, yeah," I utter confused.

Mason waves at Addie. She moves behind Alec's leg, but smiles as she peeks around his khakis. "See you later," he says. She waves back and Alec does the guy head nod thing which Mason returns. I follow him out the door, stopping when he hovers before the porch steps. He looks out at the driveway where Kellin plays basketball with Misty and Dylan.

His face is full of indecision when he turns to face me, studying me for a moment and I stand very still, waiting for him to say something. All I can think about is how attracted I am to him. How strange it feels to be so drawn to someone after so long of feeling nothing.

"I like you, Hope, and I think you might like me too," he begins. My stomach twists with nervousness. *Yes. Yes I do like you. So much.* Wait. Does he mean he *likes me*, likes me? Like I like him? Or just likes me strictly in the platonic sense? Oh, man that would suck, which pretty much sums up my life, so…yeah.

"I'm just going to be really honest right now because this is all new to me and I don't know how else to handle it." He takes a deep breath and pushes the hair off his forehead. "I like being around you. I like talking to you. When I'm not with you, I'm thinking about you." He stops there and I guess I'm supposed to say something, but I'm at a loss for words.

He's making his feelings clear, but being vague about his intentions. I don't know what he wants from me. He knows how I feel about relationships, so I'm assuming he isn't looking for one. I also made it clear that I'm still a virgin, so hopefully he isn't trying to help me cash in my V card.

Mason's a fun dude. I like being around him too. He's still waiting on my response, shifting anxiously. *He's nervous*. I like that I make him nervous. It's empowering. Something I haven't felt in a very long time. It makes me brave. "I like you too, Mason," I whisper. He grins and takes a step backwards.

"Good. That's really, really good." He turns to leave and stops abruptly, circling back to me. "Do you have your phone?"

I take it from my pocket and hand it to him in a daze. He starts keying in a number and I realize what he's doing. "Wait," I say, grabbing my cell from him. He raises his eyebrows, hand cupped in front of him as if he still holds my phone in his palm. Feeling completely stupid for my reaction, I try to backpedal. "Sorry. I have a…thing I do with my contacts. I nickname everyone." I hold the phone in front of him. "Just put your number in."

He takes it as if he's afraid I'll yank it away again. As he continues, a smile starts to form on his lips. "What will my name be?" he asks, holding the phone hostage while he awaits my reply.

"I don't know yet. You'll have to wait and see."

"As long as it's not something lame. Maybe something like Hot Stuff or Sexy Beast. I don't want your screen to say Annoying Psycho every time I call you."

I look up at him through my eye lashes. "Do you plan on calling me a lot?" I ask and I become conscious of the fact that I'm flirting with him.

His green eyes focus on me, flicking over my face, resting on my lips long enough for the cracked out butterflies to return to my stomach. He closes his eyes and sighs. "Yes. I plan on calling you a lot." He releases my cell phone and bounces down the steps.

"Mason?"

"Yeah?" He pivots on his heel and gazes up at me.

"Are you on facebook? Or Skype? Have a Twitter maybe?" He laughs and rubs his fingers along the back of his neck.

“I have a facebook account. Send me a friend request.” He starts walking away and then stops again, glancing over his shoulder at me. “I’ll sign up for Skype, and video chat, and anything else that allows me to see those blue eyes of yours.” He calls for Kellin and heads for the car waving to me before he climbs in.

I’m still standing on the porch, my cheeks hurting from smiling so much, long after he drives away.

~***~

I’m on dish duty. I’ve been on dish duty every night since I kicked Christian in the nuts. Annie comes home from cheerleading practice and starts rinsing dishes as I unload the dishwasher. She doesn’t say anything and neither do I. This has become our routine for the past three days. She helps out with the extra chores I was assigned as part of my punishment and then we avoid each other as much as possible.

I know she’s afraid I’ll ask her what happened between her and Christian. I also know she isn’t ready to talk about it. Honestly, I have no intentions of going there. Nothing would make me happier than if we never discussed it. Her situation brings up too many memories of my past. Memories best forgotten.

With the dishwasher now empty, I move out of the way and wipe down the counters as she refills it. I wish I had my iPod. Some heavy, angry music blaring in my ear drums would be great about now. Just having Annie this close makes the urge to cut flare inside me. It's like an itch that no matter how many times I scratch and dig at it, it just won't stop tingling until I'm raw and bloody. It may settle down for a while, but it never actually stops prickling and crawling below the surface. Just waiting to flare up and grab hold of my sanity again.

I throw the rag in the sink and practically run to Guy's room. A low guitar melody drifts through the partly opened door. He's had this piece of music ready for awhile, waiting for me to put lyrics to it. No matter how hard I try, I can't find the right words to match the soft, sweet notes. No matter how much Guy pushes for a love ballad for the band, I'm incapable of contributing.

I'm not going to lie; I have a shit load of love songs in my playlist. I know them by heart and sing along with them often. But to write about something I know nothing about? Impossible. Don't get me wrong, I love my foster family. Guy's more than a cousin to me. He's my best friend. I love him deeply. I also love my friends, few as there may be. I even love my car. But who wants to listen to a song about how devoted we are to possessions or our friends and the people we're ingrained to love due to our DNA or living arrangements?

Guy insists love is love. The emotion is the same even if the receiver isn't, but I'm not convinced. If I'm not convinced, I'm not inspired.

I tap my finger nails on the door and hear Guy's hesitation on the next measure. "Enter," he calls.

Pushing the door open, I shuffle in. He must read something on my face because he leans his guitar against the side of the bed and opens his arms to me. Accepting the offer, I snuggle into him and lay my head on his chest.

Guy runs his fingers through my hair, but doesn't say anything for a long time. The sound of his heart beating steadily mixed with the slow rhythm of his breathing calms me.

"You want to talk about it?"

I shake my head against his shirt.

"I think he's in love with you," Guy murmurs. "I think you could love him too. Don't be scared of him." I wonder if Guy is trying to distract me or if he thinks the Mason thing is what is bothering me.

"He's not in love with me," I whisper. I don't know why I'm whispering, but I can't stop. "He told me he likes me, though." I swallow and take a deep breath. "I do like him, Guy, and it does scare me. He scares me. But I'm not losing my shit yet." Guy's hand stills in my hair. I shrug. "I almost feel normal when I'm with him."

I feel his chest rise when he inhales a long breath. "I think he'll be good for you. You're happy when he's around. You smile, and you laugh a lot." His fingers brush through my hair again. The gesture relaxing. "I'll help you. When you start to freak out."

I nod.

"And I'll talk to Park."

I feel my eyebrows draw together as I shake my head. "Park's not my boyfriend. He'll be fine," I say.

Guy laughs. My head bounces with the movement of his torso. "It's a damn good thing you're so pretty, honey, because sometimes, you are really quite stupid."

9

Mason

Mom kisses the top of my head and touches my cheek. "Love you, Mace."

"Love you too."

"Oh, I almost forgot," she says at the door. "Straight home tomorrow. Afternoon girl quit and I picked up her hours. I have to pull a twelve hour shift, but it should be good money." She shuts the door and I slump forward in my chair, letting my forehead hit the table. *Damn it.*

Well, tomorrow is going to blow. I pull my phone out for the twentieth time since I've been home. Why wasn't I smart enough to call myself from Hope's phone? I know the answer to that question. I was distracted, wondering what she was going to name me in her contacts. I am easily distracted by her all the time.

I can't believe I'm going to have to go a day without seeing her.

I check my phone again and throw it on the table. And then I remember she was supposed to send me a friend request. I start up the ancient computer in the living room and wait for it to load. My knee bounces up and down and my fingers tap against the desk.

When I'm finally signed in, my stomach muscles clench. I click on the friend request and there she is. It's a picture of her and Guy. Her arm is around his waist, his is around her shoulders. Their shadows stretch out in front of them. Hope's looking off to the right. She isn't smiling like Guy is, but she doesn't look sad. Preoccupied, maybe. I wonder what she saw when this picture was taken. What was off camera that caught her interest? And now I'm wondering who took the picture. Is it weird that I'm jealous it might have been Park? Never mind. I know it's weird. This girl is turning me into a lunatic.

Obviously I don't mind being a basket case because I click the confirm button and start checking out her page. I don't realize she's online until I get the I.M.

I WAS GETTING READY TO NICKNAME YOU LYING BASTARD WHEN I REALIZED I NEVER GAVE YOU MY NUMBER.

I laugh as I type. UH, YEAH. THAT OCCURRED TO ME AS WELL WHEN I WENT TO CALL YOU.

My phone starts vibrating across the table and I'm thinking about ignoring it when I get a reply.

ANSWER YOUR PHONE.

I jump up and hurdle over the back of the couch. I snatch my phone up and attempt to pretend I'm not trying to catch my breath.

"Hello?"

"Hey."

"Hey."

"I'm a little concerned about your lack of male companionship," Hope says. "I mean, it would appear Guy is your only same sex friend, and he's gay, as you know. Although he is a masculine gay, you should at least have a couple more male friends. Oh, wait, there's one. Oh, no...that's a girl. She should consider waxing the mustache."

I'm grinning at the wall. "Is that a note of jealousy I detect in your voice?"

"I was going to stick with concern, but...do you really know all of these girls? It says you have over eleven hundred friends. According to your profile, you're only eighteen. How could you possibly know this many people?"

"Yours says you have three hundred and eight friends. Which mostly appear to be guys, by the way. Do you know all these people?"

"Most of them follow my blog or added me after a show. I actually only know maybe twenty of them."

"We've moved a few times in the last five years, so I've been to a few schools. That's how I know them. But I don't really *know* them. They aren't really my *friends*. It's not like I can really talk to them. Not like I talk to—*you*."

"Why?" she asks.

"I don't know," I admit. "I've never met anyone like you."

"But why me?" Her voice is low, nearly a whisper, and I have a hard time swallowing.

"I don't know," I say again. I don't want to scare her away. I can't tell her that I feel good when I'm with her. Or that she's the prettiest girl I've ever met. Or how she makes me feel things I'm not used to feeling. So I say the only truth that I don't think will terrify her. "You're special."

She makes a noise and I have no idea what it means. My palms are sweating. The girl even makes me nervous on the phone.

"What are you going to name me on your phone?" she asks. It doesn't get by me that she changed the subject. I don't know what that means either, but I go with it.

"No way. I'm not telling you until you tell me what you named me," I protest.

"I'll show you tomorrow."

Shit. "I can't come over tomorrow. Mom has to work a double. I won't see you until Friday. If I can come over Friday, that is."

"Yeah, you can come over Friday. And we're having a party Saturday night if you want to come. It's for Alec's birthday. There's going to be a ton of family and Alec's friends, so it might not be much fun for you, but having you there will make the experience more enjoyable for me." She clicks her tongue. "I can't believe I just said that."

I put my hand over my mouth because I want to laugh with joy, really freaking loudly. I can't believe she just said that either, but for a much different reason. Hell, yeah! Hope is into me. "I'm glad you did."

"Let's pretend I didn't."

"Why?" I ask.

She sighs and it sends a chill down my spine. I wish I could see her expression. I start clicking through her pictures just to see her face.

"It's embarrassing. I don't usually say stuff like that," she explains.

"You're embarrassed? Well what if I told you something humiliating about me? Would that make you feel better?"

I can hear the smile in her voice when she talks. "I don't know. I guess we can give it a try."

I chuckle. "All right. Um...okay, I buy my mom's tampons on a regular basis."

She laughs, but says, "That's not embarrassing. It's sweet in a weird way."

"Trust me, it's embarrassing. I'm a guy and she's my mom," I explain.

"Hmm. That's it? It doesn't make me feel better."

I suck on my bottom lip. "All right. When I was eleven, I went to my neighbor's pool party and her brother pants'd me in front of everyone while I was on the diving board."

She laughs, making me laugh at myself. "It's not funny," I announce. "The water was cold. It was very unflattering. I still have issues. If I even smell chlorine I tighten my belt."

"What else?"

"You want more? No way."

"Fine, but you're going into my phone as Pantsless the Boy Wonder," she says.

"That's just wrong," I mutter. "I'll tell you one more if you tell me one of yours."

She's quiet for a moment, so I wait patiently for her response.

"Okay. One," she agrees. "Then you give me one more."

"Promise."

"Ugh. I can't believe I'm going to actually tell you this. You can never, ever repeat this. Ever. Not even to me. As long as you live."

I try not to laugh. "Okay, scout's honor," I agree.

"Back when my mom was still alive, I used to buy her tampons too." She says it so seriously, I can't help the bark of laughter that leaves my mouth. "Okay seriously, not much shames me. But at our first show the band ever played, I started puking not even halfway through the first song. I dropped my drum sticks, put my hand over my mouth and took off. Guy was pissed they had to play the whole set without a drummer."

"Public puking, that's not bad," I say.

"Just as long as it's not my name in your phone."

I chuckle darkly. "You'll have to wait and see."

"Your turn. One more humiliation," she says excitedly.

I hesitate, inhaling deeply until my lungs feel as if they're about to burst. I silently give myself a quick pep talk. *Man up, Mace. She's just a girl.* But there's the real issue and I'm well aware of it. Hope is not *just a girl*. She's the first girl I have ever really liked. I want her. And for more than a pump. And that can't happen until I lay it all out for her. "This is embarrassing because I'm admitting it to you and I have no idea how you're going to react." I hesitate again, debating whether I should actually say it or not. *Screw it. Balls to the wall.*

"Go on..."

"The first time I saw you, I wanted to kiss you. And I don't mean when I pulled you away from Christian. I actually saw you before that. In the parking lot. You were laying in your car listening to music. And I thought you were overwhelmingly beautiful. I still think you're beautiful and I still want to kiss you."

10
Hope

I struggle for some kind of reply. Anything. But the silence is hitting that incredibly awkward point. I clear my throat quietly and tell the truth. “I absolutely do not know how to respond to that.”

Mason laughs into the phone. “Well, you didn’t hang up on me or cackle with laughter. Though the agonizing minute when you didn’t say anything might make this more humiliating than being pants’d.” He laughs again and I can hear the discomfort in it.

“I’m not disgusted by the idea,” I offer.

Now he’s quiet as he interprets my words. “But not open to it either?”

“I’m a pretty easy going person. I don’t close doors.”

“Hmm.” I can almost picture the grin on his face, the dimple in his cheek. “I’m starting to figure you out.”

“Oh?” *Why is he trying to figure me out?* I like it. I like it so much. Yet, it scares the shit out of me at the same time.

“Mm-hmm.”

"Like what?" I ask. I notice I'm squeezing the phone and my hands are sweating.

"It scares you to tell people what you want."

He's right. He's so incredibly right. My hands are shaking and I close my eyes. How does he keep doing this? "And you are insinuating that what I want is you?"

"I'm starting to think it's possible," he utters.

"Mason, you terrify me."

His voice lowers in a deep murmur. "I'm also starting to think that's possibly a good thing because you scare the shit out of me too."

"So what do we do?" I whisper.

"Maybe we should start facing our fears."

~***~

Thursday wasn't as bad as I had expected it to be. Mason text me periodically through the school day and gave Guy a bag of fruit flavored Tootsie Rolls to pass on to me. We sent messages back and forth on facebook until Jenny got home and I had to get off the computer. Then after dinner and dishes were done, we talked on the phone until Mason started yawning. Some people still had to get up early and go to school even if I didn't. I had told him goodbye and he whispered goodnight.

When I woke up this morning, I got right out of bed and into the shower, excited to start my day. I couldn't wait to see him after school.

I'm on my way to the basement to practice when the doorbell rings. To say I'm shocked to see Mason standing on the porch holding a package of Oreos is putting it lightly. I stand there staring at him, a ridiculous grin stretching my cheeks. "What are you doing here? Why aren't you at school?"

I move out of the way so he can come in and he offers me the cookies. "The nurse told me to leave," he says, smirking at me.

I raise one eyebrow. "Why?"

"I was so inspired by your story the other night I borrowed a few choice details from it. I told her I had just emerged from the restroom where I'd puked my guts out. Held my hand over my mouth and missed my drum solo and all. A perk of being eighteen, she sent my ass home."

"And you came here."

Mason's eyes pin me in place. "I came here."

"Hmm, well I'm glad you seem to be feeling better," I say smiling.

"It was a miraculous recovery."

I hold up the package in my hand. "You want milk?"

He nods his head. "Sure." I pour two glasses and lead him into the living room to sit on the couch. Mason sits so close to me his jean clad leg rests against my bare thigh. I crisscross my legs, set the Oreos on his knee, and my glass inside the small circle my legs make.

Mason watches me as I open a cookie and lick the center clean, and then he reaches for the two halves as I start to put them back in the plastic tray. Now I stare at him as he bites into them. I am so turned on right now for some reason and I wonder if that was his intent when he purchased them. I grab another one and we form some weird, mini assembly-like line. I open the cookie, give him one side, lick the other, and then hand that one off, repeat.

"I'm establishing a pretty unhealthy routine thanks to you," Mason says as he brushes crumbs from his shirt. "I can't believe we ate the entire pack. Seriously. The whole package. I'm afraid I'm encouraging your habit."

I laugh. "I had candy for breakfast the other day. Cookies are a step up for me."

"I'm concerned you may have a tapeworm," he says, gesturing toward me. "I don't know where else all that candy is going."

"Oh, I just throw it up. And you thought it was nerves that had me puking on stage."

He gazes at me and I can tell he's trying to determine whether or not I'm joking. I blink my lashes slowly and smile at him. Something changes in his expression. I can't quite identify it, but suddenly my stomach is tightening and my face feels hot. I can't tear my eyes away from his. This moment, whatever is happening here, is so intense, my breath shudders out of me. I feel a flash of terror roll through me. I can't do this. I can't deal with these feelings. I don't know how.

I force myself to blink and I look down at my hands. "I was just kidding," I say. My voice sounds funny, raw.

He clears his throat softly. "I know."

I stand up, the need to cut taking me into its unyielding grip. My mind shifts through different excuses, trying to find some way I can get away without him becoming suspicious.

Mason's fingers brush mine and I look down at him. "Hey," he murmurs.

"Hey," I say.

I watch a muscle in his neck move as he swallows and I'm mesmerized by the sight. He is incredibly sexy. Part of me is pooling on the floor in front of his feet, while the other part is screaming at me to run upstairs to the safety of my bathroom, to the comfort of my razor.

Somehow I reach down and take his empty glass from his hand and walk into the kitchen. I stand at the sink, rinsing the glasses and staring at the water. I inhale deeply.

"Did I do something wrong?" Mason asks from behind me.

Turning off the faucet, I twist around to look at him. "No."

He stares at me, his eyes raking over my face. "I feel like I did something to upset you in some way."

I'm grasping the counter so tightly my fingers are beginning to hurt. "You didn't," I utter.

Mason walks toward me, his gait measured, careful. He reaches around each side of me and loosens my death grip on the counter, holding our hands in between us. "Are you scared?"

My head jerks up, my body trembles. He always knows. I shake my head slowly. “Absolutely petrified,” I whisper.

“Do you want me to go?” His eyes are darting over my face again, searching for something.

All I can do is shake my head.

He steps closer to me until I can feel his breath on my face. His head lowers, our noses nearly touching. My heart is slamming inside my chest, beating much too fast. His nose skims mine and I gasp. I feel the tickling brush of his eyelashes against my skin when he closes his eyes. I tilt my neck back, bringing my chin up.

And then I slide sideways, putting distance between us. Mason turns, following my movements with his eyes. I shake my head again. “I’m not ready to face my fears yet. Don’t be mad.”

His brow puckers. “I’m not like that. I’m not going to get pissed off because you don’t want to kiss me.” He runs his fingers through his dark hair and sighs. “I read you wrong. I misinterpreted the entire situation.”

I shake my head, yet again, like it’s the only thing I’m capable of. “No, you didn’t.” I suck in a shaky breath. “That’s what scares me.” I can’t stand the expression on his face. Can’t take seeing him so confused, so torn. "I don't want you to go. I want you to spend the day with me, but I need a few minutes. I'll be right back. Please don't leave."

He nods and I flee up to my room. I close the door quietly and practically run into the bathroom. Once the lock is latched, I take a razor blade from the medicine cabinet and slide my shorts off. My hand is shaking when I bring it to my flesh and I bite down on my lip as the sharp edge sinks through the old scar tissue. I slide it over my skin and inhale sharply as I'm rewarded with the bright red beaded trail it leaves behind. I sigh as I feel the release. Closing my eyes, I imagine my fear rising from the open cut like smoke and fading away as it mixes into the air. It's enough for now. Wiping it away, I stick a bandage to the fresh wound and wash the razor before replacing it.

This is the part I hate the most. That moment it sinks in that I've sliced myself open. When the rush and release are over and I'm left with the knowledge of just how fucked up I am.

I put myself back together, making sure all evidence of what I did is cleaned up, and then I go back downstairs to find Mason.

There's a quick moment of panic when he's not where I left him, but I find him on the couch and breathe a sigh of relief.

Grinning at me, he holds a DVD up. "Wanna watch a movie?" I start laughing as I pluck A Nightmare on Elm Street (the remake) from his hand.

"Mason Patel, your pants are on fire. You don't watch it when it comes on HBO. I can't believe you *own* this!" I put it in and settle back on the couch beside him, incredibly grateful he didn't take off on me and even more so that he didn't let things get weird.

I have no idea what I'm going to do about this boy.

Chapter 11

Mason

I screwed up big time. Hope told me she was scared and I pushed her anyways. But I'll be damned if I don't learn from my mistakes.

I'm cautious all day. I make sure to keep just enough space between me and Hope. Even though my whole body aches to reach for her, I make no attempt to touch her again. I keep my glances short, careful not to get caught up in her eyes or hunger for the taste of her mouth. I make sure our conversation is fun and lighthearted. And I try to make her laugh every chance I get.

I think she expected me to leave, but after she told me she wanted me to stay, there was no way in hell I was leaving her. I wanted to prove to her that I won't abandon her. That she can trust me.

Now we're making sandwiches and I'm learning even more about her as I watch her scoop out a heaping spoonful of peanut butter. She smears it across the bread, making sure to get every last section covered evenly. Then she smothers another slice with chocolate frosting in the same manner before sticking the two pieces together.

"Don't judge me, Mason. It's delicious," she says as she spoons out more peanut butter and licks it off. I think she's trying to kill me. I tear my eyes away from the slow torture and make a simple PB and J sandwich like a normal person.

"Do you ever eat anything healthy? Fruits? Vegetables?"

She laughs as if it's the most ridiculous question ever asked. "Other than pineapple on my pizza? Uh, no. Well, that's not true I guess. I eat cornbread and mashed potatoes. Oh, and I like juice. Do fruit snacks count?"

"I don't think most of those count," I inform her.

She snaps her fingers. "What about French fries and onion rings?"

I roll my eyes and bite into my sandwich. "I'm utterly confused how you are walking around. You do understand that your entire diet consists of that tiny portion on the tip of the food pyramid? You know, the part you are only supposed to eat in moderation?"

"I don't like being told what to do. Remember? Besides, has that thing even been updated in the last forty years?"

I shrug. How the hell am I supposed to know? "I think this will be my new mission. I will find a way to integrate fruit and veggies into your diet."

She snorts. "Yeah. Good luck with that. Oh, what about chips?"

I cock my brow and frown at her in what I hope is my best "you are not serious" look.

"What do you want to do now?" she says, still laughing. I have to look away from her because that is the worst question she can ask me. I can't tell her what I really want to do, which involves me, her, that container of chocolate frosting, and figuring out exactly which body parts it tastes best on. I shrug, staring at her bright pinks toes.

"Whatever. I'm easy," I say with a devious grin because if I can't touch her, at least I can flirt with her a little. Her eyebrows lift and she licks the corner of her lip. Dear God, she is a vicious sadist. Guy is very possibly correct. The girl just may be a succubus. I stifle a moan and turn away. She is literally driving me crazy.

Before Hope, I never really understood the whole falling in love thing. With all that head over heels, being tongue tied, stomach butterflies, and always on my mind shit. Now, I'm well practiced in all of it. It's funny how some things are just words until one day, it happens to you, and it's like an epiphany. Everything now has meaning. It all makes perfect sense. And I feel bad for the poor bastards that first put a name to it.

The moments she isn't making me miserable because I can't be with her in the way I want, she's making me insanely happy. If I'm not with her, all I can think about is wanting to be.

And now I've been facing the wall way too long while I contemplated all this. She's going to freak out again. I glimpse over my shoulder.

"You want to swing?" Hope asks.

"Swing?"

"Yeah. Come on." She takes my hand. *She takes my hand*. I feel lame as hell that I'm as excited about this as I am. Opening the side door off the kitchen, she pulls me outside and leads me back to a huge swing set.

Hope releases my hand and I watch her slide onto a swing. I take the one beside her, but I just sit on it. I haven't swung since I was in third grade. Instead, I observe her as she pumps her legs, swaying higher and higher. She has this look on her face... All I can do is stare at her. Her fingers are gripping the chains, her bare feet kicking in and out, and the wind is pulling at her hair. I bite down on the inside of my lip hard. Everything she does captivates me. How she can make a swing sexy is just so damn wrong.

It's probably a good thing Hope doesn't let me kiss her because I don't think I'd be capable of stopping there. I shouldn't have left school. I should have kept my ass at my desk where I was a safe distance away from her.

What's worse is she doesn't even know what she's doing to me. She doesn't realize how amazing she is. How attractive.

My hands squeeze the chains tight enough to pinch the skin, but I don't loosen my grip. I need to get a hold of myself.

Hope's toes skim the thinning grass as she slows herself. Her cheeks are pink, her eyes bright. Holy shit, that smile is making my heart race. She twists round and round until the chains are intertwined and then she picks her feet up, spinning until she's twisted back up the opposite way.

"When I was little my mom and I lived across the street from this park for a few months." She tucks a chunk of hair behind her ear and her voice pitches low. "I woke up one morning and she was gone. Just...gone. She was there when I went to bed, and then I woke up and—gone. She didn't come back for four days. I spent the time at the park, swinging all day long." She peers down at her feet and wiggles her toes. Something quivers inside my chest, that tingling rush of adrenaline when something is scary. I feel it now and everything else seems to fade. I'm sure birds are still chirping, lawnmowers still buzzing, car doors still slamming, but I don't register any of it. It's just her. Just Hope's quiet voice.

"That's where I was when she pulled up in front of the apartment with her flavor of the week," she continues. "I watched her go inside, but I stayed on my swing. I was so *mad* at her. I watched as she ran back outside looking up and down the street. I watched her *panic* and I knew I should get off the swing and go to her, but my feet wouldn't do it. She looked over at the park and right at me and then she went inside. I like to think that she was sure it was me. That she saw me there and knew I was okay. Knew it was all right to turn around and go into the apartment.

"When it got dark, I went home. She didn't say a word about where she was or why she went. She didn't bother to apologize." Hope finally looks up and shakes her head. "She handed me one of those Dum Dum suckers and sent me to my room." She laughs bitterly and shrugs. "As if that stupid sucker made everything better."

I close my mouth that fell open at some point during Hope's story. I can nearly hear it as another piece of the Hope puzzle clicks into place. My teeth clench. I'm angry. No. I'm way beyond angry. How could her mom do that to her? I clear my throat and inhale deeply.

"How old were you?" I ask gruffly.

"That time? I was six," Hope whispers.

That time? "She did it a lot?"

She meets my eyes, one shoulder raises slightly. "All the time."

"That's fucked up." I don't mean for it to come out so disgusted, but my outrage toward her mom seeps into my voice. I picture a six year old Hope, scared, alone. So tiny, innocent, fragile. And I think about the total mind fuck her mother's afflicted her with all these years. "God, Hope. I'm sorry that happened to you." I've never been so sorry for anything, ever.

She stands up and moves in front of me, using her knee to push my knee to the side. As she steps in between my legs and bends forward, I go still and I notice I'm holding my breath. I let it out and inhale her scent as she leans into me and presses her lips against my cheek. Then she steps back and nods her head at the house. "Come on. You need to pick up Kellin."

12

Hope

I keep stealing glances of Mason. Something's flipped inside of me. Like some little Hope switch has been moved to the ON position. Nobody has ever told me they were sorry for the things my mom did. Not even Guy. Definitely not my mom. As completely messed up as it may be, I want to tell Mason more. I want to tell him all the shitty parts of my childhood just to hear him apologize for it. To express regret for something he had nothing to do with. I know it's stupid, but it felt good when he uttered those simple words. It made me feel like I wasn't alone anymore.

It's like I can breathe better. Stand taller. Smile easier. It's ridiculous. I have this sinking feeling I'm going to regret this. That this boy is going to end up inflicting the worst pain I've ever felt.

But right now, I'm nearly floating with ease. I place my hand inside his. He smiles at our intertwined fingers before turning his grin on me. I wonder if he senses a difference. Does he know how his words affected me? That they were the exact right words I needed to hear?

The sun is touching his face and turning his eyes an amazing shade of emerald. They almost glow as they regard me intently. I want to know what he's thinking. *What's inside that head?*

Kellin opens the car door and slides in the back seat. He gives me a weird look and I feel my eyes go big. *Shit.* I shoot a look to Mason, but it's taking him longer to realize our mistake. I turn around with my knees on the seat and stare at Kellin. "You're still cool, right, Little Man?"

He nods, but it's obvious he's speculating.

"Then you can keep a secret, right?"

"Yeah…?"

"Shit," Mason says, finally getting it. "Kel, I left school early. Don't say anything to Mom and I'll give you a free day next time she works a day shift."

Kellin beams at Mason. "You skipped school?"

"He was sick," I say with a smirk.

"Uh-huh, sick. Right. I won't say anything, but you better not forget my free day."

"I'm certain you'll make sure I remember," Mason sighs.

~***~

We make it back to the house just as Park pulls in with Guy and Chase. “Hey, Hope,” Chase calls as he climbs out of the car. He holds a bag up above his head. “Can you do my hair?”

“Sure. What color?”

“Green.”

“The color of money,” Guy states dryly. “Because it’s the only way we’ll ever see it.”

Park comes around the car. I feel my heart thump wildly. I turn and start heading to the house. Mason and Kellin plop down on the steps to wait for Misty. I decide I’m going to sit and wait with them, but Park takes my wrist before I get there. He swings me around into his chest and slides his hands into my back pockets. His lips slide over my neck and panic hits me. I’m not with Park technically. I’m not with Mason. But I freeze, unsure what to do. I feel wrong. I sense that I’m *doing something* wrong.

My hands hover in the air at my sides. Someone takes my arm, pulling me away from Park and it’s not until I turn that I see it’s Guy. “Break time’s later. Miss Love’s hair expertise is needed.” He winks and releases me.

"I'm thinking just the tips this time," Chase says. I keep walking, not looking back at Park, but I glance at Mason. He's looking at Kellin, nodding at whatever story he's being told. I exhale a long breath, relieved he didn't witness Park's display. He looks over as I pass him. Our eyes meet and I realize he did see it. He gets up and follows me inside.

"Where's the dye towel?" Chase asks.

"Laundry room. On the shelf," I say. Mason steps in front of me as Chase turns away. He puts his hands in his pockets, but leans into my personal space.

"That kind of sucked for me. I think I'm going to head home."

"I don't know what to say," I admit.

"I don't either. I know it shouldn't bother me, but it does." He takes a deep breath, moving his hand, gesturing from him to me. "I don't know what we are, but I think there's something here."

"I don't do relationships. I told you that," I say defensively.

He takes a step closer to me and I have to force myself not to back up. "We both know that's bullshit." He rubs his face and sighs. "I don't wanna rush you or freak you out." I can nearly hear the missing "again."

"But what you have with Guy, that's a relationship. It may be friendship, but it's still a relationship. How you are with Dylan, you treat him like a little brother, that's a relationship. The way you protected Annie, doing Chase's hair, comforting Archer the other night, those are all relationships, and you're good at them. And Park, he's your boyfriend, whether you know it or not. That guy puts his hands on you any time he feels like it. Every time he does, he's claiming you as his."

I stand there in shock, searching for some argument to disprove him. He shakes his head. "I'm sorry," he says suddenly. "Damn it. I'm sorry. I don't care. I'll deal with it. I had no right to say those things. I'm cool now." He runs his fingers through his hair and shakes his head again. "Fuck. Say something, Hope."

"I still don't know what to say," I whisper.

We stand there staring at each other until Chase comes back. He looks back and forth between us. "Did I interrupt something? I can go…"

"No, man. S'all good," Mason says. "I'll see you tomorrow?" He says to me and I nod, letting him leave and do what I do best. I push everything away as I work on Chase's hair.

~***~

I stare at my phone, debating. It's a good argument between me and myself. In the end, I win. So I text Mason.

Me: SO DID U KNOW THAT WHEN UR LITTLE COUSIN ASKS YOU TO DYE A STRIP OF HER HAIR NEON GREEN THAT U SHOULD ADAMENTLY DECLINE?

Me: CUZ I DIDN'T.

Him: NO YOU DIDN'T.

Me: I DID. SHE BEGGED ME.

Him: WHICH COUSIN?

Me: …ADDIE.

Him: HOW MUCH TROUBLE ARE YOU IN?

Me: UG. WAY 2 MUCH.

Him: WHAT'S THE SENTENCE?

Me: I HAVE 2 PERFORM AT THE PARTY.

Him: THE BAND?

Me: THE BAND WAS ALREADY GOING 2 PLAY. BUT NOW I HAVE 2 PLAY SOLO FOR EVERYONE. PLUS SING.

Me: I WILL PROBABLY BE SMASHED BY THE TIME U ARRIVE.

Him: SMASHED? WAIT. YOU SING?

Me: SMASHED AS IN HAMMERED. SHIT FACED. INEBRIATED. DRUNK. AND NO, I DO NOT SING. THAT IS THE PROBLEM. JENNY IS TORTURING ME.

Me: I'M CHANGING HER NAME TO EVIL STEP MOTHER.

Him: HEY THAT REMINDS ME. YOU NEVER TOLD ME WHAT U NAMED ME.

Me: GUESS U WILL JUST HAVE 2 WAIT UNTIL TOMORROW.

Him: SUCCUBUS.

Me: PANTSLESS THE BOY WONDER.

Him: PUBLIC PUKER.

Me: HEY MASON, WILL U BUY ME SUM TAMPONS?

Him: WILL YOU EAT A CARROT?

Me: DO U SMELL CHLORINE?

Him: DO YOU SMELL COMMITMENT?

Me: WOW. U WENT THERE.

Him: I DID.

Me: U WIN THIS ROUND. WELL PLAYED SIR. WELL PLAYED.

Him: I CAN'T BELIEVE YOU GAVE UP SO EASILY.

Me: I DIDN'T GIVE UP. I GAVE U THE WIN. IT'S CHARITY BCUZ I PITY U.

Him: OUCH. THAT HIT RIGHT IN THE EGO.

Me: I THINK THEY HAVE A PILL FOR THAT.

Him: YOU ARE THE MEANEST PERSON I KNOW.

Me: R U SURE? CUZ U KNOW 1,100 PEOPLE. 1 HAS 2 BE MEANER THAN ME.

Him: NO. I'M SURE.

Me: I SHOULD WIN SOMETHING THEN.

Him: WHAT DO YOU WANT?

Oh dear Buddha. What do I want? That is such a loaded question and he knows it. He's the one who pointed out that I have issues admitting what I want. I think he's testing me. My fingers are practically begging for me to hit the U. But maybe he's just testing the waters after what happened this afternoon. Maybe it's an innocent question. So much time has gone by without me answering. What's he thinking while he's waiting for my reply? Is he nervous? Irritated? Is he even waiting? Maybe he's playing Halo or watching TV.

Me: I'LL HAVE 2 GET BACK 2 U ON THAT 1.

Him: I'LL BE WAITING.

What does that mean? Great. Does he even understand the mind games he's playing with me? Yes. Yes, I think he does. I think he also enjoys it. The sad thing is I do too. *Damn*.

Me: NIGHT.

Him: GOODNIGHT HOPE.

Yeah right. I doubt it.

13
Mason

Mom drops me and Kellin off at Hope's before she goes to work. Guy gave me the option of staying the night or having Park take me home. I haven't made my mind up yet, but the prospect of sleeping in the same house as Hope is excruciatingly appealing.

There are cars parked up both sides of the street. The driveway's full. And there are even several vehicles in the front yard. Mom gives me a hard look. "This is a birthday party for her dad?"

"Foster dad, yeah."

"Don't get in any trouble and keep an eye on your brother," she says.

"I'll guard him with my life," I promise.

Guy's dad has good taste in music. Old southern rock plays loudly from the backyard. Kellin trails behind me as I head for the gate following the party sounds and the lines of white Christmas lights.

I stop just inside the yard as I take in the scene. There are small round tables everywhere, more white lights looping throughout. A buffet table is set up alongside the garage and there are large speakers on either side of a makeshift stage. It reminds me more of an outdoor wedding than a birthday celebration.

The music cuts off and as I turn, my breath catches and something sticks in my throat, like a lung, or my heart, or something. Hope stands center stage wearing a light blue sundress that sways just above her knees and reveals a small amount of creamy white cleavage. Her hair is pulled up in a series of twists and braids showing off her neck and shoulders. And I'm pretty sure I can see traces of make-up on her face other than her usual lip gloss. She's so pretty.

Guy unfolds a chair and Hope sits, gliding her dress up her thighs as he then hands her a cello. She places it between her legs and sits up straight. The moment is surreal. I've never seen anything more heart wrenchingly beautiful. Nothing, nobody has ever affected me as she does now. I can't take my eyes off her. I don't want to look at anything else ever again. I reach into my pocket and pull out my phone. I click several pictures before she even starts playing.

And when her bow touches the strings and the first note sounds, the entire yard goes still. Everybody stops there idle chatter, enthralled with the sweet sounds infecting their senses. I click more pictures because Hope's face has changed. Her eyes are closed, but there is this freedom that relaxes her features. A small smile plays at her lips.

I am absurdly in love with this girl.

The song ends, but Hope stays where she is. Everyone erupts with applause. Her cheeks flame with embarrassment and I smile. The rest of the band climbs on stage. Guy picks up his guitar, Chase takes the bass, and Park holds a microphone. I don't know what I expected, but for some reason, I thought Guy was the lead singer. Now as Park stands behind the mic stand, everything about him screams rock star. The ripped skinny jeans, the faded Ramones tee shirt. The stick straight hair strategically styled in a messy, just-woke-up way. But mostly it's his confidence. Like the stage is his home. His comfort zone.

Park smirks at Hope, holding her gaze as she lifts her bow, the cello leading them into their first song. And they're good. Really good. I'm in awe as I listen to each piece that makes up the band. Hope's hands are a blur as she transforms her classical cello into an instrument of rock. Park sings the lyrics, that I know came from Hope, in a smooth tenor that somehow reflects an internal aching. Halfway through the chorus, I decide I'm a fan. *Maybe It's a Catastrophe* might be my new favorite band. By the second song, when Hope takes a seat behind the drum set, I confirm it.

Kellin tries to talk to me, I think to say how good they are, but I wave him off, desperate to hear every second of the music. The hour flies by and Park announces their last song.

He holds out the microphone as Hope moves around to the front of the stage. Strands of loose hair stick to her neck with sweat and I swallow tightly, nearly groaning with want—no the need—to run my tongue over her neck. I click one more picture, never wanting to forget how sexy she looks.

I snap out of my ogling as she accepts the mic, her hand shaking nervously. I cringe internally as Park kisses her cheek and jumps off the stage not far from me. He crosses his arms and stares up at her, nodding when she meets his eyes pleadingly.

Hope clears her throat. "Hey everyone," she begins. Her voice trembles as she continues. "I had a lapse in judgment yesterday, so in retribution, I have to sing for Alec. I'm supposed to take requests, but since it's his birthday, he gets to choose." Her eyes move over the faces, seeking out her foster dad—uncle—whatever she calls him. She sees me then, her gaze pausing on me and she smiles before moving on. I can tell the moment she finds him. She tilts her head slightly and waits.

"The beautiful song," Alec calls and Hope smiles widely.

Chase sets his bass down and hops off the stage throwing up his thumbs reassuringly. Guy switches out his electric guitar for an acoustic and heaves himself onto the folding chair. Hope puts the mic on the stand and lowers it between them.

Guy strums the strings as Hope's voice fills the air.

"Pink lips, and rosy cheeks; eyes so light and hair that shines. They tell me that you're beautiful."

The way she sings it, soft and low, it's something I'll never forget, striking at my core, and changing something inside of me forever. My feet are moving me as if of their own accord. I drift forward, her voice compelling me closer. I can't fathom why she doesn't like to sing when she does it so well.

"Five foot nine, size two dress, bones protruding from your chest. They tell me that you're beautiful.

"Inflated breasts, extended hair, pigment perfected. They tell me that you're beautiful."

Hope tips her head up, her eyes closed. The music grows faster, my heartbeat with it.

"Shape me, mold me, manufacture me, and tell me that I'm beautiful. Wax me, dye me, chop and dice me, and tell me that I'm beautiful. Choose me, use me, take me, break me, and tell me that I'm beautiful. Bleach it, cover it, go ahead and remove it.

"Erase all that is beautiful." She nearly shatters me with one song. Her words echo in my mind. When she opens her eyes, she stares at something only she can see.

"Starving, purging, implanting, and *medicating*. Erase all that is beautiful. Pretend, *ignore, deny*, ratify, inculcate. Tell me what is beautiful.

"Tell me. Tell me. Tell me what to be.

"Shape me, mold me, manufacture me, and tell me that I'm beautiful. Wax me, dye me, *chop and dice me*, and tell me that I'm *beautiful*. Choose me, *use me*, take me, *break me*, and tell me that I'm *beautiful*. Bleach it, cover it, go ahead and remove it.

"Break me. Break me. *Break me* to fit you."

Guy strikes the last chord. It thrums through the silence as Hope looks at me and whispers the last line.

"I don't want to be *beautiful*."

Everyone claps and Guy grins up at Hope proudly.

****

I'm still star struck as the evening wears on. I try not to say much, but I tell her that they were great. I tell her that I loved her songs. I tell her how wonderful she plays the cello. I tell her she's beautiful whether she wants to be or not. I finally shut up when Park makes his way over.

He hands Hope a bottle of water. "You better start drinking that now or you'll end up hung over tomorrow," he says.

I watch her carefully. She doesn't seem drunk. Her voice isn't slurred, she isn't stumbling. I don't even smell anything on her. She nods and takes the bottle.

"You want a shot?" Park asks me. I shake my head.

"No, man. I'm good. I've got my brother here."

He looks back to Hope. "I got to get Jessie's equipment back to him. I'll be back later." He touches his fingertips to hers and smiles. "You were awesome tonight." His lips brush against hers and I turn my head. I don't look back at her until I know he's gone. When I do, she's staring at me. I stare back.

"Blow bubbles," Addie says, shoving a bright orange bottle at me. I look down at her and she takes a step back toward Hope as if she's still unsure about me.

I accept the bottle and blow through the wand. Bubbles float in the air and Addie giggles. She and Hope race to catch them, so I blow more and more until my head is light. "I need a break," I say rubbing my forehead.

"Mason's about to pass out Addie," Hope says. "Let's give him a breather."

"You blow," Addie insists.

Chase laughs from his seat a few feet away, nearly choking on a piece of pizza. "Yeah, Hope. You blow," he chuckles.

She rolls her eyes as she dunks the bubble wand into the bottle. "Just for a little bit, Add. There are perverts present." She shoots a disgusted look at Chase, making him laugh louder. Addie eyes him seriously, tucking her streak of green hair behind her little ear.

"Chase is nice," she declares.

"Yeah," he agrees. "I'm nice."

Hope licks her lips as they round in an O shape and she blows softly across the little plastic stick. It's right about now that it occurs to me that I'm a pervert too, because this is hot. This whole night has been a slow death.

She looks over, and without taking her eyes off me, she hands the bottle to Addie. "All done. Go ask Chase to blow some for awhile since he's so nice." Taking my hand, she pulls me toward the house. We're barely through the door when she turns to face me.

"Do you still want to kiss me?" Her voice is just above a whisper, her breathing accelerated.

Hell yes I do. I nod, staring at her mouth. "More than ever."

She looks up at me through her long dark lashes and I don't think I can live another second not knowing how she tastes. "Then kiss me," she murmurs.

14
Hope

Mason doesn't hesitate. His hands slide up my neck, his fingers brushing gently over my jaw line. He cups my face and leans in. I close my eyes in anticipation.

"Have you been drinking?" he asks, his mouth so close to mine I can feel the warmth of his words.

I open my eyes and nod. "I had a few shots, but that was hours ago."

"Are you drunk?"

"No," I say firmly. I'm not. I'm feeling good, but I'm not at all drunk.

He smiles. "Good." His lips caress my jaw, he plants light kisses, moving toward my mouth.

"Hope—oh, hey," Annie fumbles, her eyes wide, brows raised. Mason and I pull away from each other like we were doing something wrong. "Sorry. Mom sent me to get you. We're doing the cake." She gives me an apologizing look and mouths, "Oh, my God. Hot."

I burst out laughing and Mason shifts beside me. "I will be right out," I manage to say. He presses his head against my shoulder with a frustrated groan and I laugh harder. "Come on. I need some cake."

He reaches out as I turn and glides his fingers across the back of my shoulder, over my tattoo. “Hey. A blackbird. That’s what I named you in my phone.”

I look up at him trying to determine if he’s joking. “What? Why?” I love that song. There was a time I honestly felt like it was written for me, but there’s no way he could know that. I’ve never told anyone how the lyrics touch me.

He smiles at me as he opens the door. “The first time I saw you, you were wearing that Beatles shirt with the blackbird. I think about that moment a lot, so I thought it fit.” He nods at me as I move past him. “And now that I see your tattoo, I think I made a good call.”

He grins at me proudly and I can’t help but smile back.

We make it just in time to sing Happy Birthday. Alec blows out his candles. Yes, Jenny put all forty candles on his cake. I let the birthday boy, and all the little kids get a piece of cake before I secure slices for me and Mason.

“Are you ever going to tell me what my name is?” Mason asks. He licks icing off his finger and I watch his movements carefully. My body is so aware of everything he does. Especially when it involves his tongue.

I pick up my plate and bite my lip, contemplating what I'm about to do. His green eyes meet mine and I take a deep breath, steadying myself. "My phone's in my room," I say slowly. I stand up and move in a determined line to the house, hoping he's behind me. What if he thought I was just running in to grab it? What if he didn't understand that I want him to come with me to the privacy of my room? What if he did get it? I don't know which makes me more nervous.

The door closes behind me and I glance over my shoulder. Mason meets my gaze and for probably the first time since I've met him, he isn't smiling. I feel my cheeks warm as I move up the stairs. In my room, I place my paper plate of cake on the desk and turn around to face him.

Mason's eyes shift around the bedroom, moving slowly over my side. I turn the lock on the door. I don't want Annie walking in on us again. The click causes him to turn his attention in my direction. He glances at the door knob then back to me. My stomach flutters and a chill skitters down my back.

I don't move. I'm not sure I'm capable. "Kiss me," I whisper.

His long legs have him across the room in front of me before I can even force myself to exhale. One of his hands touches my cheek, the other grasps my lower back, his fingers bunching the material of my dress. I look up at him and I have only a second to comprehend that I'm not scared. My heart is racing, my pulse pounding, my stomach is a mess of nervous excitement, but I'm not afraid of him. Then Mason's mouth is on mine. My shoulders crash against the door as he presses into me.

His lips are surprisingly soft and warm as he uses them to part mine. I open my mouth for him and his tongue slides in slowly. I skim my hands up his arms and into his hair. His grip on my back tightens, pulling my body flush with his and he moans quietly. I feel the vibration on my lips and my whole body responds.

I don't know what comes over me, but I like it. I push against him, guiding him backward until we fall across my bed, our lips separating only from the impact. I bring my legs up so I'm straddling his hips and he pulls my head back to him. I gasp as his fingers slide under my dress and sink into my thighs. I can't believe I'm allowing him to touch me like this. I can't believe I like it as much as I do. The way Mason makes me feel, the comfort I find in his warmth, it's unnerving, but in this really great, crazy way. I know I'm risking everything. Taking the chance he'll discover my secret.

Mason moves his mouth to my neck, his tongue sliding over the sensitive skin and he growls. "You taste so good," he murmurs, his voice husky. I love his voice. I move against him, setting off another moan and I like that I can do that to him. I like making him feel good and I decide he may very well be worth the risk.

We find our way back to each other's mouths and as I run my tongue over his bottom lip, he smoothes his palms down my sides. He takes hold of my hips and now I moan as he presses against me.

With a groan, Mason breaks away gasping. "We need to stop," he pants. "Or I'm going to take this too far."

How far is too far? How far do I want this to go? I don't know, but I don't want to stop. Not yet. He feels too good to stop. Too right. I nod my head like I'm in agreement, but crush my entire body against his, embracing him as I caress his neck with kisses.

"Oh, my God," he breathes. Then his hands are under my dress again, grazing the skin on my back. He pauses. "You're not wearing a bra."

"Hm-mm. Not with this dress." He grunts and his hands clamp around my arms.

"I think we need to stop. Now. Because I'm nearing the point where I won't care you have a yard full of party guests."

I sit up, but I stay on his lap, looking down at him. His cheeks are pink, his hair messy. He's adorable. I shake my head. "I trust you, Mason." His eyes rake over me—my face, my body. "I trust you," I whisper. The fact that I mean those words scares the hell out of me.

My chest is rising quickly with my breathing. I can clearly see the agony on Mason's face as he struggles to make a decision. I'm about to implode when he finally sighs and clasps my fingers. "Show me what you named me in your phone," he says hoarsely.

I swallow my disappointment, appeased only by the longing and regret evident in his demeanor. But just to verify that I'm reading him correctly, and maybe to tease him just a little, I shift slowly against him as I wiggle myself off his lap. He sucks in a breath and I try to hide my smile.

"Succubus," he hisses. I laugh and hand him my phone, watching as he takes his own from his pocket. When his ringtone sounds, I scan his face intently. First he reacts to the song, his mouth opening in surprise as *Blackbird* plays, and then he laughs when he reads the screen.

"Skittles? You named me Skittles?"

"I had to. That was the moment."

"The moment?" he asks. He pushes himself into a sitting position.

"The moment I decided I really liked you."

He grins at me and shakes his head. "And *Blackbird*?"

"You played it on the way to the store," I explain.

"I played it because of you. Because of your shirt." He laughs again. "This is kind of frightening."

~***~

"What are those?" Mason asks, gesturing to my little squishies.

I pick one up, a pink pig, and press it between my finger and thumb. "I used to get these from the machines outside of this store my mom shopped at. We'd go there to pick up toilet paper and laundry detergent. After she paid, she'd hand me a quarter and I'd be all excited to see which one I'd get." I poke my finger through the box. "I keep trying to recall which one I bought last, but I can't remember."

"Which one's your favorite?" he asks softly.

"Penguey," I say immediately. Damn, did he just use my trick?

"Penguey?" he asks amused.

I smile and sift through the animals until I find the tiny blue and white penguin and hold it in my palm for him to see. "He's my favorite."

Mason plucks it from my hand and examines it. "Why this one?"

I shrug. "I don't know. He's cute."

"What's your favorite animal?"

"I guess penguins. What's yours?"

He brushes his hair off his forehead and smiles. "Elephants. Don't ask me why. I just like them. Favorite song?"

"Don't have one. I love too many. Favorite color?"

"Blue," he says and I don't miss how he stares into my eyes. Normally I would find that cheesy, but the way he nearly breathes the word, the intensity of his gaze, it has me melting right here on my bed. "And yours?"

“Purple,” I say honestly. “Even though I’m seriously considering changing it to green.” His eyes still have a hold of me. I’m not sure who moves first, maybe we move at the same time, but suddenly I’m lying back. Mason is above me and our lips are once again fused together.

15

Mason

Hope and I are sitting in the grass, our knees pressed together as we play the hand slap game. She's winning. I may be letting her win a little bit. I can't help it if my hands are reluctant to leave hers, even if it ends with heated red marks across my skin.

"You're really bad at this," Guy states with a smirk in my direction. I shrug as he leans back on his palms, his head nearly touching Hope's shoulder. "Honey, you do know he's doing this on purpose, right?" He winks at Hope and her brow puckers. Her next slap is hard. Really, really hard. I jerk my hands back.

"Damn it," I hiss.

She leans forward until her butt comes off the ground. Her face is so close to mine I can feel her heat. I want to close the minimal distance she's left open. Her eyelashes drop as if in slow motion and she peers up at me. I love when she does this. "If you can't handle pain, you may not want to play games with me," she taunts.

There are multiple ways I can interpret this, but I go with the belief she's flirting with me. I let one side of my mouth curl up in a devious grin. "I can take whatever you offer me." I drop my eyes to her mouth, still so close, and suck in my bottom lip. My teeth drag across the soft skin as I watch her gaze focus there. She looks around us quickly and before I have a chance to register what she's doing, her warm breath is against my ear.

"You have no idea how much I'm prepared to offer you." Her tongue skims along the outside of my ear before she sucks the lobe into her mouth. With her this close, I can hear the small squeak that escapes as my hands shoot out and grip her waist.

I turn my face in so I can whisper into her ear. "Then give me a clue."

She laughs softly, but not enough to hide the nervous tenor. "I thought I was."

We pull away enough to look at each other, but the amount of space between us is minute. Intimate. I give her my best smile, and wink. "I'm a slow learner. I may need more to go on."

"Oh, for the love of all that is holy," Guy grumbles.

"Seriously," Chase grunts. "Get a freaking room already."

"They just came from a room," Annie says flatly.

Hope drops her forehead to my chest. I laugh as I run my fingers down her bare arms. Her skin is hot and smooth. Just this simple, innocent touch has my heart thumping wildly.

"I would say it's cute if it weren't so nauseating," Guy sighs and shakes his head. But he's smiling, making me wonder if he actually approves. He winks at me before leaning his head back to look at the sky.

"Yeah, well, Park isn't going to think it's cute," Chase says matter-of-factly. "He's going to kick your ass, Mason. And I'm not saying that to be a dick." He shrugs his shoulders slowly, a sympathetic expression on his face. "It's just fact. He's going to be raging. Hard core."

Hope lifts her head, steadying a glare on Chase. He holds his hands up in defense. "You know I'm right, Hope. Hell, he flips out when guys look at you, let alone..." He waves his hand, gesturing at us.

I feel my body go rigid. I don't know how to react to this. I figured there might be issues. But the way Chase talks, it seems like Park is going to be more of a problem than I anticipated.

"Park won't flip out," Hope says quietly.

Annie laughs loudly. "You are in serious denial, Hope." She rolls her eyes at the raised brow she receives. "You know when other guys are around and Park keeps touching you, and hugging you, and kissing you? Well, he's telling those guys that you're with him, without actually saying it out loud. He's going to flip. And it isn't going to be pretty."

"But I'm not with him. I'm not *with* anybody."

Guy stands up, straightening his dark jeans. "I'll take care of Park," he says. "But I just want to know exactly what I'll be taking care of him for." His eyes dart from me to Hope. "I mean, what is this? Do I tell Park you're seeing both him and Mason? Or are you just seeing Mason now?"

Good question. I turn my gaze on Hope. She curls her hands into fists in her lap. A muscle twitches in her throat as she stares at the ground. My stomach aches as I wait for her to respond. I want to know where I stand as well. I don't want to share her, but I'll do it. God this is so messed up. I cannot believe I am willing to do that. But I knew she had a fear of commitment. And I haven't asked her for one, so it's not like I can complain. Ugh.

But the idea of his lips touching her now since mine have...it makes me sick. I want her to myself.

Slowly, Hope raises her eyes to meet mine. She stares at me for so long, I don't know if I should say something or not. I suck my bottom lip into my mouth and bite it. *Choose me.*

Hope lets out a breath, long and slow. She looks at Guy, her eyes settling somewhere on his chest instead of his face. "Don't say anything to Park right now. What I do, and who I do it with, is my business." She stands up and brushes her dress off. "I'm going to change."

I watch her walk away. When my attention focuses back on our circle, everyone is looking at me. *Thanks a lot Hope*. "Can I get a ride, Guy?"

"Yeah. No problem," he murmurs. "I, uh, don't drive. But Chase can take us."

I find Kellin snuggled up next to Misty on the porch swing and wave him over. "We're leaving."

His brows crinkle and he frowns at me. "I thought we were staying the night."

"We're not. Chase is taking us home, so come on," I say. And I hate the sound of my voice. I hate that I'm pissed off. I hate that my chest burns and my throat feels clogged like I'm about to choke. None of this should bother me. None of this should matter. So, Hope wants to see both of us. So what? So, Park's hands will touch her body. So, his mouth will be on hers. So fucking what?

"I don't want to go. I want to stay," Kellin whines.

"Just get in the fucking car, Kellin. DAMN IT!" I shout. He flinches away from me and I close my eyes tightly. Why am I such an asshole? This went from being one of the best nights of my life, to being...just *shit*. But it isn't Kellin's fault. He waves to Misty and stalks toward the driveway.

Guy rides along, sitting in the backseat behind me. Chase keeps the music down and I sense I'm about to get a lecture or something. Maybe they're going to tell me to back off their friend's girl. I'm not in the mood. I just want to go home, punch something, and go to bed.

Guy clears his throat and sits forward. *Great. Here we go.* "Don't give up on her," he says. That's not what I was expecting. I turn around so I can see him, read his expression. His face is passive, giving nothing away.

"What?"

"She does this," he sighs. "She will do shit to push you away. It's just another one of her stupid tests, but I don't think she even realizes what she's doing. You're good for her, Mason. She's happy when she's around you. She said you make her feel normal and that's *huge* for Hope. I'm telling you not to give up on her. Don't let her scare you off because I think you two could have something good."

Um, wow. "Isn't Park supposed to be your best friend? Why are you telling me this?"

Guy and Chase exchange a look in the rearview mirror. "He is my best friend, but so is Hope. She told me she likes you, but liking you is scary for her. She's had a hard life. Things you can't even imagine. I love the girl more than I can explain and if you're the one that can make her feel like that shit didn't leave a permanent mark on her, then I'm rooting for you."

"What kind of shit?" I ask, my voice scratching my throat. My fingers tighten into fists.

Guy glances over at Kellin. "Shit I can't talk about. Shit no one should have to talk about."

I look at Chase. "Do you know?"

He sucks in a breath and holds it for several seconds before releasing it in a rush. “I’ve pieced some of it together, but no, she’s never told me.”

“And this shit, is it what caused her aversion to relationships?”

Guy nods slowly. “Some. Most.” He leans back and pinches his eyes shut. “Hope has an aversion to love. She says she doesn’t believe in it. That people can’t romantically love each other unconditionally.”

I rub my face. “So, what exactly do you suggest I do? Let her see us both?”

“For now,” he agrees. “Park won’t be able to handle it, he’s had her all to himself for too long, but if you’re the one who sticks it out...” Guy lets the sentence float between us.

“You’re giving me a headache.” I heave a sigh, turning my attention to the window. I press my head to it. “I like her. Way too much honestly. I just need to decide if she’s worth all this.” It’s a flat out lie because I already know she is. I also know I’m going to go along with what she wants. And I’m pretty damn sure it’s going to turn me into a raving lunatic. Hell, I’m already questioning my sanity.

“She is,” Guy says quietly.

16
Hope

Sometimes I think my veins run with poison. We're all slowly dying, right? From the moment we're born, our time dwindles away. Like some countdown we're not privy to. We can die at any moment. I could be walking down the street one day, minding my own business, and then, BAM. Hit by a truck, massive heart attack, some random disease, shot in the chest, stabbed in the back, aneurism, cancer. Who knows? *Anything*. Anything could happen at *any* second.

So why bother? Why bother meeting people? Making friends? Caring about someone? Falling in love? It's just going to end. Taken away, ripped from my hands. Tore from my heart.

I have enough scars.

This is why I'm standing in the middle of my bathroom, naked, clutching a razor blade between my thumb and finger. I need to release the poison. The fear. The anger. I want the pain that festers inside of me—*out*. I want it on the outside. On my flesh. Where I say how I hurt. Where I say when. Where I say for how long. Where I say stop. Where I *can* stop it.

I'm so ugly.

I am so fucking ugly.

My insides are disgusting. There is nothing good inside of me. I'm not a nice person. I'm not smart. I'm not funny. I am selfish. Mean. There is nothing special about me. I can't stand the sight of myself. I hate myself. I hate everything that makes me, *me.*

I have enough scars.

I do not have enough scars.

Light hits the blade of the razor. I twist my hand, allowing it to pass over my face. What would happen if I cut there? Right across my face where everyone could see. Everyone would know. Maybe someone would finally stop me.

I shiver. My secret is all I have.

Pressing the razor flat against my stomach, I take a deep breath. Push my belly out to shove against my savior. I could mar all my skin. Then nobody would want me. Nobody would look at me. My outsides could mirror the sickening rot that lives beneath.

I pull up on the grip so the sharp edge is poised against flesh. I need the bite of this instrument so badly.

My phone sounds. I jump, the blade nearly going to work before I'm ready. Blackbird plays, filling the bathroom with its soft melody.

And I lose it. I lose my shit as I drop the razor into the sink. It makes a tinkling sound as it bounces and slides across the porcelain.

If I answer it, he'll know I'm crying. He'll want to know why.

I don't want him to know.

I want him to know.

He will probably hate me. I don't want him to hate me.

I want him to hate me.

"Hello?"

"Hope? Hey."

"H-Hey."

"You all right? You sound upset?" Mason's voice trembles over the last word. *Why does his voice tremble?*

"…I'm…I'm…*fine*." I'm whispering. Like maybe he'll believe me if he can't hear me well. I don't want him to hate me. I don't want that at all because he makes me feel like I have someone I can talk to. That I can trust. That I can love.

My breath catches. I am incapable of loving like that.

The mere fact that I want to love him, that I can imagine myself loving him… My stomach clenches. I drop the phone and flip the toilet seat up as I begin emptying the sad contents of my stomach. Cake and tequila.

Awesome.

My forehead feels hot in a majorly uncomfortable way. Sweat beads on my neck and above my lip.

My cell phone shouts my name, muffled by the pale pink rug in front of the bathtub. I wipe my mouth on Annie's towel—she's going to be pissed—and I pick up the phone.

"Mason?"

"Are you okay? Are you sick?"

"No. No. I mean, yes. I just got sick." I pause here because I want to say something, I think. I want to tell him about the cutting. That he just stopped me from doing it. That he's the reason I was getting ready to do it. But that last part isn't true, and how do I say something like that anyway? "I'm fine now."

I can hear his soft breaths. I can almost feel them against my ear and my own breathing slows until it matches his. "You don't sound fine."

"I'm not."

"You're not fine?" he asks slowly. There's this tone to his voice. Low, concerned. It makes me shiver. "Go see if you can catch them."

"What?"

"No. Not you. I was talking to Kellin." There's a scratchy sound, his phone pressed against his chest. His next words echo deeply, garbled and scruffy. "Tell them we're going back." A pause. Another scratching sound. "Hope?"

"Mm-hm?"

"We'll be there in a few minutes. Did you take anything? Drink anything else?"

"No. I'm not fucked up." And then I laugh. Because I am so fucked up. I am the most *fucked up person* in the world.

"I think something's wrong with her. Hurry up. Hope?"

"Yeah, there is something wrong with me." I laugh again as tears fill my eyes. Pathetic. A sob rips at my throat and I choke on it. "There is something so incredibly wrong with me, Mason. You don't want any part of this. Of me. You can't." And I hit the end button. I stare at it until my vision blurs. The end button. Yeah, that sums it up nicely. I just hit the end button on Mason Patel.

Pushing myself up, I flush the toilet. I place the razor gingerly back where it belongs. I wash my face and brush my teeth. I put a pair of pajamas on and then I drop onto my bed, willing my eyes to dry.

I don't cry.

I didn't cry when the police officer showed up at the door and I knew something was wrong. I didn't cry when he informed me my mom had died. Didn't cry when he made me pack a bag and took me to CPS.

I didn't even cry at her funeral.

I never cried when she left me. When the boyfriends looked at me. When the asshole touched me.

So why am I crying right now?

What the hell is wrong with me?

I press my ear buds into place and turn my iPod up loudly. Something fast. Something angry. Something to numb me so I don't go back into that bathroom. I can't with Mason on his way.

I close my eyes. Squeeze them tightly.

My mom was crazy. One minute, she was this fun, caring mom. She would be happy. Smiling. Laughing. She would want to be with me. We would play games. Stupid games. Who could finish their breakfast the quickest? Who could take the most steps? Freeze dance. Hide and scream. Those times were good.

Then in the next moment, she would snap. Screaming. Throwing things. Everything was my fault. Get evicted for not paying the rent because she drank the money away. That was my fault. Boyfriend left her after spending one night in bed. That was my fault. Stretch marks. My fault. Car won't start. Ran out of smokes. Bad breath. Communicable disease. Poverty. World hunger. All. My. Fault.

And then there were the drugs. The alcohol. The men. My mom was addicted to them all. So much so, they were her first—no, her only—priority.

There was a time where my mom was pretty. I would look at her and I would think she was a princess. Her hair was thick and shiny. Her eyes bright. Even her skin was radiant.

Do you know what happens to someone's body when it's ravished by addiction? It changes. So slowly, it's not noticeable until it's too late.

Toward the end, her hair was dull and thin, showing signs of graying. Her eyes sunk into her skull, dark bags engulfing them. Her skin yellowed and sagged. She was this useless, scrawny, brittle *thing* that I didn't—couldn't—recognize.

My mom was bitter. Lonely. Sad.

There are times, I look in the mirror, and I see her. I. See. *Her*.

And the realization strikes again. I am her daughter. Mental disease is often hereditary. Often comes on quickly. Often as a person gets older. Let's face it, I cut myself. I am not a stable person. I walk a tight rope, fifty feet in the air, without a net, over sharp rocks, every single day of my life.

Pushing Mason away is like charity or something. The right thing to do. It's the *noble* thing to do. I'm saving him. From me.

17

Mason

The party's still going pretty strong when we get back to the house. We leave Chase and Kellin in the yard and I follow Guy into the house. He takes the stairs two at a time up to Hope's room. He seems worried, which makes me worried.

Without knocking, Guy opens the door. Hope is lying on her bed, arm draped over her eyes, iPod on her stomach. I just stand there, watching like some bystander as Guy crawls onto the bed. She doesn't acknowledge him until he wraps his arms around her. When his face presses against hers, she drops her arm and turns into him. He whispers in her ear and her hands knot into fists, pulling on the sleeves of his shirt, clinging to him. She needs his comfort.

I don't know what I'm witnessing, but I feel like I'm intruding. As if I'm creeping on some personal moment. I take a step back and Guy puts his index finger up, gesturing for me to hold on. So I wait with my hands in my pockets, trying not to watch them sprawled out on the bed. And I try not to be jealous. It's not like I think something's going on between them. But he has an obvious connection that I wish I had with her.

Guy puts the finger up again, this time signaling me over to him. He rolls out from Hope's embrace and guides me until I am filling his spot.

Hope's arms grip my waist, her nails cutting into my skin, but I barely notice it as she pushes her head into my neck. The room goes dark and I register the click as the door closes. I kiss the top of her head, my hands trailing up and down her back as I wait for her to say something.

She doesn't.

"Are you feeling better?" I ask. My voice sounds loud in the quiet blackness. I feel the movement of her head as she shakes it in answer. No. She doesn't feel better.

"Are you still sick? Are you going to throw up again?"

"I'm not sick." She sighs and moves her head to my chest. Her finger traces a pattern on my stomach. "I threw up because..." Her body shakes as she inhales a jerky breath. "I have to tell you something."

"Okay." I swallow hard. My throat is tight, resisting the movement. My hand stops on her back and I squeeze her, willing her to go on.

"I'm not good for you. I have so much baggage, so many skeletons in my closet, so many *issues*, I need a storage unit for all the overflow. I'm fucked up. And if you hang around me too long, I'll fuck you up too."

It's probably a terrible thing to do, but I laugh. "Everybody is fucked up. I'm already fucked up. I promise you that."

Her head moves again, shaking out a denial. "No, you're not. You're so great. You're sweet and funny. And good. You're happy and I'll take that away from you."

I close my eyes and replay her words. "I am happy. Now. But I wasn't. I mean—" I take a deep breath and blow it out. "I wasn't depressed or anything, but I wasn't happy. We haven't known each other very long, but I like being with you. I wish I could be with you all the time. I'm happy when I am."

I can hear music playing outside. Another southern rock song. Something old. Hope is quiet. Maybe listening to the song. Her fingers move under my shirt, tracing her pattern on my skin. My stomach twitches at her touch. It feels so good. I could stay like this for the rest of my life.

"I puked because I got scared again. I'm not scared of you. I don't think you're going to hurt me." She shakes her head and growls out a frustrated noise. "No. I'm petrified you'll hurt me. Not physically." Her voice drops to a whisper. I've noticed she does this when something is serious. Something she doesn't really want to say or admit. I lift my head, straining to hear her. I don't want to miss anything she says.

"I'm afraid that if I let myself feel the way I do about you, ugh, I'm so afraid you'll realize what I am, and you'll walk away. And it'll hurt me."

"What are you?" I hold my breath, waiting.

"Broken," she murmurs.

I do not have a hero complex. I have always been attracted to strong, independent women. I like a girl who has her shit together. No strings. Simple. Confident. But the way she nearly sighed the word *"broken"*—as if it was her sole identifier, as if it's branded on her somehow, as if admitting this has cost her dearly, shamed her—just killed me a little bit. I want to save her.

I want to be *her* hero. I want to make her see she is so much more than her damaged past.

"I can't walk away from you. I tried. I can't do it. Even as I was trying, I knew it was stupid. I already knew I wasn't really going anywhere. God, Hope. I *care* about you. I don't *want* to walk away." I coil my fingers in between her braids and twists, holding her head to my chest. "I'm broken, too. I think..." I lick my lips and press them into her hair. "I think we can fix each other."

"How are you broken?" she asks, her voice small.

"My dad." I swallow my words, nearly gagging on them and try again. "My dad died almost six years ago. Mom's never been the same. She can't stay in one place for too long, so we move at least once a year. Sometimes more. It's like she's always running and dragging me and Kellin with her." I start pulling clips from Hope's hair as I talk. I need to keep my hands busy or I'm afraid I might actually cry.

"I don't get close to people. I make friends, school friends, Mom's work friends. Nobody that means anything. After the first few times I had to leave them behind, I figured there wasn't much point. But I know how to smile, make conversation. I learned pretty quickly. When you switch schools as much as I do, always being the new kid, you pick it up. Girls are easy. I flirt with them. Hook up. We move and I never see them again. I'm...kind of a male whore. When I'm with a girl, it helps me not feel anything real." I laugh, but I know it's not funny. It's messed up. And I hate confessing this to Hope, but I want her to see. I want her to know I'm damaged, just like her. She doesn't comment on it, though, and I don't know what that means.

"How did he die?" Her fingers move higher, drawing across my heart and it's getting harder to breathe. The clips are gone from her hair, so I start loosening her braids.

"He got jumped by some guys. He and his friend were having dinner at this diner down the street from where we lived, back in Illinois. Right down the road. So close to home. It should've been safe. He went there all the time. These drunk guys at another table were giving the busboy a hard time. Talking shit to him, calling him a fag. The kid tried to ignore them. One of the guys walked up to the kid and got in his face, calling him stupid, retarded, a list of shit because he wouldn't acknowledge their simplemindedness. He pushed the kid and my dad had enough. He stepped in; told the guy to back off while his friend got the manager. The guys were told to leave and they left. That should have been the end of it. My dad paid his bill and left not long after." I take a deep breath, filling my lungs with enough air to finish. It's been so long since I've talked about this.

"They were waiting on him. Followed him as he started walking home. Two guys grabbed him. One of the guys had a crowbar. He hit my dad in the head, Dad went down, unconscious, but that didn't stop them. That guy hit him *twelve times* before my dad's friend realized what was happening."

Hope's hand flattens against my heart and I force another breath. "He was dead before the ambulance made it there. We were all home. I remember hearing the sirens, but I didn't know. *I had no idea*. I feel like I should have *felt* it somehow. It's been a long time, but I miss him every day. He was a good dad. A good person in general."

I don't get the usual generic sympathy statement from Hope. I guess because she's been through it. She's lost a parent. In a way, two. She sweeps a kiss over my chin. "What was his favorite band?"

I smile into the darkness. "He loved all music," I say.

"Did he play an instrument?"

"Yep. Taught me how to play the guitar. He was so good. He met my mom playing at the bar she worked at. She brought him drinks and he played her whatever she asked him to. She got pregnant with me and they got married. My dad would always tell me I wasn't a mistake. I was a miracle because my mom wouldn't have married a bum musician if she hadn't gotten knocked up." I laugh a genuine laugh. "She would have married him anyway. They were in love. I get it now. It was real love.

"They fought like crazy, but they were happy. And I remember they always touched. Always hugged and kissed. Snuggled on the couch, in bed. Held hands whenever we went anywhere. I hated it at the time. Thought it was embarrassing. She's never been the same since that night. It's almost like part of her died with him. I guess he took a piece of each of us and we'll never get it back. I'd do pretty much anything to see Mom and Dad holding on to each other again."

"Does it scare you? That you might love someone that much someday, just to lose them too?"

"Yes," I confess, "I've been scared since the first time I saw you."

18

Hope

Before I have a chance to even try to comprehend what Mason could possibly mean by that statement, Guy thrusts the door open. "Park's back. Just thought…" He shrugs as one side of his mouth lifts in an uncomfortable smile. "I thought you might want a heads up."

I sit up slowly because I don't want to hurt Mason's feelings by jumping out of bed, but I can't let Park find me snuggled up to him either. That's not the way he should find out about this. Especially when I don't know what *this* is.

"What do you want me to do?" Mason asks quietly.

Guy lingers in the doorway, I think wanting to know the same thing. I look at him. I beg him with my eyes for help. I already know what he thinks I should do. He wants me to give Mason a chance. A real one. But I feel the fear creeping back inside, warring with the anger and sadness that already resides there.

"You need to tell him," Guy says firmly. I don't know if he means tell Park about Mason, or tell Mason what I want him to do. I just sit on the edge of the bed numbly. The footsteps on the stairs cause them to make the decision for me.

Mason stands up. Guy flicks the light on and moves farther into my room. We look like the three of us are hanging out. Like friends do. Innocently.

I am a coward.

Park walks in and plops down on the bed next to me. His entire side touches mine and he plants a lingering kiss on my cheek. My eyes dart to Mason. He's looking right at me, his face is blank, expression unreadable, but his posture is stiff. He reminds me of the Buckingham Palace guards that aren't allowed to move or show emotion. Somehow that's worse than knowing how he's thinking.

"You smell good," Park says quietly against my ear. "Let's go somewhere. Alone."

I'm frozen. Like time stands still. Park's breath in my ear. Mason's eyes on mine. Guy hovering. Me, with my heart twisting into a knot, battling my stomach for most severe upset.

"Yeah, okay. We need to talk," I say. I never take my eyes off Mason and I see something flash over his face, too quickly to read. I shift my gaze to Guy. "Can you give us a few minutes?"

"We'll be outside. Partying it up with old people," Guy drawls with mock excitement.

"Have fun with that," I say. I wait until they're both out of the room and the door is shut before I turn to face Park. I can tell with one look that he understands "we need to talk" wasn't a pretense for making out. He knows…something.

We sit in silence until he finally clears his throat. "What's going on?"

I just say it. "We need a break."

He looks away, staring at the door for several heartbeats, and then he laughs bitterly. "*We* don't need a break. You do." He leans forward resting his elbows on his knees and shakes his head. "Why? Or should I say who?"

"We had a deal," I point out. My voice cracks and I know I am about two seconds away from freaking out.

"Mm, yeah. Our noncommittal relationship that isn't really a relationship. Except it is. For me. It is." He runs his fingers through his dark hair, letting it fall into his eyes. "So that's it? We're done? Do I even get to know why? What I did wrong?"

My chest is rising and falling quickly as I fight to control my breathing. This is why. This is why I don't do relationships. I don't want to hurt him. I don't want to see that look in his eyes. I glance at my bathroom where my razor awaits me. If I had just done it earlier, maybe it wouldn't be pulling me so strongly right now. I dig my fingers into my hair and yank it. It's not enough, but it helps.

"You didn't do anything wrong," I whisper. "I just need…" I don't know what I need. Space? Change? Freedom?

Mason. I need Mason.

I need him right now.

I stand up and rush to the door, flinging it open so hard it slams into the wall. Park shoots off the bed after me. His arms close around me from behind, hugging me back against his chest. "Calm down," he murmurs, his mouth against my neck. "It's okay. Just calm down."

I shake my head. I can't stop shaking my head. "No…it's…not okay." I can barely breathe. "Get Guy."

Park releases me and I slide down his body to the floor. "I'll be right back."

I watch him leave, listen to his descending footsteps as they explode down the steps. I just hurt him and he still cares about me. I can't even stand that. I can't.

I lay my cheek to my bent knees and concentrate on breathing. And Mason. And breathing. And Mason.

Am I doing the right thing? Is it ever right to hurt someone? But is it right to stay with someone when you want to be with someone else? Which one would hurt more? If my mom had just stayed any of those times, I would have felt better, right? But if she stayed when she felt the need to run, would her blow ups have been worse? Was it secretly a blessing when she left?

It's too much.

Mason. Breathing. Mason. Breathing.

Footsteps.

"Honey," Guy says softly. "It's bad tonight, huh?"

I nod, my head jerking around until I find Mason. Guy follows my gaze and holds out his arm, offering Mason the glorified position of taming the crazy girl. I nod again, needing him to be close. I don't know why I want him. Need him. It just makes it worse. The panic blooms, rising higher, higher. Mason kneels in front of me. I wrap my arms around his neck and breathe my first good breath. Fill my lungs with his scent. Breathe. Mason.

"This is why?" Park says stiffly. I meet his glare over Mason's shoulder, letting him read it in my eyes. I can't bring myself to say it aloud. "I knew it."

Park chuckles darkly. He steps into my room and crosses his arms. He looks seriously pissed and I shrink back. It's not like I think he'd ever hit me, although he looks like he kind of wants to, but I have seen this expression more times than I can count. He's on the verge of lashing out. He wants to hurt me and he's going to do it.

His brows lift, his mouth turns up in a malicious smirk. "Does he know?"

My mind goes blank for half a second, but Park scowls and it hits me. He only has one thing he can use against me. I try to stand up, but my legs won't cooperate. "Don't," I choke. *Please. No. Don't do this to me.*

I draw back from Mason. My body trembles with fear and anger. So much anger.

Park's smile widens. He's standing above me, grinning. Ready to ruin my life. I catch Guy take a step toward him from my peripheral. "Hm-mm. He must not. You think he'll still want you when he finds out?"

"Dude, what the fuck?" Mason spits. "Back the fuck off."

"NO! You back the fuck off. I'm having a conversation with Hope."

"Park, dude, let's go for a walk. You need to calm down," Guy suggests. He takes another step. Park and I are still locked in a staring contest.

His smile drops and I know this is it. It's coming. "Did you know Hope cuts herself?" Just like that. One sentence, so casually spoken, he could have been reading some random fact from a book. One stupid sentence is all it takes for this son of a bitch to crush me.

I push myself up and lunge at him. I get one good hit in before Guy is pulling me away. "You mother fucker," I utter. My voice doesn't shake. Not a single quiver. It's cold and even. "Get the fuck out."

"Check her inner right thigh." Park turns on his heel and glides out of my room, slamming the door behind him. Guy's hands drop and I sink back to the floor.

Nobody moves. Nobody says anything. I'm not sure if anybody even breathes. I don't know if it's seconds or minutes, but then I feel a hand gripping my ankle. I don't understand at first, but I look up and Mason is stretching my leg out. He reaches for the hem of my shorts.

"No." I try to pull away, but he tightens his grip as he takes hold of the fabric. "NO!" I struggle with him. Try to squirm away. Try to kick out at him. He can't see. He can't see. He CAN'T SEE. "NO!"

And then he does see. He gets my shorts up nearly to my hip and shifts my leg. Angry, ugly, pink and red scars stretch across my flesh. Three of them covered with fresh scabs. Nine of them older.

Guy gasps and the room goes still again. I can't look at either of them. I don't want to know what they think. What they see. How could Park be so cruel? How could he tell? How could Mason believe him without even asking me? How could he use his strength against me? Overpower me so he could see my secret. How could Guy let him? How could he look?

I am alone.

Without a word, I slide my shorts back into place. I want to run to my bathroom, lock myself in, and make myself feel better. But Park took that from me.

Mason stands up and stomps around my room, shuffling things on my dresser. He heads into the bathroom. Cabinets bang, unknown objects clatter. Guy sits behind me, his legs on either side of mine, and pulls me against him. He presses his cheek against mine and rocks me from side to side soothingly.

Mason's feet stop in front of me. "Is this what you use?"

I look at his hand. A silver razor blade lying flatly inside his palm. I nod once. He shoves it into the box with the rest and slips it into his pocket.

"Is there anymore?"

I shake my head. Then clear my throat. I almost tell him how sometimes I use scissors. Occasionally tweezers or a knife. Razors are just easier. But I don't tell him. I can at least have that secret.

"There's some in the bathroom I share with Dylan," Guy says. "I don't know about my dad's."

"Do you really think you can just take away the razor blades and I'll magically stop being in pain? Do you think I'll just quit? I can get more. I can do other things. I can…" I stop. I shouldn't be saying this. I should let them believe whatever they want.

"You have to stop, honey. You can't hurt yourself like this anymore."

"Why? You don't even get it, Guy. I've done this since I was twelve years old. I'm not hurting myself. I'm making myself feel better. You can't take this from me. I won't make it."

He sucks in a breath and I realize how he must have taken that. I'm not suicidal. I'm not going to kill myself. I just don't want to go completely insane.

"I don't know what to do," Mason admits. His eyes flick between me and Guy.

I laugh soundlessly. "There's nothing you *can* do."

19

Mason

I haven't seen Hope since Saturday night. She kicked me and Guy out of her bedroom. And when Kellin and I went home Sunday afternoon, she hadn't left the room once. I spent the rest of Sunday alternating between texting and calling her. Both of which she ignored, so I talked to Guy a few times. Apparently she wasn't speaking to him either, but Annie assured him she was all right. Just really pissed off.

I lean against my car, ear buds in place, and wait for her to pull into the school parking lot. It's hard to believe it's only been a week. It's hard to believe it's already been a week. Time has meant nothing lately. Up until yesterday, that is. God, yesterday stretched out so long. It was the first time I haven't seen or spoken to her since the day we met.

I freaking hated it, which is screwed up. The whole thing is screwed up. Hope told me she was damaged. Said she would fuck me up. And she was right. I don't know if she realized she'd fuck me all up just by refusing to talk to me. But she has.

The old Bel Air pulls in and I sigh loudly. Not sure how she'll react today, I head toward the doors to wait for her. She looks like she always does. I don't know why, but I expected her to be different. I don't know. Sad or something.

I move in beside her and brush my shoulder into hers. "Hey."

"Hey." She doesn't look at me.

"How are you?"

"I'm fine."

"What did you do yesterday?"

"Worked on a couple new songs."

"Oh, what about?"

"Just lyrics like I always write."

I stop and take her hand. "Look at me."

"What?" Her voice is neutral and calm and I've learned quickly that isn't a good sign. Her eyes meet mine and she looks at me like she always does only there's something cold in her gaze.

"I don't understand why you won't talk to me," I say. She rolls her eyes and pulls her hand away.

"I am talking to you."

"But you're not saying anything. I called you twenty times yesterday. Text you."

She takes a step closer to me and my stomach tightens in response. I want to pull her against me. I want to hug her and breathe her in. "I'm giving you your out." And then she turns around and walks away. *What the hell?* I don't want an out. She's playing her damn games with me again. Pushing me away. Assuming. Making my choices for me.

Well fuck that.

I push my way through the hallway traffic and grab her arm, guiding her until her back is against the lockers. "I still want you."

Hope's eyes squint into a glare. "I'm not a pity project."

I shake my head at the ceiling. "Park put that shit in your head. I don't pity you. I liked you before I knew. I still like you."

"Then there is something seriously wrong with you." She pushes off the lockers, trying to walk away, and I push her back with my body. She's starting to piss me off.

"There *is* something wrong with me. I freaking know that. And there's something wrong with you. I don't give a shit. I feel good when I'm with you. I want you so bad I can't even think straight. You are one of the coolest girls I've ever met and I want to know you. Stop using bitchiness as a form of self defense and let me in."

"You didn't even ask me. You shoved yourself on me." She takes a breath that shakes her small frame. "You held me down and looked. You pulled up my shorts." She's struggling to speak now and I'm staring at her in shock. A cold shiver runs over me as dread sets in. I didn't mean it to be like that. I wasn't trying to hurt her or scare her. I didn't think. Maybe one of the biggest, most important pieces of the Hope puzzle is revealed in her frantic eyes.

Who made her like this? What happened to her?

"Hope..." I don't know what to say.

She shoves me away. "You should have trusted me."

I laugh dryly at that. "Maybe I shouldn't have handled it the way I did, but don't say I should've trusted you." I lean my face close to her ear. "Your point is moot since you are, in fact, a cutter."

"I hate you," she spits and propels herself off the wall past me. I let her go this time because I can't believe she said that. At the same time, I know I deserve it. I thrust my fist into the locker. The clang of flesh against metal rings throughout the hall. People turn to gawk at me. I kind of want to tell them to fuck off, but instead, I do an about face and go to class.

****

I walk into Biology fourth period and Hope is already sitting at a table. Her feet are resting on the chair in front of her. My chair, though she wouldn't know that since she hasn't been in school since I started.

I place a box of grape Nerds on top of the table and slide it toward her slowly. Her eyes narrow on the candy before she swipes it onto the floor. Twisting her lips in disgust, she opens her book and adamantly ignores me.

I scoop up the candy and shove it in my backpack. Message received loud and clear. Her feet drop as I reach for my chair. I sit sideways and clear my throat.

"Hey," I say.

Besides the stiffening of her shoulders, Hope makes no indication she hears me. "Hope," I say louder. "I know you're pissed, but—"

She looks up quickly, her gaze sharp enough to slice me in half. "Don't."

I freeze. Half of me is relieved that she's showing some kind of emotion, even if it's anger. The other half hates that it's directed at me. "I screwed up," I say. "I get it, all right?"

Both brows rise and she scoffs at me. Her voice is low when she speaks. "You don't get shit, Mason. That's the point."

"I would if you talked to me," I fire back.

She shakes her head. "Just leave me alone."

But I don't want to leave her alone. I want to make her see that I wasn't trying to hurt her. I want her to understand that I would *never* hurt her. I open my mouth to tell her, but she shoves her chair back, plucks her book bag from the back and strolls out the door just as the bell rings.

The girl beside me smiles and scoots her seat closer to mine. I force my own smile before fixing my eyes on the door, waiting for Hope to come back.

She doesn't.

20
Hope

I'm shaking when I close myself in the bathroom. It took everything in me not to hit Mason with my book bag.

I can't believe I actually allowed myself to feel anything for him. I told him things. I got close to him. I know better than that. I trusted him.

I trusted him.

Maybe it's my stupidity that's bothering me most.

My legs go weak and I sit heavily on the disgusting floor. It reeks in here, like urine, cleanser, and about fifteen different perfume scents. I don't want to be here, but I can't go back in that classroom and stare at the back of his head.

Like a ten year old with a diary, I pour my feelings out onto the pages of my notebook in the form of lyrics. When the bell finally rings, I gladly pack up my things and go to lunch. Until I look at my usual table. My stomach twists when Mason's eyes meet mine from across the room. Guy follows his gaze back to me and I turn around, walking out the way I came in.

I can't hide forever. But I'm not ready to deal with either one of them yet.

So I skip Art, too.

By the time I get home, I'm in a hellish mood. Guy bringing the Patel brothers to the house doesn't help.

"We need to talk," Mason says as I retreat upon his arrival.

I keep walking and when he lifts his hand like he's going to grab my arm, I flinch away from him so quickly I bang my elbow on the wall. There is nothing humorous about hitting your funny bone. "Damn it," I hiss, clutching my pounding arm.

"Jesus, Hope." His eyes are wide, his cheeks pink. "I'm not going to *hurt* you."

I shudder at his words and I don't know if it's because I don't believe him or because he says it so softly, so sincerely, I want to believe him.

So I say the only thing that I am sure of. "You already have." His eyes flash and something passes over his face that makes my heart skip a beat. But he lets me go without another word.

~***~

The whole week has been the same. I get to Biology before Mason. He relentlessly sets candy on my table each day. He's annoyingly persistent. He doesn't say a word, just places it gently in front of me and takes his seat. I stopped slapping it to the floor yesterday—after I got sick of feeling bad for being so mean. But I'm not ready to be nice yet, either, so I still ignore his apology in the form of sweet snacks. Even when I really don't want to. Skipping lunch is getting to me. Every day, I sit in the library, my stomach growling, wishing I would have accepted whatever candy he brought me that day.

Today is especially difficult because I was running late this morning and skipped breakfast. That Snickers bar is just sitting there, staring at me, and taunting me with its chocolaty goodness.

If I pick it up and eat it, then he'll take that as forgiveness. He'll smile smugly and start talking to me.

I do not miss his smile. I do not miss his voice or the way it sounds when he's speaking just to me, all soft and low. And I definitely do not have a crazy attraction to him.

I find myself reliving the night of the party. The hours before everything went to shit. The times he kissed me. What's messed up is when I think about the way he grabbed a hold of my leg, I have a mini meltdown, but the second my mind flips back to that first kiss, I am not at all repulsed. I find myself wanting to do it again. Thinking I should just explain why I freaked out and exonerate him.

I have *got* to remember to pack a lunch tomorrow. My hunger is obviously getting to me.

Carly Reeves leans into Mason's arm, pretending she doesn't understand the assignment. I stifle an eye roll. She's a straight A student. I hate when girls dumb themselves down for a guy.

If I'm being honest with myself, I guess I kind of hate her because Mason didn't tear her heart apart. He's looking at her with those stupid green eyes that I do not miss, trying to explain it in a way he thinks she'll comprehend. His dimple peeks at me three times before I look away.

My foot bounces as I glare at the clock. I swear the second hand just moved backward.

Carly giggles at something Mason says and I cringe. I hate when girls giggle like toddlers. I need out of here before I laugh at her and draw attention to the fact that I've been taking in their whole interaction.

The moment the bell rings, I'm out of my seat and out the door.

Art is worse than Biology because I have to sit right beside him. I have to sit here, smelling Mason's scent that's all clean boy and laundry detergent. I have to feel the warmth coming off his body that is much closer than it needs to be. I have to hear every single time he asks a question, or clears his throat, or breathes.

I feel him steal glances, but I keep my eyes to my side of the table.

He doesn't bring me candy in this class, but today he pulls a sandwich from his backpack and holds it out to me.

"Peanut butter and chocolate frosting," he says quietly. He smiles and I do not melt a little. "I thought you might be hungry since you keep skipping lunch." When I just look at him, he sighs and sets it in front of me. "I'll sit somewhere else from now on. You don't need to skip lunch to avoid me."

I don't pick up the sandwich, but I do stare at it until it blurs out and I'm not really seeing anything. Damn him for being so sweet and making me feel like shit for being upset with him.

I feel myself getting angry. Bitchiness is always my go-to place when I'm confused about the emotions whirling inside. I shouldn't feel guilty over this. He should. He's the one that pulled my shorts up. He grabbed me when the last thing I wanted was to be touched. He made me feel twelve years old again. He made me feel things I never want to feel again.

I pick up the sandwich and his eyes absorb my movement with bright anticipation. "I didn't ask you to make me a sandwich and I didn't ask you to sit somewhere else at lunch." I drop it on top of the still-life he's working on. "Just like I didn't ask you to man handle me in my bedroom."

He clenches his jaw like he's pissed off, but he's staring at me like I kicked his puppy. "I don't know how to make you believe I'm sorry. I fucked up. I made a huge mistake. Again. I know that, but I also know there is way more to what happened than you're telling. I was freaked out and I wasn't thinking clearly, but I would never purposely hurt you, Hope. Ever. I didn't even kiss you until you asked me to. I would never…" He trails off and shakes his head. Hurt etching his features, he leaves his work, with the sandwich still on it, and says something to the teacher before walking out.

Sometimes watching someone walk away from you sucks pretty badly.

~***~

"What? No Mason today?" I ask Guy sarcastically when he tromps through the front door.

He pauses, tossing his books on the counter. "No. He just dropped me off. He didn't feel comfortable coming in." He grabs a bottle of water from the fridge and kicks the door shut with his foot. "Besides, we need to have a talk. Don't you think?"

"No," I say immediately. We stare at one another, neither of us willing to give in. I hear the bus pull up out front and when the door opens, I try to use the distraction to sneak up to my room.

Guy's on my heels, stopping my door from closing in his face. "You aren't the only one who gets to be mad."

I feel my eyebrows scrunch in annoyance. "What do you have to be mad about? You didn't have your best friend stand there and do nothing while you were mulled."

He rolls his eyes. "You were not mulled, first of all. And second of all, you've been *marring* yourself for who knows how long and hiding it from me. How is there even a question as to why I'd be mad?"

I don't respond, mostly because I'm shocked and don't know what to say. In retrospect, it makes sense. Of course he'd be pissed that I've been keeping secrets from him and even more pissed that I'm cutting. But I'm still pissed too, and I'm selfish, so my anger trumps his.

"I waited all weekend for you to talk to me. Then I waited all week. You had no intentions of explaining anything to me. Did you?"

I say nothing.

"I looked some stuff up about self-injury. You're not doing it for fun." He lowers himself to my bed and rests his elbows on his knees. His blonde hair falls across his face as he stares at the floor.

"I know why you do it. What I don't understand is why you couldn't trust me with it."

"You would have tried to stop me," I whisper, my voice hoarse with emotion.

He lifts his head and regards me sadly. "Of course I would have tried to stop you, but I would've helped you, too."

"Maybe I don't want to be stopped. Maybe I don't want help."

He winces. "Maybe not yet, but you can't do this forever." I bite down on the inside of my cheek because just the thought of never doing it again scares the shit out of me. Guy knows me too well. "It might be scary now, but there will come a day that you'll be ready to quit. You'll need help. From what I read, it's pretty hard to do on your own."

"Don't act like you understand just because you spent twenty minutes on Wikipedia," I say coolly.

"I've spent *hours, daily*, on multiple sites. There's this one where you can talk to other people that cut. People that went through something similar to you."

I don't want him bringing *that* up. "I'm not going to do some group therapy online chat."

"You don't have to. I didn't…I didn't say you had to do it. I just want you to know it's an option. There's help, too. Counseling. Specialists. And I'll be there for you."

"I'm not ready."

"That's okay," he says carefully. "When you are ready. *But you can't do it anymore.*"

"You can't stop me," I say defiantly because the way his voice quivered makes me want to cry.

"I'm not trying to fight with you, Hope. I'm trying to help. What would you do if it were me?"

I don't know. I can't even imagine. "I'd sit beside you and do it with you."

Guy narrows his eyes. "Fine. Let's go." He stands up and I take a step back.

"What?"

"Show me how it's done. I'll cut with you and you can watch me." He motions at me to hurry up.

"Don't patronize me."

"If it's the only way to get through to you, I'll do it. Maybe if you see me slicing into my flesh something will click up here." He points to his temple. "Maybe if you see the scars that are left on my legs it will make you as sick as it makes me."

"I'm sorry you're so disgusted by me. Maybe you shouldn't have looked when Mason took it upon himself to hold me down and show off my repulsive disfigurement."

He shakes his head. "Get over yourself. I meant I've been sick with worry over you. What would happen if you went too deep or it got infected? I don't want to lose you."

I close my eyes. "You aren't going to lose me."

"You don't know that," he says quietly, voice cracking.

"You can't promise me I'll never lose you, either. Anything could happen."

"Yeah, but I'm not walking around looking for ways to end my life."

"Neither am I," I shout. "I know it's fucked up to cut myself. I realize there are risks, too. I'm always careful. It's not like I do it every day and I am not trying to kill myself." I take a deep breath and lower my voice. "If it makes you feel better, I haven't done it since Mason stole my razors."

"It does, actually." He sweeps his hands over his face. "Can you at least try to come to me first from now on? Talk to me before you hurt yourself?"

"No. I won't promise that." I move toward him. "Look, I do come to you sometimes, but there are times when you can't help."

His face pales. I know what he heard was me telling him he's not enough.

"Then promise me you'll at least look at the website I found." He hurries on before I can respond. "You don't have to do anything. Just look at it." Tears make his eyes shine and I can't breathe. "Just give me something, Hope, because I feel like I'm drowning.

Pretend roles are reversed and you know I'm hurting myself. What would you want me to do?"

"I'll look at the site," I promise.

"I'll take what I can get."

"You aren't going to tell anyone, are you?" I have to ask. I trusted Park and that didn't work out so well.

He stares at me, an unsatisfied expression on his face. "I can't promise you that anymore than you can promise me you'll stop cutting." He tugs on my hand, pulling me into a hug. "I won't say anything unless I feel like I have to."

I nod against his chest. "I'll take what I can get," I mimic him.

"Don't keep shit from me anymore."

I nod again.

"I love you, craziness and all."

I huff out a surprised laugh. "Love you too. Pushiness and all."

He releases me and steps back. "You should talk to Mason."

"One step at a time, dude."

He chuckles and shrugs. "He's a good person. And he cares about you. The dude has been seriously mopey since you've stopped talking to him. Just think about it."

"Are you talking to Park?"

Guy clears his throat. "Uh, no." I arch a brow. "He's supposed to be my best friend and he didn't tell me what you were doing. That's fucked up on a whole different level."

I don't say anything else because I'm not going to try to talk Guy into forgiving Park. That's his business and I'm still mad as hell at Park anyway. But I want him to realize he shouldn't be telling me to do something he isn't willing to do.

"I will though. Once he suffers long enough to know not to pull that shit again."

I smirk, liking the sound of that. "That's exactly what I'm doing with Mason."

21

Mason

I stayed away from Hope's house all weekend and it freaking sucked. I spent my time lying around watching made-for-TV movies with Mom and playing video games with Kellin. Mom was ecstatic yesterday when she got the whole day with us. I was miserable, not that I don't like hanging out with her, but there is only so much Lifetime a guy can take. And I just missed Hope.

She has been on my mind way more than is considered healthy. I text Guy probably fifty times to check on her. He was cool about it, but I'm expecting harassment charges to be pressed any moment.

When I get to school I automatically look for her car. It's habit now. And though I know she isn't going to acknowledge me, I wait by the doors for her. It's fucking pathetic, standing there like a dog, hoping she'll throw me a bone and look in my direction.

I do it anyways.

Today I'm trying something new. I've given her space. I've even kept my mouth shut for the most part. That didn't work.

I don't hide it as I watch her walk up the steps toward me. Her eyes meet mine and I hold them, putting everything I'm thinking into that gaze. At least I hope that's what I'm doing. I hope I don't look like some creepy, psycho, stalker.

Her cheeks turn pink and she drops her eyes. I chuckle lowly as she passes. Yeah, I think I may have played that right.

****

In Biology I place the daily denied candy on her table. Usually I sit down and mind my own business. This time I wait until she looks up at me and then I smile at her.

"Hey, Hope," I say softly.

"Hi, Mason."

I didn't expect that and it throws me off. "Did you just talk to me?" I know I sound shocked, but…I am.

She laughs quietly. "Yeah. I said hi."

"Hi." *Hi?* I need my ass kicked. *Talk to her, dumbass*. I sit down and turn sideways in my seat. "How are you?"

"Better. I had a good weekend."

What does that mean? I'm glad she had a good weekend, but is it because I left her alone? Are she and Park back together? "What'd you do?" I ask. God, I sound like a douche bag.

She laughs again and my stomach tightens in response. "Not much. Watched TV, played Candy Land like forty-four times."

"Even your games involve candy?"

She smiles, but doesn't answer because Mr. Roberts starts class. I'm happy as hell the rest of class until she slips out as soon as the bell rings. The candy I brought her still sitting on the table.

When I get to lunch I sit with my locker groupies. They're more than happy to oblige since I'm not blowing them off for once. I'm barely listening to them as I watch the doors.

Hope never shows and by the time I get to Art, I'm a little irritated. How long is she going to make me suffer? Can't she kick me in the balls and forgive me. I think I'll suggest it to her.

Note to self: Never piss Hope off again.

"You can come back to the lunchroom," I start as soon as I sit down. "I moved tables."

She tucks a lock of hair behind her ear and the fine strands slip right back into her face. I fist my hand in order to restrain myself from fixing it. "I told you not to worry about moving. I'm not avoiding the cafeteria just because of you." Her eyes flick over my face and settle on my mouth. I swallow with difficulty as she licks her lips. She's trying to kill me.

"Ah, but I'm part of it."

She shrugs, smirking. "You were. I'm trying to get over it."

I don't fight the grin, but I don't push my luck either. I keep my mouth shut and work on my project.

****

Kellin made me late this morning and I missed Hope before school started. I nearly run to Biology in my hurry to see her. I drop a pack of Skittles in front of her.

Her gaze lowers to the candy and she pushes herself up straighter, dropping her feet from my chair. I chose this particular candy purposely; wanting to remind her of that moment she decided she liked me. I see it in her eyes—she's thinking about it as she reluctantly tears the package open and puts one in her mouth. A purple one. She doesn't thank me or even acknowledge me, but it's a start.

I take my seat and sigh. I swear her eyes are burning a hole in the back of my head. Good. I turn around and catch her gaze. "Do you have an extra pencil I can borrow?" I have about ten pencils in my backpack, but it's a reasonable excuse to talk to her.

She places another purple Skittle on her tongue, holding my gaze. "Yeah." She rolls her pencil across the table to me.

"Thanks," I say and turn back around.

The pencil smells like raspberry lotion. I have absolutely no intentions of returning it now. Not when a part of her is so clearly on it. I hold it under my nose knowing I look stupid as hell, but I don't give a shit. The girl next to me glances over and giggles. Yeah, she giggles. I can't freaking stand gigglers. I just look at her.

"Are you smelling your pencil?" she asks with another annoying giggle.

"It smells like raspberries," I say loud enough for Hope to hear me.

"Let me smell," the girl, Carly, I think, says. She moves as if to take it and I pull back. And then I realize I'm protecting a *pencil*. Seriously? I have got issues. And Hope thinks she's fucked up? She cuts herself because it's her way of dealing with the messed up shit she went through when she was a little kid. All things considered, I don't think that's all too crazy. But sitting here sniffing a pencil, refusing to share it as if this girl could alter the scent somehow, that's just...insane.

Carly scrunches her brows, obviously thinking the same damn thing. I'm still not willing to share, though. She rolls her eyes and turns her attention to the front of class. "Whatever then."

Hope snorts behind me and I smile. A yellow Skittle lands on my book in front of me and I slap my hand down on it before it can roll away. I glance back at her as I pop it into my mouth. She leans forward, so I lean back.

"It's black raspberry vanilla," she says quietly.

I grin wider. "I like it."

"I'll remember that," she states, and the tone of her voice sends a pleasant chill down my back. I let my head fall back on her table and stare up at her. She puts a Skittle in my mouth and pushes my head away. When I sit up, I catch another eye roll from Carly. I smile at her, chewing on what I assume is Hope's peace offering, or at least acceptance of mine. Finally.

"Are you, like, with her?"

My smile falters and I raise an eyebrow. "What?"

Carly huffs and rolls her eyes yet again. "Are you dating Hope Love?"

I glance over my shoulder. Hope's head is down as she scribbles in her notebook, but I'm fairly certain she heard the question. I look back at Carly. "No, but I'm working really hard on it," I admit. "First I have to get her to forgive me for being an asshole."

Carly's eyes go wide in surprise, then disgust. And I have never, ever wanted to hit a girl, but I kind of want to at least trip this one. "Gr-oss."

I shrug my shoulders. "Actually, she's delicious, but I have a very selective taste pallet." And clearly I lose Carly. English is apparently a difficult language for her to understand. Her eyes squint in confusion and Hope snorts again. I almost want to thank Carly for being such a pretentious bitch, but Mr. Roberts walks into the room and begins class. Doesn't matter. I got Hope to laugh twice and very possibly forgive me.

Best day in over a week.

22

Hope

Carly Reeves is a bitch.

I want to punch her in her stupid face. I would do it too if it weren't for the little detail that I just came back to school last week. Of course, if she glares at me over her bony shoulder one more time, I don't think it will matter much to me.

Mason shifts in his seat, blocking my view of Carly. Purposely, I'm sure. I throw another Skittle at him. It hits him in the head and he turns around to look at me. That adorable dimple is out and I bite down on my lip. I'm still mad at him for how he acted at Alec's party, but he was right. How can I be mad at him for not trusting me when I obviously don't deserve it? And to be completely honest, I'm actually kind of glad he knows my secret. We are definitely having a discussion about his overpowering me. I don't like that shit and I won't put up with it.

His eyes focus on my mouth, take in the way I'm biting my lip, and like he knows what I'm thinking, he licks his own lips slowly. I drop dead. Well, not really, but damn. Our first kiss flashes in my mind and I want to do it again. Like right now.

He turns back, trying to pay attention, I guess. I keep staring at him. His dark hair is shiny. Remembering how it felt to run my fingers through it… I clear my throat to cover the sound I involuntarily make. Why am I lusting over him in the middle of Biology? I'm mad at him. I mean, I think I am. I was.

He leans back and stretches his arms over his head and my eyes run over his nicely shaped, sun-kissed arms. A piece of paper falls from his fingers right in front of me. He did not just do the 90's stretch and note drop. I'm smiling. He is so cheesy.

I unfold the paper and feel my cheeks rise higher.

I HOPE I DON'T PISS YOU OFF MORE, BUT I'M GOING TO FAIL THIS CLASS. AFTER YOU TORTURED ME FOR OVER A WEEK, ALL I CAN THINK ABOUT IS HOW CLOSE YOU ARE AND HOW MUCH I WANT YOU TO ASK ME TO KISS YOU AGAIN. PLEASE TELL ME THAT WILL HAPPEN EVENTUALLY.

I don't write him back. Instead, I tuck the note into my book—I'm keeping that shit. He doesn't need confirmation that we're in the same state of mind. I shove a handful of candy in my mouth and attempt to listen to the lecture.

~***~

I went to the cafeteria yesterday. Mason sat at Bailey Grove's table with Annie and the other cheerleaders. I wasn't exactly jealous. I was just—jealous. Dear Buddha, I was so ridiculously jealous and I had no idea how to handle it.

I still don't. All I do know is that I miss him, and I can't stop thinking about him. Guy's talking to Park again like nothing ever happened. Maybe I should take a cue from him.

Maybe.

Like yesterday, Biology is filled with playful flirting. He makes it way too difficult to concentrate in this class.

The bell finally rings and I put my things in my backpack. Mason does the same before looking back at me. "Can I sit with you at lunch?" He says it carefully, like he's afraid of spooking me.

"Abandoning your pom-poms already?" He quirks a brow and I laugh. "It's your table too."

"I wasn't sure if you wanted me there since I told you I'd move."

I shoulder my bag. "I want you there." He smiles at me, but it falls as his eyes lower to my lips.

I usher us into the hallway and head toward my locker. Mason follows, stopping beside me as I dump what I can. "Are we all right?"

My hand pauses on my Algebra book. "Yeah," I say. "Pretty much. But I swear to whatever god you believe in, if you ever use your superior strength on me again, I will cut off your nuts." His eyebrows rise, hiding under his hair. "And I obviously don't want you to tell anybody about, you know, the thing." I shake my head and sigh. "Not that that means anything. Park wasn't supposed to tell and we know how that ended."

"I'm not Park," Mason says firmly. "I won't do that shit to you. And I'm sorry. I didn't mean to use my super strength against you."

"Superior strength," I correct.

"Potato, patato." He grins at me for a second before getting serious again. "I wouldn't ever hurt you. Not physically and not on purpose. I need you to know that. You can trust me."

"I want to," I say. I want to so badly.

He smiles and that urge to kiss him is back and it's strong. The bell rings, but I'm motionless, caught in his gaze. Mason knows my secret. He knows one of worst things about me and he's still here.

I slip my hand behind his neck and pull him into me. He leans in easily and our lips meet. I nearly sigh into his mouth. It feels so good. He presses against me gently, a soft murmur sounding in his throat. I drop whatever book I was holding and grip him with both hands, arching my body into his.

"Mm. Hope," he utters against my mouth. I pull back and look at him, gasping for air. "I really like the way you forgive me. We don't need to go to lunch. Do we?"

I touch my fingertips to my lips. "I don't need to eat," I say softly. Mason leans slowly toward me again.

"Mason." He and I both flinch at the intrusive voice. "Are you going to sit with us today?" Bailey Grove. Ugh. I hate the way she says his name and the way she looks at him. Like he's her property. Bailey is the embodiment of evil, popular cheerleader. I don't know how Annie can stand her. She's hated me from the moment I started school here. The feeling is mutual, but only because she decided I was the equivalent of gum stuck to the bottom of her shoe.

Bailey flips her strawberry blonde hair over her shoulder and smiles up at Mason. I bend and pluck up my book, shoving it into my locker. I suddenly have an overwhelming desire to not be in the general vicinity.

"Uh, no, thanks," Mason says slowly. "I'm sitting with Hope and Guy."

Bailey's eyes slide over to me as if just now noticing I'm here. She arches one thin brow and looks me up and down. "Oh." Her nose scrunches up like she smells something bad and she blinks. Once. Twice. Three times.

I slam my locker door.

"Tomorrow, then," she says, turning her devouring gaze on Mason.

He shakes his head, smiling apologetically. "They have me all week. Sorry. I'll see you later." He pulls me toward the cafeteria and I look back in time to catch the appalled expression on her face. I can't help it, I laugh, which isn't the smartest thing to do.

Bailey glares venomously at me. I stop walking and turn all the way around. Mason gives me a quizzical glance before following my line of sight. "Do you have something to say to me?" I ask.

"Nope," Bailey says through her teeth. "I don't associate with trash." I glower back at her. *She did not just call me trash.*

"Did you just call her trash?" Mason grinds out. He marches deliberately back to her. "People that sling insults are trash. I don't know what made you such an ugly person, but trying to hurt people isn't going to make you any prettier."

"I am *not* ugly," Bailey seethes.

"Oh, trust me. You are."

"Fuck you, Mason! You don't know me!"

He turns around and stalks away. "I'm lucky like that," he throws over his shoulder. He pulls me along and all I can do is grin stupidly at him. Give the man another ten—no—twenty cool points.

"I really wish I could've met your dad," I say. Some people might not be so quick to jump to another's defense after their dad was killed for doing just that, but not him.

Mason tilts his head, eyebrows drawn together. "I do too."

"You turned out to be a pretty amazing person." He stops abruptly and hauls me into a hug.

"Jesus, Hope." He squeezes me to the point I'm having trouble breathing. "*You're* amazing. That girl is a stupid bitch. You know that, right?"

I laugh against his chest. “Yeah, I recognize a bitch when I see one.”

“Asshole,” Bailey spits as she glides past and all but rips the cafeteria doors off the hinges.

“You’re not an asshole,” I whisper.

“You’re not trash.”

“I’m sorry I said I hated you. I don’t. I actually like you a lot,” I confess.

“I know. I like you too. A lot.”

“I know.”

“I’m going to kiss you again.”

I smile. “I know.” And then he does.

~***~

Lunch is almost back to normal. Park still doesn’t sit with us. He’s two tables over with some guys that attend our shows. We make eye contact as soon as I take my seat. And just like yesterday, I look away first because honestly, I can’t stomach to look at him. Shifting my body, I open my oatmeal cream pie and tear pieces off.

“Did you get me one?” Chase asks.

I pause, sucking cream off my thumb. “Um…”

Chase rolls his eyes dramatically, sighing loudly. "I always get one for you when I buy one for myself. *Always*."

"I'm…sorry…? I didn't know we had some agreement to purchase snack pies for each other," I say exasperated.

"No, not an agreement. An *understanding*. Just like Guy always gets extra fries for you to steal, and Mason always feeds your candy habit, and Park always keeps you in chocolate milk. We get one another cream pies!"

"Cheese and rice, Chase. Fine! I will go get you a damn oatmeal freaking pie!" Mason and Guy laugh like this is the funniest thing ever. *Whatever*. I shove my chair back and stomp off to the lunch line. Again. *Freaking baby*. I grab the stupid pie, and then grab another one just in case. I don't want to piss anyone else off who believes we have some sort of silent snack arrangement.

"You forgot Chase's cream pie?" Park asks suddenly beside me. My body stills.

"Don't talk to me," I mutter.

"I'm sorry. I feel like shit," he says anyway.

I whip around to face him. "You should. I can't believe you did that to me. We were friends before we were... I never would betray you like that." I turn away and move up in line.

"I know," he sighs. "I'm a dick. If I could take it back, I would."

"You can't. That's the thing. You put it out there and now it's too late." I stare down at my shoes. My lace is coming untied, part of it dragging on the floor. "I don't think I can forgive you."

"You broke my heart." My head snaps up. He smiles at me sadly. "I cared about you. I *care* about you. I wanted to be with you, really be with you. And then Mason shows up and you start acting weird. Ignoring me. It's no excuse, but when I saw him hugging you…" He rubs his hand over his face. "He was calming down your panic attack. I've never seen anyone do that, but Guy. *I* could never do that. It fucking killed me to see some douche bag you've known for an hour able to do that for you. I wanted to hurt him. I wanted to hurt you. So I said the only thing I knew would break you as much as you broke me."

"I'm sorry I hurt you. I'm so sorry for that. I tried to make it clear from the beginning that I wasn't ready for a serious relationship." I close my eyes. "You were the only person that knew about me. The *only one*. You were special. Now I can't stand you."

23
Mason

"Not to sound like a complete jerk, but why does the majority of the female population at school dislike you so much?" I ask Hope as I drop beside her on the couch. It's something I picked up on my first day and has become more apparent now that she's been back from her suspension. Girls steer clear of her for some reason. And when they have to be around her, they treat her as if she isn't even there, or act bitchy like Bailey. I can't fathom it because I'm completely drawn to her. She's pretty, funny, and passionate about music. I don't get it.

She shrugs. "I don't have a clue. They just always have."

Guy hands us Popsicles and falls beside me. "That's because all the girls know their dickhead, jock boyfriends are thinking about you while they're with them." He slides the orange Popsicle into his mouth and wiggles his brows.

"You're disgusting," Hope groans.

"Yeah, I don't want to hear that shit," I state dryly. God I hope that isn't true. I know she isn't my girlfriend, but I'd like her to be. Besides, she is a girl and she is my friend. I just don't want guys thinking about her like that. "What I don't get is how they all seem to like Annie, and Annie likes you. So why don't they? Girls like that usually follow the leader."

"Honestly?" Hope blows at the hair in her face. "I don't care. I don't like them either, so it's all good."

"I told you why," Guy says. He licks dripping juice from his knuckle. "They're jealous."

"Yeah, of my rainbow hair, bad grades, and lack of friends."

"No, smartass," Guy sighs. He sits up and jabs his frozen orange treat at Hope. "They are jealous that you draw the attention of every guy at our school, including the jock assholes that date the cheerleaders and act like you're a freak. All the straight dudes think you're hot. I should know, they tell me all the time." He rolls his eyes. "'Hey, Guy, how can you be gay when you live with that?' Or my favorite, 'You should give Hope a try. If anyone can turn you straight, it'd be her.'" He licks the Popsicle before pointing it at her again. "That came from Christian Dunkin right before he proceeded to ask me where my dress was. Like I'd wear a stupid ass dress. I'm gay, not a cross dresser." He leans back and continues to eat pensively.

Hope laughs quietly. "Was that before or after I kicked him in the testicles?"

He cocks his head to the side. "That was today in gym class."

She has no reaction to this other than the lift of her eyebrows. She opens her Popsicle and puts it in her mouth. But it pisses me off. I can't stand the thought of people talking about her that way, even if she has the star role in all my fantasies now. I know how guys think and I know how they act with their friends. I can guarantee Hope is the talk of the locker room.

"I'm pretty sure you just made him that much more interested in you," Guy explains. "Some guys like it rough." He grins at Hope. "I know I do."

"Okay, I'm sorry I asked," I say before taking a bite.

"Way too much information, Guy. Seriously." Hope shakes her head, laughing. "So what are we doing today?"

"I got plans," Guy says.

"What? With who?"

He smiles. "With Samuel. I'm meeting him for a movie."

"That dude you Skype with all the time?" Guy nods excitedly. "Ew. You aren't seeing a movie. You're hooking up with him in a movie theater. What is your obsession with public oral sex?"

I raise a brow. Yeah, too much info, for real. Guy chuckles. "Well you have seen him, right?"

"Yes, and he is cute, but can't he come here, or you there?"

"You are totally asking me to make a joke with that statement," I say.

Guy laughs. "Don't worry Hope; I'll make sure he comes lots of places."

I try to suppress my amusement, but I can't help the way my mouth turns up. I discreetly flip my hand out and Guy gives me five.

"Ugh. I do not need to hear about your sex life. Just make sure you at least sit in the back this time." After a moment of thought, she adds. "And tell him I said hi. I feel like I know him after all that I've seen of him." And I'm not sure I even want to know the situation in which she saw so much of Guy's play toy.

"Seeing someone's penis doesn't make him your best friend," Guy declares.

"Oh, man," she sighs. "I've been making friends incorrectly this whole time."

He tips the Popsicle stick at her. "And that's why all the girls at school hate you."

"This feels like the longest joke ever," I say, laughing.

Guy stands up and bends at the waist, bowing. "That is what you call wit."

"Not what I call it," Hope murmurs.

"See? Wit." Guy musses her hair as he walks past. "I'm jumping in the shower."

"Wait. How are you meeting him?" Hope asks. "Who's taking you?"

"Chase. He's meeting some girl at the mall."

I watch Guy disappear around the corner and turn to Hope. "So, why doesn't he drive?"

She grins, tucking hair behind her ear. "I'm not supposed to talk about it. Let's just say there was a very traumatic incident involving Guy, Alec's car, and a very dead raccoon his first time behind the wheel."

"Oh," I utter.

"Yeah. Never speak of it," she warns seriously, but her eyes are bright with amusement and she winks at me.

"Probably best if I don't make raccoon references either."

"Mm, probably."

"Where'd Kellin and Misty go?" I ask, just now noticing they aren't at the kitchen table.

"They went outside with Dill Weed. Probably playing basketball."

"So, we're alone?"

She smiles at me, her lashes dropping, hooding her eyes. "Yep."

"Want to go to a movie?" She looks up at me, glowering and I laugh. "Kidding. Unless you want to. To see a movie. For real, I mean."

"I'm not sure if you're asking me out or asking for oral sex."

Uh... I seriously was joking up until her perfect lips formed the words oral sex while looking directly at me. My dick twitches against my pants with the thought and I clear my throat, shifting on the couch. *Focus*. "I'm trying to ask you out, just not very well. Do you want to go do something? The two of us? Like a date?"

"*Like* a date?" She obviously finds this humorous.

I run my fingers through my hair. It drops back into my eyes and she brushes it aside with the tips of her fingers. *God that feels good*. I catch her hand and hold it. "Will you go on a date with me?"

Hope grins and twines her fingers with mine. "Yes. When?"

Okay. She said yes. I feel like an idiot because I know I'm smiling manically, but I can't help it. "Mom's off on Sundays. Unless I can find someplace for Kellin to go. He hangs out with the neighbor sometimes. That might work. I'll figure something out."

"He could stay here and hang out with Misty. Guy could keep an eye on them. Not tonight, obviously, but whenever."

"That would work," I agree. "I'll set it up."

"All right. So what do you want to do now?"

I gaze at her. I cannot answer that question. I'm completely content just sitting on the couch with her, but I also want to taste the cherry on her lips that's turned her mouth red. But it doesn't stop there. I want to devour Hope. All of her. I want to make her mine. I want to kiss the scars on her thigh. I want...

I bend my head to hers, but I don't kiss her. I want her to do it, like she did at school. I want to know she wants me like I want her. That I invade her thoughts and fantasies even half as much as she does mine.

"I want you to be with me," I say, my lips brushing hers lightly as I talk. "Just me. Like your boyfriend."

Hope's lips form a smile beneath mine. "*Like* my boyfriend?"

Now I smile, nodding. "Or, you know, your boyfriend." I run my palms down her sides.

She shivers and pushes her mouth against mine, kissing me gently. *Finally*. I growl as she deepens the kiss, my fingers gripping her ribs. I must tickle her because she squirms and pulls away. "No," I complain. "Come back."

She moves closer, but she doesn't kiss me. She stares up at me. Her eyes are so pretty. Bright and blue, framed in those long, dark lashes.

"What would that involve?" she asks quietly in her whispery voice she reserves for the scary or important conversations. "Being your girlfriend."

Holy shit. She's considering it. I didn't think she'd go for it. We haven't even had our first date yet. I don't bother to hide exactly how happy that makes me. I grin at her. "Well, I guess it would be like it is now, except, everyone would know that I'm yours." I let my gaze pass over her face, suddenly afraid how she'll take my next words. "And that you're mine. I know how you feel about the whole relationship thing, but I want to commit to you. Which is so—it's not normal for me. But I like you and I only want you. And I want everyone to know it."

"That sounds like ownership," she says slowly. Unsure.

I shake my head and sit forward. "Kind of. I don't mean I own you. You would be *my* girlfriend. Nobody else's. I wouldn't own *you*. Just like...your..." I trail off because I can't say love. I haven't told her how strongly I feel for her. That would scare her off for sure. And I definitely am not assuming that she could love me already. I'm fully aware of how strange this all is.

"Heart?"

Our eyes lock and I can't breathe. That's so close to the same thing. "Yes."

Hope tugs on my shirt sleeve, pulling me toward her. "Okay," she whispers just before her lips meet mine.

And I'm the happiest I've been in six years. Maybe ever.

I can't believe she said okay. I pull back, needing to verify. "Okay? You want to be my girlfriend?"

"Yes," she says. She looks down at her hands. I notice they're shaking. Closing one hand over hers, I pull her chin up with my other.

"I won't push this if it's not what you want."

"I tried the no commitment thing before. It didn't work out so well. I like you. And I like—" She bites her lip and closes her eyes. Without opening them, she continues. "I like that you want to commit to me. It makes me feel..."

Good? Happy? No, Hope's never really had someone committed to her before. Reluctant? Scared?

"Safe?"

She blinks her eyes open and they're glossy with unshed tears. "Yes," she breathes.

Damn, she is breaking my heart and filling it at the same time. And I realize she will never have to worry about ownership because she thoroughly owns my ass. I will do anything, *anything* for her.

"So this is it?" She smiles at me and squeezes my hand. "We're official?"

"Yes." I feel like running. Or shouting. Or laughing really freaking loudly. But I don't do any of those things. Instead, I pull her into my lap and kiss her until we're both gasping for breath.

24

Hope

Mason is my truck. I have no idea what happened, or how, or even why. I was just walking through my life one day and, BAM. Mason smashed into me. Into my mind. My body. My heart.

He's filled every fraction of me. Every minute, of every day, Mason is a part of me.

Does this scare the living crap out of me? Oh, hell yes. But you know how roller coasters are really fun because they're fast, unpredictable, and terrifying? Yeah, that's the equivalent to our relationship. He's impulsive and candid. His sense of humor is twisted, but he makes me laugh like it's something I do all the time. Let's not forget he's so gorgeous he makes me liquefy in his presence. There's also the little fact that he has a messed up past as well. He knows what it's like to lose a parent. Above all that, Mason makes me feel protected. Like nothing, nobody, can hurt me. Sometimes I catch myself believing we can work.

That's the truly scary part.

I don't believe in forever. I don't trust it. But I trust Mason, which means now I have a boyfriend. It means that I am through fighting my feelings. My mind and heart have stopped battling. The peace treaty has been signed and we are now a joined force.

I smile as he pushes away from his car and saunters over to Neko. I love the way he walks. Mason has so much confidence it shows in every move he makes. It's like Park's stage presence, only it's all the time, in every single thing he does. He ducks into my window, flashing the dimpled grin that makes the muscles in my stomach squeeze happily. Before I have a chance to return the smile, his mouth is moving against mine. I lean back, tugging on him until his body spills through the window and lies on top of mine.

Mason laughs against my lips causing goose bumps to burst across my arms. The way his weight presses me against the seat is making my heart race. I swear, I think there is a whole army of gymnasts doing somersaults in my stomach. His hands move over me slowly until they're both cupping my face, fingers splayed across my cheeks. He brushes his lips gradually across my collar bone, then over my throat and I am so blissfully happy.

"I don't wanna go to school now," he murmurs against my skin. "I wanna stay right here, all day."

"Okay."

Mason raises his head and his green eyes regard me dubiously. "Really?" There's a distinct hopefulness in his voice. How can I possibly deny him?

"Yeah. Why not?" I say. He opens his mouth to say something, probably to list the many reasons why not, but I don't want to hear them right now. I lift my head, his fingers sliding over my face and into my hair, and I trail my tongue over his lip. He accepts the invitation eagerly, nipping my tongue and pulling it into his mouth to meet his.

My toes curl. Literally.

A sound, somewhere between a moan and a cry bubbles up from my throat. Mason responds to this by deepening the kiss until I want to scream with pleasure. Nobody has ever kissed me like this. I didn't even know anybody *could* kiss like this. But oh, dear Buddha, I know right at this moment, Mason was wrong. He does possess me. He owns me in every sense of the word. I am his. As much of me for as long as he wants.

A tortured sound escapes from Mason as he pulls away gasping. I stare at him, panting. "I want to be a good guy with you," he says, his voice is deep and husky, and I shiver. Even the way he sounds makes my body want in a way I've never experienced. "But Hope, you are making it so hard for me."

We both explode with laughter. "No pun intended?"

He nuzzles into my neck, burying his face in my hair. "Ahh. I want you so bad."

I sigh. The feeling is mutual. I run my fingers through his dark hair, loving how the soft strands feel. "Maybe we should go to class," I say reluctantly.

"Nooo," Mason whines. "I'll be good. I promise." He kisses my cheek and pushes himself up so he's sitting on the driver's side. "So, where are we going?"

"I thought you wanted to stay right here?" I tease, batting my lashes.

"Don't make me come back over there," he says, slitting his eyes and raising one brow. Oh, cheese and rice. He is so freaking sexy. I pull my hair over my shoulder to get the heat off my neck.

"That's a terrible threat. It's like telling me you'll give me extra candy if I don't eat my dinner."

A devious smile spreads his lips and he lunges sideways, grasping me around the waist, and lugging me against him. "I'm your extra candy?" He skims his nose down my neck and I can't seem to answer him yet.

Instead, I tilt my head, giving him free reign. His lips brush my shoulder as he inhales deeply.

"Sweet like candy to my soul. Sweet you rock and sweet you roll," I whisper.

Mason's arms tighten around me. "Good song," he utters.

"Mm-hm."

"I love when I discover something new about you."

"What did you learn about me now?" I ask.

He clenches me to his chest and clears his throat. "This is the second time you've talked to me through song lyrics. I like it."

"Hmm. But lyrics mean different things to different people. What if you're interpreting my meaning incorrectly?" I shift so I can see his reaction.

He starts my car and puts his seatbelt on, gesturing at me to do the same. "Okay. Then why don't you just tell me what you meant?"

"I like candy. I like you," I say, smiling innocently.

He glances at me as he backs out of the parking space. "Some would say you have a candy obsession."

I scrunch my brows. “It’s a healthy addiction. I am not obsessed with you. Or candy. Candy for me is, like, comfort. It makes me happy. Makes me feel good. It’s been my friend through some shitty times. I love candy—” What. The. Hell. Did. I. Just. Say?

The space between us feels smothering. I see Mason turn his head to look at me from my peripheral, but I can’t bring myself to look back. How could I say that? How could I compare him to candy and then say *I love candy*?

I can’t breathe.

Mason places his fingers in between mine and squeezes. “I love M&M’s. Hard outer shell, sweet and soft inside. They’re a vulnerable candy. I mean, they have that protective casing, but they’re still capable of melting so easily.”

“But only in your mouth, not in your hand,” I say, my voice raspy.

“So they claim,” he says.

I finally look at him and he smiles at me. “You’re always smiling.”

He shakes his head. “Only when I’m with you.”

I turn to my window, putting my hand out and catching the wind until it forces my arm back. "So, where are you taking us?"

"I'm just driving. Any suggestions?"

I think about it as I kick off my flip flops and prop my feet on the dashboard. We pass over the bridge taking us out of town and an idea pops into my head. "Keep going straight," I say. "When you hit the first stop light, take a right."

"All right. Are you going to tell me?"

"Nope."

~***~

Mason puts the gear into park and looks out at the water. He shifts his attention to me as I open the door. "What is this place?"

"It's The Pond." I slam the door and walk toward the water.

"I see it's a pond, but who owns it? Are we trespassing?" He catches up to me easily.

I glance at him and arch my eyebrow. "It's not *a* pond. It's *The Pond*. And I have no idea who owns it. Are you scared?"

He gives me a look. “I don’t scare easily,” he grunts. *That’s the truth.* “Just curious.”

I smile, letting my eyes blink slowly. “You know what they say about curiosity?”

“I’m not a cat. I think I’m safe.”

“I wouldn’t be so sure,” I trill as I lift my tank top over my head and drop it onto the grass, not breaking my stride. I don’t stop until I get to the muddy edge of the water.

Normally I wouldn’t be willing to wear a swimsuit, let alone my underwear in front of anybody, but this is Mason. He’s the only one I can be like this with. The only one that can look at me like I’m a buffet set up just for him.

I unbutton my shorts and slide them down my legs before I realize he isn’t with me. Turning around, I find him standing a few feet back, his hands interlocked atop his head, staring at me. I feel my face warm under his intense gaze.

“What are you doing?” I ask quietly.

He clears his throat and swallows, his Adam’s apple moving slowly. “Just watching you. Wondering how much you plan on taking off.”

I peek down at my plain, black underwear. “That’s it.” I force an eye roll, feigning nonchalance. “It’s no different than wearing a swimsuit.” It is.

He takes several slow steps until he’s standing right in front of me. “It’s different. Trust me.” He takes a breath and blows it out through his mouth. “It’s painful how beautiful you are.”

I take a step back and into the pond. “Take your clothes off, Mason,” I say, my voice soft as I continue to back into the water. It’s warmer than I expected. My toes stick into the mucky bottom and I pause. Or maybe it’s because Mason lifts his shirt up over his head and I get my first look at his naked chest. His skin is golden and smooth. I stifle a sigh at the sight of him. Normal people shouldn’t have abs like this. Park has a nice six-pack, but this… Mason is… Am I still breathing?

Unhooking his belt draws my attention from his chest. My eyes focus on the way his hands move expertly over the buckle before trailing up. His eyes are trained on me, taking in my observation of his unclothed gloriousness. *Damn.* When did I become one of these people? I’m ogling my boyfriend. Openly. And I am not ashamed.

I give him a grin and continue into the water. Mason drops his pants, revealing white boxers with tiny four leaf clovers all over them. "Cute," I call. "I can't wait to see those after they're wet."

He takes a step into the water and grins back at me. "I feel so violated. I'm not a piece of meat, ya know."

"Damn it. I was ready to take a bite of you."

He lifts his brows. "I'm lying. I am absolutely loving this." He wades out to me, wrapping his hands around my waist. "You can sink your teeth into me anytime you want. I'm all yours."

My heart beats in double time. I can't explain how much I like the sound of that. Mason is mine. I inhale a deep breath, attempting to regain control over myself and take another peek at the boxers. "Feeling lucky?" His eyes widen, but I grasp for something else to say before he can answer that question. "So, this is all right? No pantsing flashbacks?"

He shakes his head slowly, one side of his mouth lifting. "Nah, no pool, no chlorine, no diving board. I'm good."

"Okay. That's, um, good." The last word comes out a little breathless and I bite my lip.

“Are you nervous, Hope?” Mason’s voice drips with a sexy gruffness. His hands snake around my back, locking me in place. The muscles in his arms flex with the movement. He has *great* arms.

I peer up at him, meeting his eyes. “Yes,” I admit.

“Don’t be.” His hands run up to tuck my hair behind my ears, water trickles down my neck sending a chill through me. “I don’t want anything you aren’t ready for. I promised I’d be good.”

I hold his gaze and breathe my next words out. “I never asked you to be good.”

25

Mason

Well, hell. How am I supposed to respond to that? I'm pretty sure not with words. So I kiss her. I kiss Hope like I need her lips to breathe. And it's true, in a way. I need this girl. I want her. I love her. And she loves me. Or candy. I'm still debating that one. But when she looks at me like she has today, when she kisses me like she is now, it feels like love.

Hope's fingers work their way into my hair and she pulls as if she's afraid I'll break away. Yeah, not happening. I teased her about being obsessed, but that's me. She's my first thought when I wake up every morning. I fall asleep each night with her on my mind. My day consists of the time I'm with Hope and the shitty minutes until I will see her again. I consider her when I get dressed, wondering if she'll like a specific shirt. I've even contemplated buying something purple just so I can wear her favorite color. Every time I'm at the store I stop in the candy aisle. I'll stand there for ten minutes mulling over which to choose based on her mood, what candy she already ate that day, and which candy she's mentioned. The girl's turning me into a freak. And I have zero problems with that.

This is real.

I feel so good right now. Swimming and kissing. Everything feels right. I'm happy. And I don't stop to think. All I know is I need to tell her. I need her to know what's inside of me. Separating from the kiss is agonizing, but necessary. Keeping my arms around her, I let my lips graze her ear. "I love you," I say softly.

Hope's whole body goes rigid as she ducks her head. And then I realize my mistake. Why am I always fucking this up? The one thing I want more than anything else in the world and I can't stop destroying it. This has to be some kind of Karma. What did I possibly do in my past lives that was so bad?

"I didn't say that," I stumble over my words. "I didn't mean to. I didn't mean it—" And then I stop, because I did mean it. I don't want to freak her out or cause her to run away from me. Or, hell, make her want to cut herself again. Who tells someone they love them after a couple weeks? But I don't want to hide it. Yes, it happened quickly. And, yeah, some people may not understand it, but she does. I know she does. She's just scared.

I shake my head and tighten my grasp on her. "Shit. I probably shouldn't have said that yet, but I did mean it. I love you, Hope. I don't expect you to say it back. And...just...don't flip out. It doesn't change anything. I won't repeat it, I swear. Just look at me, please."

Hope tilts her head up, squinting against the sun. I hold my breath, waiting. She will either make me or break me with her next words. If she pushes me away again... Are my legs shaking? If I wasn't waiting execution I would be appalled with myself.

"I'm hungry," she says at last.

Okay. Okay. Okay. I can work with this. I slap my thighs. "I have candy..." Twisting around, I rush out of the water for my pants. I put a pack of Rollos in my pocket before I left the house this morning. She told me last night on the phone that caramel was one of her favorite "non-fruity flavors". Snatching up my pants, I turn around just as my fingers close around the candy.

"Oh," Hope breathes.

My eyes flick to hers and I follow her line of sight down to my translucent boxer shorts before returning to her. I chuckle at her shameless staring.

"Well," she laughs, finally looking me in the eyes. "I guess they are lucky. For me, at least." She grins wickedly and I let my pants slip from my fingers. I stalk toward her, gliding through the water, ripping the candy wrapper open as I go. I smoothly place a piece in between my lips, holding it with my teeth and bend my head to hers. This I can do. This is easy. If Hope wants to keep our relationship physical for now, I am more than willing to oblige.

She seizes my shoulders, pulling herself up to meet me. Her nails dig into my skin and I nearly whimper with yearning as her mouth surrounds the candy, stealing it from my lips.

Gazing up at me, she licks the corner of her mouth. "I love candy," she whispers.

Okay. Am I still the candy? Damn it. This girl is so confusing. Is she freaking talking about Rollos or is she trying to tell me something? Am I reading too much into her words? *Shit.*

"Do you want to go to my house?" she asks. "I think I need some real food."

And that. Does she really want to go home and make a sandwich or is she inviting me back to her house for more than brunch? I shrug. Screw it. It doesn't matter. I'm grateful she's still with me, inviting me in any manner. We don't need to rush this further right now anyway. I think I did that enough already for one day.

"Sure," I agree. "You don't happen to have a towel in your car, do you?"

"Actually, I think I might have one of Guy's beach towels in the trunk. Don't ask. You don't want to know."

"Uh, all right. It's clean, though. Right?"

Hope raises her brows and lifts one shoulder in a lopsided shrugging gesture. "Clean enough." I stand where I am as she trudges through the mud.

"What does that mean?" I call.

She dips into the car, plucking the keys from the ignition. "It means," she says as she opens the trunk, "that it's good enough to dry off with." I ring myself out as she pats the Spiderman towel against her arms. Hm-mm. I'm not using it.

“Stay back there. I’m going commando,” I warn before sliding my boxers off and thrusting my legs into my jeans.

“Yeah, um, just so you know, I can totally see you.” I can hear the smile in her voice. I glance back as I button up and it’s not just a smile. It’s a heart stopping, sexy as hell smirk. The wind blows her long hair across her face. She catches it and it flutters across her throat, her collar bone, her chest. Goosebumps stand out on her pale skin. I move around the car, not taking me eyes off her. As she points her leg out to dry it, I spot the scars on her thigh. Without consciously deciding to, I reach out and run my fingertips over one of the jagged lines.

Hope inhales quickly, a hissing sound through her teeth. The muscle in her leg twitches at my touch. I kneel in front of her, taking the towel from her trembling hands, and smooth it over each leg. I look up at her, catching her gaze as I lean into her, pressing a light kiss to each scar. Her body convulses, quivering, and she cinches her fingers into my hair. I trail my hands across her thigh one last time.

“Why did you do it?” I ask softly.

Hope sinks to the grass as if she's unable to stand. She pulls her legs to her chest and my breath hitches in my throat. This is the most beautiful thing I've ever seen. How her back curves over her pale legs, her ankles crossed gracefully over each other, chin resting on one knee, the wet ends of her hair clinging to her arms, big blue eyes bright with pain. I don't know a word meaningful enough for this beauty. How is it possible the entire world isn't in love with her?

Probably the worst timing ever, but I have to capture this image. I dig my phone out of my pocket and snap a picture causing her to scrunch up her face in confusion and glower at me at the same time. I almost take another because I've never seen this combination on her before, but I refrain.

"Sorry," I say. "I couldn't help myself. You're beautiful."

She shakes her head and looks at her feet. "I hate when you say that."

I tilt my head to the side, trying to get a better look at her face. "Why?"

She positions her hands on her shins and shakes her head again, angrily this time. "Because I'm not."

“That’s bullshit.” I settle back against the car and steady my gaze on her profile. “Inside and out, you are the most attractive person I’ve ever met. You’re like a siren, drawing me to you.” I shrug and smirk at her. “Face it, Hope. You’re hot.”

“So you want to get in my pants. That doesn’t make me beautiful.”

I’m not going to deny I want in her pants, but I don’t have to confirm it right now either. “You’re not wearing pants. And I’m entitled to my opinion. I say you are.”

Hope shifts uncomfortably. “I don’t want to be.”

I feel my brows merge. “You don’t want to be what? Beautiful? Why?”

Closing her eyes tightly, she bites her lip. I pry one of her hands from her leg and squeeze it, assuring her I’m here, listening. Without opening her eyes, she takes a deep breath and sighs.

“I don’t like attention.” She clenches my hand tightly. I move closer to her, letting our sides make contact. The trembling in her body scares me. Unease fills me and I don’t know if I want to hear what she’s about to say. But, Jesus, that is so selfish. Running my free hand through my hair roughly and pressing closer yet, I rest my head against her shoulder.

"What happened to you?"

Her voice is broken when she answers. "His name was Andy." She spits his name like it disgusts her to have it pass through her lips. "Fucking Andy. Sounds like a sweet, dorky dude, right? He even looked like it. Tall and skinny, glasses." I feel her shake her head again, her body jerking with the motion. "But he was wiry. Is. He *is* wiry."

I grind my teeth as I shake with rage. But I don't say anything. I won't rush her. I won't stop her. So I wait.

"I was twelve when he and my mom started dating. Back then, I wanted to look like her. I was happy I resembled my mom. She was still pretty, not like she was before she started using, but still, I was *proud* I shared her looks." She huffs a frustrated laugh.

"The very first time I met Andy I knew something was wrong with him. The way he looked at me made me nervous. Everything about him was so intense, but he treated me like an adult. Made my mom back off me when she'd lose it. I started to like him because when he was around, things weren't so bad. He brought food to the house. Good food, too. No Ramen noodle bullshit. Name brand cereal. Fresh bread. He kept my mom happy for the most part, helping her with some of the bills, kept the alcohol flowing. Two weeks. That's how long it took." Hope shivers and inhales a quivering breath.

"She passed out, drunk or high, I don't know which. I was in the living room watching the movie he rented." She opens her eyes finally and a tear rolls down her cheek. "Don't ever ask me to watch Happy Feet." It takes her second to continue and in that moment, I feel the anger coiling inside of me.

"Andy carried my mom back to the bedroom and then... I shouldn't have been wearing one of my mom's old nightgowns. I was a kid. I should have been in flannel pajama pants or something. I should've gone to my room when she passed out. I knew better than to stick around her boyfriends. I—I should've... He sat too close, but I kept watching the movie. I could smell his cologne. It was so strong it burnt my throat, stung my nose. I still remember that smell.

"When he put his hand on my leg I realized I had made a mistake, but it was too late. I was alone. All I could do was stare at his long fingers as they slid the nightgown up. I didn't stop him until it was around my waist. I don't know why I let him get it that far. I should've—I should've *stopped* him."

Hope pinches her eyes shut and more tears fall from her lashes. I wrap my arm around her shoulder and crush her against my chest. The need to jump up and beat the shit out of something is so strong. I think I might puke. My eyes burn and I know I'm shaking as bad as she is. I don't want to know. I need to know, but I don't want to hear it. I'm going to kill this guy. I'm going to hunt him down and I am going to *fucking kill him*.

She sniffles, tearing me away from my murderous thoughts. "I smacked his hands away and he laughed. He fucking laughed at me because he knew I was weak. He touched me, Mason. He touched me everywhere. And the whole time I begged him to stop, he kept telling me I was beautiful. Like it was my fault he was a filthy fucking pedophile. Like he couldn't help himself." She pulls away from me, her chest rising and falling too quickly as if she's fighting for breath.

"He made me touch him. He took my hand, controlled it. Controlled me. Forced me to do what he wanted. I had never kissed a boy, but I was jerking my mother's boyfriend off in our living room while a cartoon played in the background. All while he explored my twelve year old body with his disgusting fingers. There were things about my body I didn't know about; parts I had never thought to touch, but Andy introduced me to them all."

Hugging her arms around herself, Hope drops her head, staring at the scars on her inner thigh. "I didn't even understand what happened when he got off. All I knew was he let go of me and I ran into the bathroom. I locked the door and I went nuts. I tore the shower curtain from the rod. I threw every bottle of my mom's hair shit, all her make-up, anything I could get my hands on. I destroyed the room. I was so angry. Because if I was angry, if I was pissed as hell, then I wasn't giving him the satisfaction of my tears.

"I punched the wall over and over again and the pain started to calm me down, so I kept slamming my fist into anything solid. My knuckles were bloody and I don't know why, but I wanted more blood. I needed more blood to leave my body. Like the memory would leave with it. I pounded on the mirror until it shattered and it cut the shit out of my hands. It felt so good, Mason. It felt *good*. I felt nothing but this insane physical pain. I was numb to the rest. For that moment, it was like what Andy did—it didn't happen. Do you know the only thing worse than what he did to me is?"

I don't think she expects me to answer. I couldn't anyway if she did.

"My mom was pissed about the bathroom. She didn't ask me why I did it. Didn't even care about my fucked up hands. All she said was: Clean it up.

"You asked why I did this to myself." She moves her leg so I can see the marks of her suffering. "This makes me forget. It releases all the torment that lives inside. It erases him. It makes all the things that remind me of him easier to deal with. It draws it out and makes it disappear for a little while.

"I'm not beautiful. And if you knew what's contained within me, you would see the truth. This—" She jabs her leg hard enough to turn her pale skin whiter. "This is so much uglier inside."

It hurts to swallow and it takes several tries. Twelve years old. Kellin's age. I grit my teeth as I work my jaw. My eyes are wet and I press my palms to them.

"Mason, I'm ruined. I can never give you what you deserve. I'm incapable of loving someone like—like you want. I will never be able to do it right. I will never deserve to be loved."

My breathing is erratic. I shove myself to my knees and grasp her arms, pulling her toward me once again. "Sometimes never is a distorted perception. *I* love you, Hope. And I'm not the only one. I know you care about me. I see it in your eyes. I feel it. Everybody needs love. *Everybody*. And some people need it more than others. You're a liar if you say you don't. I'll do that for you. I'll love you. All you have to do is let me."

The wind whispers against my back as if giving me a nudge toward her and I take it as a sign. I propel myself into her, pushing my bare skin to hers. I need to feel her. I need her to feel me.

This is real.

"I'm so sorry that happened to you," I whisper.

With a broken sob, Hope twines her arms around my neck. She claws at me in her attempt to secure her body to mine. My chest aches as my heart drums with a mix of sadness and bittersweet relief. I can feel her racing pulse against my flesh, matching my own.

“It’ll be all right. You can trust me. I won’t hurt you. I won’t let anyone ever hurt you again.”

I feel her nod as her tears run down my neck. “I do. I trust you. I...I—need... Mason.” I don’t know what she’s trying to say, but I can feel her struggle to get it out. “I love Skittles.”

26
Hope

While we wait for Kellin, Mason tells me about the different places he's lived. Eight different schools in five years. Nine homes. Four states—Illinois, Indiana, Michigan, and Ohio. Sixteen "girlfriends," he *thinks*. Six part time jobs ranging from a weekend dishwasher to working concession at a movie theater. The way he talks, with a distant look and small frown, it sounds like he wants to settle somewhere permanently. But it sounds nice to me. Getting a fresh start, seeing new places. I'd love to do that. My mom and I moved around a lot, but always within the same twenty mile radius in Ohio.

"Where was your favorite place?" I ask.

"Home. Illinois. I had friends there. I went to the same schools my dad did. We lived a block from the house he grew up in. That's why Mom wanted to move. Everything reminded her of him. She couldn't stand it, but she didn't realize how much I needed those reminders. Kel doesn't even remember most of those places. They were a part of Dad and he'll never know them."

"Maybe you can take him sometime," I suggest softly.

"Yeah. I've thought about it. I planned to move back when I turned eighteen and he could visit, but I couldn't leave them. They're the only family I have left." I understand that. I don't have any family unless you consider my absentee father, which I don't. If I had someone, I wouldn't be able to leave them.

"What are your plans for after graduation?"

He glances out the window staring at the kids pouring out of the school. "I don't know. I stopped applying to colleges because we kept moving. Probably just go somewhere close while Kel's in school. Pick up a job that'll work around my schedule. Dad had a life insurance policy, nothing big, but Mom took what was left after the funeral and split it up between me and Kellin. It's more than enough to cover community college. If Mom hadn't kept it in trust until I turned eighteen, I probably would've wasted it on a car by now." He turns to regard me. "What about you? Any big plans after you graduate?"

"I wanna go to school. I don't wanna end up like my mom. But my grades aren't good enough to go anywhere, so I'll do the community college thing too. I have no idea what I wanna be when I grow up, though." I flash a smile.

"You don't wanna do something with music?"

"I don't know. Maybe? I love music, I just don't know if I want to *have* to do it. Don't read into this, but I kind of like kids, so if I could do something with kids and music, that'd be cool. I'm pretty much a C student, though. I don't know if I'd make a very good teacher."

"You wouldn't necessarily have to work at a school. You could do something like musical therapy maybe."

"If I could help kids with emotional issues by using music, I think that'd be my dream job."

"I think you'd be good at it. Kids and music."

"Guy and Chase count on the band making it big. I don't even know if there still is a band now with Park and everything. I don't want to rely on it. And I don't want to do it forever. I need to find a real job, and soon. Alec and Jenny get money from the state for fostering me. Once I turn eighteen, they'll lose that money. I can't be a burden."

"When's that? Your birthday?"

"Not 'til November, but I'd like to have something more saved than the ninety-four dollars in my dresser."

"November what?"

I raise a brow. "Tenth." He nods at the steering wheel.

Kellin stops outside the car with the raise of his eyebrows. The gesture is so Mason, I smile. "What's going on?" he asks. "Where's Mom's car?"

"At school," Mason explains. "We'll pick it up on the way."

I wait for Kellin to get in the back before I shift in the seat. "How was school, Little Man?"

He buckles his seatbelt and grins at me. "I got my schedule changed. I have lunch and a free period with Misty now."

I arch my brow and give him a knowing nod. "Did you ask her yet?"

"Ask her what?" Mason inquires as he pulls onto the street.

"No. Not yet," Kellin says slowly. His cheeks turn pink and he fumbles the zipper on his backpack.

"Why not?" I ask.

Kellin shrugs his thin shoulders. "What if she says no?"

Oh. Boys can be clueless. "What if she says no to what?" Mason grunts, obviously irritated that he doesn't know what we're talking about. "And can you put your seatbelt back on, please?"

I flop onto the seat and buckle up. "She won't say no, Kel. I promise."

"Say no to what?" Mason hisses.

"How do you know?" Kellin asks.

With a look in Mason's direction I say, "He wants to ask her out. You know, *like* a boyfriend." My lips curl up in an evil smile, teasing him before I glance into the backseat. "And I know because I'm a girl and I see the way she looks at you. It's pretty much the same way you look at her."

"How do I look at her?"

Mason laughs. "Like you're a starving dog and she's wearing a skirt made of meat." Kellin's face morphs into a brighter shade of pink, but he laughs as well.

"Like your teacher just assigned a pop quiz and Misty has all the answers tattooed on her face," I add.

"Like you've been in the desert for a week and she's a bottle of ice cold water," Mason continues.

Kellin grins at Mason in the rearview mirror. "Like you look at Hope?"

I feel my face heat up now. Mason's eyes dart from the mirror to me and back again. "Yeah, exactly like that," he says. "Damn, Kel. You've got it bad."

Kellin leans into the seat and sighs. "I know."

I clear my throat and smile at him encouragingly. "Just ask her. She likes you. After you leave every day, all she does is talk about you. It's annoying, really. And just imagine, dating an older woman. You'll be a legend."

Mason quirks his brow at me. "A legend?"

I shrug. I don't know. "It sounded good."

"If you like the girl half as much as I think you do then tell her," Mason instructs his brother. "If she turns you down, which I don't think will happen, then at least you'll know where you stand. And if she does what I expect she'll do and says yes, well, then that'll be awesome. Right?"

"But how do I tell her?"

"When you think about her, what comes to mind?" Mason asks.

Kellin considers this for a moment. A small smile forms and he lets out his breath slowly. "She smells good. Like cookies or cake or something."

"Vanilla," I offer. "I got it for her for Christmas last year."

"Yeah, that's it. When we play basketball, her sweat mixes with the vanilla. I try to steal the ball just so I can smell her. And her hair's soft. Her ponytail rubs against my arm sometimes and I wanna run my fingers through it."

Mason clears his throat. "You can start by telling her that," he says. "Maybe not as detailed, but soft hair and smelling nice is good. What else?" I notice he has this expression on his face that I can't interpret. But Kellin goes on, pulling my focus away.

"She's smart. She helps me with my homework. She's really nice. And she does this thing when she's thinking, where she sucks on the corner of her lip. It makes me wanna—" He stops abruptly. His cheeks are bright red now and I stifle a laugh.

Damn. Kellin wants to make out with Misty. I turn my head slowly and meet Mason's eyes. He doesn't bother to hide his amusement.

"Let's stick with asking her out for now," he suggests.

~***~

Annie lies back in her bed and checks the alarm on the nightstand. "What's going on with you and Mason Patel? Did you break up with Park for good?"

"Uh, yeah. Park and I are done. Mason and I… He's my boyfriend." The word sounds strange coming from my mouth.

"Really? Like, officially?" I nod and she returns the gesture. "He's hot as hell. 'Course, so is Park. Everybody's talking about it at school. Half my friends hate you for breaking Park's heart after keeping him off the market for so long. The other half hates you for taking Mason."

"What's new? You're friends have always hated me," I mutter.

"Yeah, but before they hated you because they wanted a piece of Park and you had dibs on his ownership papers. Now they have twice the ammunition." She examines a bottle of nail polish I left on the stand. "Can I borrow this?"

I nod dismissively. "What do you mean? First of all, I was never *with Park*, but besides that fact that nobody can seem to accept, we're done. He's free to date whoever he wants." The idea of Park with another girl causes a slight twinge in my stomach. For the past year he showed no interest in anyone but me. I don't know how I'll feel seeing his arms around someone else. I think of Mason and that helps relieve my panic, but I recognize the dull pain burning in my chest, marking the end of whatever it was Park and I had.

"Rumor has it, Park is holding out."

"Holding out for what?" I ask, confused.

She looks at me incredulously. "He's waiting on you, Hope. Your whole 'no commitment' thing?" She bunny ears her words. "He doesn't think this thing with Mason will last long."

"He's wrong," I say, irritated. Huh. Did I just say that? Yes, and I meant it. I grab my cell phone off the charger and storm out of the room, heading outside so I'll have some privacy.

Park picks up on the second ring. "Hope?"

"Yeah. We need to talk."

"All right," he says languidly. His voice is soft, low. "Talk."

Taking a deep breath, I forge on. "I care about you and I don't wanna hurt you."

"I care about you too."

"But," I continue, ignoring him. "I am so mad at you for telling Guy and Mason about—*my vice*. We can never be what we were before. I'm with Mason now. I'm *with him* with him."

The silence stretches out and I close my eyes.

"You're with him?" He hisses the words into the phone and my eyes pop open.

"Yes. He's my boyfriend."

"Great. Congratulations. I need to go."

"Park, wait," I murmur.

"What, Hope? What?"

"I'm sorry."

"Fuck you. And fuck Mason. I hope you're both fucking happy together." The line goes dead and I stare at my phone.

Well that went well. But at least it's done. He has his closure. I have mine. The girls at school will have theirs.

I sit on the step and text Mason.

Me: U STILL UP?

Him: YEP. WHAT'S UP?

Me: JUST THINKING ABOUT U.

Him: REALLY? WHAT ABOUT ME?

I smile as I key in my next text. Me: I CAN'T GET THOSE BOXERS OUT OF MY HEAD.

Him: COME OVER. I HAVE ANOTHER PAIR.

Me: RIGHT NOW?

Him: YES. PLEASE?

Me: REALLY?

Him: DON'T MAKE ME BEG YOU.

I bite my lip. I'm already outside. Everyone else is in bed. I doubt they'd miss me. I text Guy to cover for me before I respond to Mason.

Me: DIRECTIONS?

27

Mason

It takes Hope ten minutes to get here. I open the door before she has a chance to knock. I don't want Kel waking up. She smiles at me and I have a sudden bout of nerves. This is the first time she's seeing my house. I move out of the way, giving her space to get through the door.

There are still boxes piled along one wall, waiting to be unpacked. Her eyes brush over them. She circles the living room, her fingers skimming across the couch, the desk, the ancient computer.

"You want something to drink?" I ask her because my throat feels too dry.

She nods. "Some water?"

I turn into the kitchen and she follows me. "Oh, wow. Your kitchen's really clean," she observes.

I chuckle. "It's just the three of us. Mom's usually sleeping or working and Kel and I are at school or your house. Pretty easy clean up."

She takes the glass I offer her. I gulp mine down while she sips hers. "Where's your room?"

I stare at her over the rim of my glass. She does that thing that drives me crazy, dropping her lashes leisurely and looking at me through them. I take the glass from her, setting both on the counter, and take her hand. She pauses halfway down the hall and I think she's changed her mind, deciding she's not ready to be alone in my room with me, but when I look back she's examining a picture on the wall.

"Your dad," she says. It doesn't sound like a question, but I nod. "You look just like him, except the hair obviously. Does your mom have your dark hair?"

I nod again and she moves around me. "Which one?" she whispers.

I point at my door and watch as she opens it, moving inside. I reach for the light switch at the same time she does and I hear her quick intake of breath as our hands meet in the dark. "Sorry," I say barely audibly.

She takes another step in and let's her gaze drift around my small space. Her fingers trail over the books and movies on my shelf and she smiles. It's mostly horror, her favorite. She moves on to the shelf of CD's. "Hey, you know *Dead End Days*?"

"Yeah. I'm from Illinois, remember?"

Hope scrunches her nose. *So freaking cute*. "He's from Ohio. The lead singer is, I mean."

"But he lives in Chicago now," I correct her. "I'm surprised you know them."

"Female drummer. Of course I know them. Great band."

"Yeah, it is."

She finally turns to the bed and walks right over to it, kicking her shoes off and sitting in the middle. "Great bed," she says so softly I almost miss it.

I swallow hard. "Yeah, it is."

I watch as she lies back on my pillow. Her shirt rides up as she rests her arms above her head just like she did the first time I saw her. Hope lying on my bed is the most perfect thing I have ever seen. Straight out of my fantasies and into my room. "It smells like you."

I dip my chin. "What do I smell like?"

Propping herself on her elbows she manages a slight shrug. "Like boy soap and fabric softener. I like it. It's nice." Hope gazes up at me, her eyes boring into mine with fascination. "Why am I here, Mason?"

That throws me off. I stare at the exposed strip of pale stomach. It amazes me that this little piece of skin can turn me on as much as seeing her at the pond in her underwear, dripping wet, her hair sticking to her... "What was the question?"

She sits up. "I was promised shamrock boxers. Are you going to deliver?"

"I can't get in that bed with you," I say as it dawns on me. "Being good, remember?"

Peering up at me, Hope slips out of her shirt. The light pink bra she's wearing makes her look so girly. So soft. So incredibly gorgeous. I realize I'm not breathing and suck air in quickly. Extending her arm, she drops the tank top to the floor and lies back once again. "And you remember I didn't ask for you to be good. I want you to touch me." Dear, God. She has no idea how much I want that too.

And then she throws my words back at me. "Don't make me beg you," she breathes.

Her words set me on fire, causing my body to burn with need. Nothing could stop me now. I crawl up the bed, moving over her little by little, dropping kisses on her legs. Taking my time on her smooth stomach. Paying special attention to her belly button. My fingers graze the indentations between her ribs.

Her breathing speeds with every move of my lips. I meet her eyes as I reach for the front clasp of her bra, giving her time to tell me to stop, but she doesn't. Her chest rises faster and faster and I'm about to lose it just watching her reaction to me. I slide the lacy material away and taste her bare skin, my eyes still locked with hers. With one last kiss, I let my gaze drop and my hand replaces my mouth. My thumb skims her tightened pink nipple.

Hope wiggles under me while pulling on my shirt at the same time. She works us into the position she wants and draws my mouth to hers, whimpering as our tongues meet, and my eyes threaten to tear up.

Warm hands slip under my shirt releasing a loud moan from me. Somehow she gets my shirt off with minimal separation. Her knees shift to either side of my hips. I fall into place between her legs and she makes a sound in her throat.

As she glides her hand between our bodies and unbuttons my jeans, it occurs to me that I'm letting her guide. I've never done this before, letting someone else set the pace. I've just done whatever felt good and the girls seemed to enjoy it. I've never been led. And I really like it.

I move my hands everywhere, desperate for the sensation of her body against my palms. Hope pushes my pants down as far as she can and I scramble out of them. It's obvious how much I want her, the sudden restriction of my boxers evident. She squirms out of her shorts and I sink into her. There's not enough fabric between us. I can't handle this much longer. It's becoming too great a need to join our bodies. I want her. I want her right now. I pull back and rest my head at her neck. She smells like raspberries and I think I die a little inside.

"You feel so good," I groan. It's difficult to breathe and I really don't want to say what I know I need to say. "We should probably stop."

"No," she pants. "I don't want to stop. I want you. I need you." Her voice is breathless, cracking over several words. Pleading almost desperately.

Shit. I have no willpower. Not when I know exactly what she means. "We don't have to do this," I protest, but it sounds weak even to my own ears. I want to. So badly.

"I know."

"It'll hurt," I explain. I don't want to hurt her. Didn't I just promise her I wouldn't?

"I know," she repeats. Her hand cups my jaw, thumb caressing my cheek. "But in a good way and our next time will feel better."

Our next time. I've never had a next time with somebody. And now my mind is filled with all our next times. I desperately need to know what her face looks like in the height of physical pleasure.

This is real.

"I need to say it. I know I said I wouldn't say it anymore, but I need to know you understand before we go further."

She blinks slowly and fixes her eyes on me. I can feel her heart slamming against my chest. I press my palm to her skin, mesmerized by the power. Hope trails her tongue along my throat before pressing a kiss there. "I love you, Mason," she whispers. "I don't know how this happened to me, but I'm trying not to fight it anymore." Her eyes shine as they find mine again. "Make love to me."

I try to say something, but I have no voice. Too fast. This happened too fast. She's going to regret it tomorrow and then she'll disappear from my life. But she said she loved me. She said it. Not candy. Not Skittles. Me. She said Mason.

I grin at her, unable to pry my eyes away. "I love you too."

And this all seems wrong. I love her. I want better for her. Should her first time be here at midnight in my messy room? No. It should be—I don't know... In a nice hotel. With candles and roses. I glance around. Not here in this shitty house.

Hope ushers my attention back to her and I sigh. "It's not supposed to be like this. Your first time needs to be special."

"This is special."

I shake my head emphatically. "No it's not. You deserve a nice place. Nice things."

She laughs, her lips turning up in a way that makes me want to kiss them again and again. "The place doesn't matter. It's the person. It's you and it's me. That's the important part. I happen to love where I am.

In your bed that smells like you, surrounded by the things that make you you."

This is why I love her.

This is real.

I reach under the bed where I hide the box of condoms from Kellin. This is happening. My hands are shaking, my heart pounding, matching hers.

"Tell me again," I say just above a whisper. I need to hear it. I want to hear it over and over.

"Lost for you. I'm so lost for you," she sings quietly and then presses a kiss to my cheek letting her lips brush down my chin. "I love you."

"I love you, Hope."

28
Hope

The contrast between my creamy arm resting on Mason's dark golden chest is the most compelling thing I've ever seen. There's a strange beauty that I cannot tear my eyes away from. Another difference between us that somehow compliments the other.

Mason's soft breathing, the slow rise and fall of his chest, his familiar scent, it all lolls me into a peaceful bliss I'm unaccustomed to. The low ache in my body is a far away thought. I'm happy. The realization is startling. Over and over, he makes me feel. He makes me enjoy feeling.

I rest my chin on my hand and smile at him. His fingers stroke the hair away from my face and he smiles back. He looks content. Happy, like me. That realization is even more startling. I make him feel good too. In some distant part of my brain I know this shouldn't be so shocking. Most people feel good all the time. Most people aren't like me. Am I becoming part of the average? My normal has always been abnormal. I like it there. I'm pretty much the only affiliate.

Eh. I don't care. I'll give up my membership to the lonely hearts club for Mason. I'd much rather be here with him then go back to empty. Empty or overloaded. Same difference. Here is nice. Here is good.

"What are you thinking about?" Mason asks brushing the tips of his fingers over my shoulder and leaving a trail of goose bumps.

"That I like this. You. Being with you."

He grins widely and I feel so warm, in a good way. Have I been walking around cold inside this whole time?

"I like it too." His expression clouds for a moment, his eyes seeming to look through me for a just a second. Blinking several times, he focuses on me and his next smile is off. As his eyes dart over my face, he squeezes my waist. He looks…anxious. His heart thundering under my palm verifies it.

"What?" I ask slowly, suddenly scared.

"Are you all right? I mean, this," he lifts his arms, indicating us in the bed. "It didn't…bring up memories or… You aren't going to…" He rubs one hand over his face and closes his eyes tightly.

"Am I going to cut myself? Am I thinking about—*him*?" I sit up quickly and grope the floor for my clothes awkwardly. Who does that? Why? Why would he go there? Why would he summon the memories knowing how awful they are? My stomach churns.

Mason grabs my hand, but I jerk away from his touch. "Whoa. Hey. Hope, calm down. I'm sorry." He goes for my hand again and I slap his wrist away. I can't be touched right now. His brows merge and his teeth grind out a sound that makes me cringe. "It's a legitimate question. I want to know you're okay. If you freak out and regret this," he shakes his head, jaw working, "regret *us*, it'll crush me. Just tell me how you feel right now." He stands and shoves his legs into his pants, not bothering to button them.

I get my shirt adjusted before I respond, needing the layer of protection. My hands shake as I push them through my hair, yanking until I can breathe easier. "I was fine. I was happy. Then you go and *ruin it*. Why would you bring *him* up right after we have sex? What the hell is wrong with you? Do you want me to think of him every time we're together?"

Mason glares at me and I flinch away from his anger. "Of course I don't want you to think of that piece of shit when you're making love to me. Jesus. I was worried it might have brought up the memories because—because…similar—because we had sex."

"Nothing about this is similar to Andy you dumb asshole. He is a pedophile. I didn't care about him. I didn't want what he did to me. I wanted you, Mason. There is a huge difference. I never—he didn't… You are the only one that I've done this with. My mind was so far away from that shit until you went and brought it up." I slam my fist down on my thigh as hard as I can, trying desperately to erase Andy's face from my mind. I should never have talked about him. It's too fresh. Too raw. I just want it to go away. I want a razor so badly. I need it. *Shit. Shit. Shit.*

I get my shorts on and spin, looking for my shoes. I find one, slip my foot in, and drop to the floor on my hands and knees. I need to get out of here. *Where the hell is my other shoe?* Flipping the blanket away, I search under the bed.

"Hope? Calm down," Mason murmurs. His hand brushes my arm and I jump back, smacking my back against his dresser. One of the knobs digs into my spine, setting off a shooting pain. I take a deep breath, sighing. Papers flutter around me. Something rolls off the dresser, thudding loudly on the floor. I do it again, this time on purpose. The sensation so satisfying, I do it again.

Mason wrenches me away from the dresser, his hands forming vice grips around my wrists. He shakes me once. I look up into his daunted eyes. “Don’t,” he growls. “Don’t.” Strong arms enclose me in a hug. “I shouldn’t have said anything. I’m sorry.”

Something hot slides down my cheeks. Am I crying? I didn’t realize. My back is so sore. “It wasn’t just once,” I mumble into his collar bone. “He did it for months. I tried to stop him after that first night. I tried to fight him. Tried. And tried. And tried. Until I quit trying. I hated him. I hate him. You are nothing like him. Don’t ever bring him up again. Don’t ever do that to me again. Don’t ask about him again. Don’t ever.”

He shakes his head. “I won’t. I swear. Never again.”

“I can’t find my shoe,” I say gravelly.

He leans around me and comes back with it in hand. “Let me see your back.”

I gently pry my shoe from his hand and turn around. He lifts the back of my shirt and inhales through his teeth. “Jesus Christ.” I stand up quickly, pulling my shirt into place. “FUCK!” I jump at his outburst, my eyes refusing to meet his. Mason punches the dresser, rocking it back and sending more papers and other miscellaneous items flying. I jump again and take a step away from him.

His gaze is burning into me and I finally meet it reluctantly. Immediately wishing I hadn't because there it is. The horror. The repulsion. The regret. My feet move of their own volition, backing me up until I can't go any further. Mason moves to stand in front of me, blocking me with his body.

"I won't let you do this to yourself anymore. I said I won't let anyone hurt you ever again and I was serious. That means you too." The determination on his face makes me swallow my retort. "I know this is my fault. I shouldn't have said that. I hate myself right now and I can't explain how sorry I am." There are those magic words yet again. He closes his eyes and brings his mouth to mine, hovering just a breath away. "I want to make it go away. *I* want to make you forget. *I* want to make you feel better." I want that too. His tongue traces my bottom lip and I open my mouth for him, letting my eyes shutter. I need this. I need to feel Mason. To know it's him and me. As the kiss deepens, he twists his fingers into my hair, tugging it in a way that makes my knees go weak. Working through my hair, he grazes his palms down agonizingly slowly, applying a perfect amount of pressure. He's just on the edge of hurting me. Drifting along the line between pleasure and pain. Something I'm overly familiar with. His touch is rough, but sensual.

I gasp as he drives his fingers into my hips, nails digging into my flesh. His teeth nip my lip, my tongue, and I moan loudly as I grab onto him. He turns us around quickly, walking me backwards and bending me onto his bed. I watch in dazed captivation as he peels my clothes away and moves his lips over my body, his teeth biting gently at all the right places.

I expect him to remove his own clothes, to make love to me again, but he doesn't. He captures me with his ravenous gaze as his fingers work me into a frenzy. I bite my lip to keep from screaming and Mason presses his mouth firmly to mine as his fingers press against me, releasing an explosion of ecstasy throughout my body. It's over quickly, but little pulses tingle throughout me and I loosen my grip on him, suddenly very tired. Sated.

His kiss softens, turning tender and it finally clicks what he did for me. He pulls away enough to look at me. "Your back is bleeding," he says gruffly. "We should clean it up."

~***~

I take my seat in Biology, ignoring the irritated glares from Carly I've been receiving all week, and pull out my notebook. I know the moment Mason comes in because Carly turns in her seat, facing the chair to her left. I look up just as he leans down. He kisses me, a soft brush of lips, but it lingers. He pulls away slowly and produces a package of Twizzlers from behind his back.

The corners of my mouth turn up as I take them. "Thanks," I say. He grins and dips his head with one nod before dropping into his chair. My phone buzzes in my pocket and I wiggle it out to look at the screen.

"Why doesn't Guy have a nickname?" Mason asks, his lips pouting out in confusion.

"'Cause he's Guy," I say. I press the button and try to hide my cell underneath my hair. "Why are you calling me during school?"

Guy sighs. "Obviously because it's important. We got offered two hundred bucks to play Warren Grant's party Friday."

"Warren Grant can't afford two hundred bucks. He spends all his money on *herbs*."

"His stepdad is paying. Guess the dude's loaded and sucking up to Warren, trying to bond or some dumb shit like that. The point is that's like… How much is that a person?"

"Fifty," I sigh.

"Exactly. Fifty bucks a person. We all need the money. Plus, it's Warren Grant's party. Everybody will be there. We could develop a whole new following."

Mason raises his brows, only getting half the conversation and apparently curious about the other half. *Nosy*. "Yeah, everyone will be there," I mutter. "Warren hangs with all the *assholes* in this school." I look pointedly at Carly as she glowers at me.

"It'll be good for the band," Guy whines.

I turn sideways in my seat, away from Mason. "Is there still a band? I had a pretty unpleasant conversation with Park last night. He's pissed. Like, seriously pissed."

"How pissed is seriously pissed, exactly?"

"Shut up. Talk to Park and Chase and get back to me."

"Already did. They're all for it. Park just has one condition," Guy says quickly.

I freeze. "What is the condition?"

He clears his throat and I know he's uncomfortable relaying this information. "No Mason." Something flutters in my stomach and I feel like I could throw up. I don't like that sentence one bit.

"What does that mean? Like at all, or during the party?" I glance at Mason. He's watching me closely, an obvious annoyed expression plastered across his face. I frown at him. He couldn't have heard Guy. Could he?

"During the party." Not that it really matters because my answer would be the same either way.

"No."

"Come on, Hope. I know it's stupid and he has no right to be a prick, but it's the only way he'll do it. We need this."

"No. Goodbye." I end the call and shove my phone back into my pocket. There's no point arguing about this. I will not give Mason up, even for one night.

"When did you talk to Park?" Mason asks immediately.

"Last night," I say trying to understand where his clipped tone is coming from. "Why?"

He leans on my table, hugging his elbows. "Before or after you came to my house?"

"Before. Again, why?"

"Well, gee, I don't know, Hope." He leans closer, dropping his voice. "Maybe I'm just curious if my girlfriend was talking to her ex-boyfriend before or after we had sex for the first time."

Oh. "Okay. One, I can talk to whoever I want. Park's been my friend for a long time and just because I'm pissed at him doesn't mean he doesn't matter to me anymore. Two, he's not my ex-boyfriend and you know that. And three, he is the lead singer of the band I'm in. We are going to see and speak to each other a lot."

"All right. Fine. But you could have mentioned it to me." He pulls back, crossing his arms in front of his chest and looks at me expectantly.

"Really? I need to give you a detailed summary of every conversation I have with Park? Or does it even stop there? Do you want a report when I talk to Guy and Chase too?"

"No. Just Park. And just the general idea."

He's serious. Is this normal? I honestly don't know. I never did this whole boyfriend thing before. Park never cared who I talked to. Of course, I never really talked to anyone. *Damn it.*

I raise a brow and purse my lips. "Fine. Annie said he didn't think you and I would last. He was waiting for you to get tired of my lack of commitment. I set him straight. He didn't take it well. Happy?"

Mason's lips twitch like he wants to smile, but thinks better of it at the last second. "Yes. Thank you." He stops fighting it, freeing the dimpled grin. "So what's going on?" He gestures at me, indicating my phone call with Guy, I assume.

"Have you always been this nosy?"

"Yes."

I roll my eyes. "Warren Grant is having a party Friday and wants us to play." I stop there because I have no intentions of going.

"Well, that's good. Right?"

Mr. Roberts calls the class to attention and Mason turns around hesitantly. I consider the subject finished.

29

Mason

Hope's quiet on the way to lunch. I take her hand and receive a small smile, but it's apparent something is bothering her. I probably pissed her off with my temper tantrum about Park. Yeah, that was shitty of me. She's one hundred percent right. All three points she ticked off were legit. I'm acting like a little boy, I know, but it freaks me out. She was with him/not really with him for a year. Their break up/not really break up is still fresh. They have the band. He's Guy's best friend and Guy is her best friend. They have this history and connection that I don't and—I'm jealous. I should trust her. She's *my* girlfriend. We're together. In a real relationship. She never had that with Park. But I can't help being protective of her. Being protective of us. I'm in new territory and haven't worked out the best way to handle it yet. But I'm trying. I'm determined not to totally fuck this up again.

"Hey. I'm sorry about earlier. About Park. I was being stupid and jealous and... Well, I'm just sorry."

She smirks. "You've done a lot of apologizing since I met you."

I scratch my neck uncomfortably. I have, haven't I? "Yeah. I screw up a lot, so it kind of goes together."

"We're good," she says. I squeeze her fingers. "Kiss me before we go in there."

I pull on her hand bringing us chest to chest and lower my head. I kiss her gently and she hums happily against my mouth. *Hell.* I really, really wish we weren't at school.

"You're going to make me puke," Chase calls loudly as he passes us, moving through the doors. He glances back making a gagging gesture.

"Bite me," Hope replies. Chase pauses and does an about face, walking toward us with purpose. "You touch me with that mouth and I'll hurt you." Hope slaps at him and he laughs.

"Tease," he says with an exaggerated shake of his head.

I put my hand on his chest. "Back off my girl. I like you, don't make me have to kick your ass."

Chase huffs. "Like you could, Patel. I've been working out." He pulls his sleeve up to his shoulder and flexes his gangly arm. "Look at that." He lowers his limb and nods his head. "It's okay, I know it's intimidating."

"Like a bunny," I say.

"A rabid bunny. With fangs," Chase adds seriously. I laugh and Hope nudges us into the cafeteria.

"So, did you agree to Park's terms?" Chase asks. My brows pull together as I look at Hope for clarification. *What terms?*

She closes her eyes for a moment and when she answers, it's through clenched teeth. "No. I did not."

"What terms?" I ask and I know I sound every bit as guarded as I feel, but seriously, *what terms?*

Chase looks from Hope to me. Back and forth several times. He tucks his lips and shakes his head. "Nothing. Never mind." *Hell no.*

I throw my hand back up on his chest as he tries to walk away. "Hold up. What terms? What are you talking about?"

He looks down at my hand and then raises his eyebrows at me pointedly, but I'm not backing down. I want to know what Park thinks he can get Hope to agree to. I glare venomously at him, giving my own message.

"Not me, man. I'm not the one you have beef with, so back up." He wraps his hand around my wrist and it takes me a few tense seconds to drop my arm. My first instinct is always to fight, but he's right. I'm not pissed at him. I nod, letting him know I'm cool. He shoots Hope a look and she rolls her eyes.

"Park doesn't want you to go to Warren's party," she explains. "That's the only way he'll do it. I wasn't even going to mention it because it doesn't matter. I said no."

I may make stupid decisions from time to time, but I'm not a complete moron. I know there is only one reason Park would put this stipulation on Hope. And there is no freaking way I am letting it go. It's time I make shit real clear for the guys in this school.

I pivot on my heel, jaw grinding as I scan faces. As soon as I spot him I move toward his table quickly. I'm just itching to put my fist through something right now. Hope cuts. I fight. We all deal with our shit in different ways.

Every muscle is tense as I stop in front of Park's seat. He looks up at me and the disdain he regards me with is miniscule compared to the red hot rage I know is radiating off me. I want to beat his ass and I don't even care that he's Hope's ex or Guy's friend.

"You need to walk away from me, right now," Park says through his teeth.

Oh, yeah. I want to hurt this asshole. "You need to stop making demands. Especially when it comes to *my girl.*" I stress the end, unmistakably staking my claim for everyone around to hear. Hope's mine.

"That's not your decision to make," Park spits.

"No. It's mine," Hope says calmly. I turn my head and she's staring hard at Park.

"I don't want him there," he says, his voice low. "This is hard enough. The band is mine. I should at least get that."

All the air seems to leave Hope, deflating her. "All right." She holds his gaze. "You can have the band. Find a new drummer."

"What?" Chase says from behind me. "No."

Park sits forward in his chair, resting his hands flat on the table in front of him. "That's not what I meant—"

"That's what you get," Hope interrupts. They're locked in some kind of silent debate. It takes every ounce of strength not to step in between them, cutting off his view of her.

Park finally cracks. He drops his eyes, squinting at the table. "Bring whoever you want. I don't give a shit anymore." He gives me a fierce glance, anger rolling off him in waves. "But just so we're clear—" He stands up, his chair sliding out loudly in the eerily quiet cafeteria. I close my hand, making a fist. "You come near me outside of school, you'll regret it." And then he turns around and walks away. He turned his back on me, not only cutting off my response, but telling me loud and clear he isn't afraid of me. He should be, though, and that's what bothers me most. I outweigh the guy by at least a good twenty pounds. I have a few inches on him. I've been in my share of fights. I look at Hope and imagine losing her a year from now and the pain in my chest has me looking back to Park's retreating form. He's a man with nothing left to lose. He's in love with her and she broke his heart. For me. And I don't know how to feel. I'm not about to give her up, but I actually think I might feel a little bad for the guy. I sure as hell don't want that to be me. Ever.

****

Tonight is my first date with Hope. I'm excited as hell to take her out as my girlfriend. I originally didn't plan anything other than picking her up at six, but Mom was so horrified by this that I spent all last night detailing our date. As soon as I got home from school today, I started cooking. Everything I made has a fruit or vegetable in it. I packed it all up, picnic style and loaded it in the trunk. Hope is either going to love or hate it. I'm not even going to lie, I'm nervous as shit. As lame as it sounds, I tried on four different outfits before settling on a white button up with dark jeans. I roll the sleeves to my elbows and attempt to do something with my hair for once. I want her to know she means enough for me to make an effort.

Mom switched her shift so I didn't have to worry about Kellin and I have full use of the car. I think she's more eager about this date than I am. Well, maybe not more, but definitely as much as me. And I know she's dying to meet Hope, but that will have to wait. Maybe this weekend I'll invite Hope over for lunch. Mom will appreciate that. Is it too soon for them to meet? Shit. I don't have a clue. I've never made it this far into a relationship before.

Ten minutes on my hair and it still falls into my eyes. I give up and go out to the living room for Mom to gush.

"I'm heading out," I announce and lean over the couch to kiss her cheek. "Hope has a midnight curfew, so I'll be home a little after."

"All right. Have fun. And be careful. And responsible." Mom smacks a kiss on my forehead and combs her fingers through my hair.

"I will. I promise." I hold up three fingers, scout's honor and she rolls her eyes.

"You were never in Boy Scouts," she says. "They probably would've kicked you out." She laughs at her joke and clears her throat. "Do you have your phone?"

"Yes."

"Is it charged?"

"Yes, Mom. And the charger's in the car just in case." I open the door and almost make it outside.

"Mace?"

I sigh and turn around. "Yeah?" God, please don't let her ask me if I have condoms. It's not like she doesn't know I have an active sex life, but I still don't want to talk about it with her. Especially when it comes to Hope.

"You look handsome," Mom says with a proud smile.

I grin and step back into the room to give her one more kiss. "Thanks. Love you."

"Love you too. *Be safe*. And you know what I mean," she calls as I shut the door behind me. I was so close. She just had to get that in there. Tonight is not about sex. Not that I don't want to make love to Hope again, because it's all I think about, but tonight is about spending time with her away from school and her house. However, I pull my wallet out at the car and verify that I do have protection, just in case. I shake my head. I am not getting with Hope in the back of my mom's car. Though that image is now in my head.

I rub my face and take a deep breath. And then another. I start to put the key in the ignition and notice my hands are shaking. At this point I'm not sure if it's my nerves or anticipation. Maybe a little of both. Or a lot of both. I get the next six hours with Hope. Alone.

30
Hope

"He's early," I exclaim. Annie pushes me back down on the computer chair and continues to curl my hair. She's been working on it for the past forty minutes and I have to admit it looks pretty good. I decided I've spent too much time hiding. I want to look nice for Mason. For our first date.

"Oh, my God. Look at you smiling," Annie says. She grins as she runs her fingers through my hair, loosening the curls. "Mason Patel is your bitch Kryptonite."

I don't even respond. Because she's right. Mason makes me happy.

Annie folds a tissue in front of my face expectantly. "Blot."

Guy peeks his head in the door as I press my lips around the tissue. His eyebrows jump up and he smirks. "Your date is here."

"I know. He's early. Go entertain him for me. I just have to change and I'll be down."

Guy nods. "You look nice," he says, his hand circling around his face. "Different, but good."

"Thanks."

"Nice? She looks amazing," Annie says insulted. She hands me the sundress that's hung in my closet, untouched, since Jenny bought it for me last year. I never even thought about wearing it until today. First of all, it's white and I'm not really the white dress type, but it's also shorter than any dress I've ever been willing to wear. Plus, it's a dress and I just don't do dresses unless it's a special occasion. I decided tonight is special.

Annie shoos Guy and closes the door. I go to our bathroom to change, not wanting her to see my scars. I really don't want to go there tonight. As soon as I open the door, she squeals and shoves her hot pink flats at me. "Wear these. You look so pretty. Mason's not going to recognize you."

I take a look at myself in the full length mirror. My stomach flutters. The pink shoes match the pink in my hair almost perfectly. I thought the white would wash me out since I'm already so pale, but with my dark hair, it actually contrasts nicely. The dark eyeliner makes my eyes look bluer and the thin straps show off my shoulders and collar bones. Areas I know Mason likes for some reason. I tug the bottom of the dress afraid when I walk my scars will be visible.

I sigh. He already knows about them. He's touched them. Kissed them. I feel the heat move up my neck and over my face with the memory. I take a deep breath and turn away from the mirror.

"Get down there," Annie urges. "I can't wait for him to see you."

She heads down before me, nearly running so she doesn't miss Mason's reaction, which is exactly the one she was hoping for. He stops, midsentence, as I round the corner. Eyes go wide as they slowly study me, head to toe and back up again. My heart beats quickly, waiting for him to say something.

Standing from the couch, Mason clears his throat. He doesn't look away from me as he says, "I'll see you later, Guy."

Guy chuckles. "Don't do anything I wouldn't do." He frowns as I laugh. "No, seriously, there isn't much I wouldn't do. Shit. Don't do anything I would do, either." He takes two steps after us, running his hands through his hair. "You aren't going to a movie, are you?"

I bite my lip and glance up at Mason. He's still staring at me. He takes my hand and shakes his head. "Nah. No movie."

"Okay. Good," Guy sighs. "She has to be home by twelve."

Mason pauses, finally looking at him. "I know. I'll have her home on time." He smiles at Guy's disheveled appearance. "I'll take care of her. I promise."

"Bye, Dad," I tease as I kiss Guy's cheek.

"Ha. Ha. Ha. You're so funny, Hope." Guy crosses his arms, but kisses the top of my head. "Have fun," he says.

~***~

As soon as we hit the bridge, I realize where Mason's taking me. I smile at him and he squeezes my hand. "The Pond?"

"The Pond," he agrees. "I like it there."

"I do too." A shiver runs through me as the memory of our first time there replays in my mind. I glance up at the dark clouds and wonder how long we'll have before the rain hits. Maybe it'll pass us by.

Pulling to a stop, Mason turns to me. "I don't really know what to say about this." He gestures at me before brushing his fingers over my hair. He regards me nervously and my stomach tightens. "I want to tell you

you look beautiful, but I know you don't like that." He dips his chin toward his chest and presses his lips together. "Is it all right if I say that I couldn't breathe for a minute when I saw you? Or that it took every last ounce of self restraint to not start making out with you in front of Guy and Annie? Because the only thing that held me back was the idea you wouldn't like that very much."

I grin at him and make a show of looking around. "They aren't here now."

Mason leans into me, trailing kisses from my ear to my jaw. When he moves to my chin I drop my head so he meets my lips instead. I open my mouth against his, parting his lips in the process. He murmurs something indecipherable and sinks into the kiss. I twist my fingers into his hair and he groans, pulling away slowly.

He licks his lips, one corner pulling up, showing off the dimple that I will never get enough of. "I'm all for staying in the car kissing you, but I packed you a picnic. Are you hungry?"

Oh, yeah, but not for food. "Starving," I whisper.

Mason stares at me so intensely my pulse picks up. I watch his throat as he swallows and a little high pitched noise bubbles in my own throat. My chest is moving quickly as my breathing accelerates. The desire building in this car is overwhelming.

We move at the same time, crushing into each other. Mason's hands cup my face as he kisses me hard. I scramble closer until I'm in his lap, the steering wheel against my back. He slides his fingers down my neck, my chest, my stomach. Glides them under my dress. Over my thighs, around my hips. He grips my back and pants against me.

"I cooked for you," he says in between kisses. His voice is thick, causing goose bumps to raise the hair on my arms.

"You cooked?"

He nods, his lips moving against my neck. "Ravioli." He flicks his tongue over my pulse. "Bread." He nips gently at my shoulder. "Chocolate." He skims his nose over my collar bone.

"Chocolate?" I breathe.

"Mm-hm." His warm tongue slides into the indent below my throat and I tremble. "I could feed you and then I could kiss you. I wouldn't mind doing both at the same time. I want to taste chocolate from your lips."

Oh. Hot. Damn. Yes, please. I nod as his mouth devours mine.

"Best date ever," he utters. I laugh and climb off his lap. "Wait here while I set everything up."

I watch Mason as he spreads a dark blue blanket out on the grass and then empties the contents from a large box. He lights candles, placing them along one side of the blanket and I smile. He's trying so hard. I can't believe he cooked. I didn't even know he could. After he's satisfied with everything, he turns back to the car, opening the door for me.

"This is awesome, Mason. I love it."

He arches a brow and sighs. "Don't commit to that just yet," he replies. He guides me to sit and opens a container. "Mushroom ravioli with homemade tomato sauce."

I try not to recoil from the evil container, but seriously, mushrooms. I cringe and Mason laughs that full body laugh. "I told you I was going to introduce you to veggies."

"Mushrooms are fungus," I squeak. "Not food. We can readdress this when I have an infection. And even then, I think I'd rather die."

He laughs again as he wraps his fingers around a fork. "Just take one bite," he says softly. "If you hate it I'll take you to get a cheeseburger."

I watch him poke at a ravioli and shiver. "Promise?"

"Promise." He brings the fork to my mouth and I hesitate for only a second. I don't want to hurt his feelings. I pull up my big girl panties, close my eyes, and take the bite.

I open one eye and peek at his uneasy expression as I chew. Then I open the other eye. "Mmm. Oh, my Buddha, this is really good."

Grinning, Mason leans in for a kiss, licking sauce from my bottom lip. "Delicious," he mumbles. He hands me the fork and I dig in. He's cute, funny, and he can cook. I think I'll keep him.

"You said something about bread…?"

He nods, opening another container. "Zucchini bread. Also homemade." He rips a chunk off the small loaf and offers it to me, laughing at the irate look I give him.

"You put a vegetable in the bread? That's just sick." I pluck it from his fingers and smell it uncertainly. But it smells incredible. I take a small bite. It's almost gooey and tastes more like cake than bread. It's so good. "What the hell? You're a wizard."

"I prefer warlock," he says leaning in for another kiss. He apparently wants to taste everything on my lips. "I brought your grape juice as well."

"Not homemade? I'm so disappointed."

"Maybe next time. I'll buy a juicer first thing tomorrow."

"Where did this come from?" I ask between bites. "The cooking, I mean."

He shrugs. "Mom's Italian. She loves Italian food, but she can't cook to save her life. Dad and I used to find recipes and try them out. Some of them I've made so many times I know them by heart."

"Like mushroom ravioli?"

"No. Like homemade sauce and noodles. Mom hates mushrooms."

I shoot him a look. Funny. Jerk. "Do you cook a lot?"

He looks out at the water and shakes his head. "Not a whole lot. I've taught Kel how to make a few things. Mom does most of the cooking now. Our menu is pretty small. We're restricted to the few things she doesn't burn." He chuckles and finishes his last bite.

"Thank you for cooking for me," I whisper. "I love everything. I love the food. I love this place. I love this whole night." I tuck a curl behind my ear and glance down at my now empty bowl.

His fingers brush my cheek before lifting my chin. He caresses my lips with his thumb. I open my mouth enough for him to feel my tongue as I kiss his smooth skin. "I love your hands." Mason's body trembles in a way I've never seen, encouraging me to continue. I work my way over his palm, then wrist, leaving kisses up his arm. "I love your arms." When I'm cut off by his shirt, I move to his neck. He growls and I feel it against my lips. "I love your neck."

He shifts, taking hold of my head, fingers tightening into my hair. He brings his mouth to mine and kisses me with urgency. I lean into him, pushing him back until we're lying down. "I love you," he breathes. "I love you. I love you."

I feel a drop of cool water hit my shoulder. And then another. I ignore it, too absorbed in the way Mason makes me feel. More drops hit my skin, picking up speed and I finally pull back. Rain hits my face and I hold my hands out.

"Of course," Mason groans, "it would rain." He sits up and starts shoving everything back into the box while I blow out the candles. By the time we get the blanket folded, thunder rumbles in the sky. He takes my hand and pulls me toward the car. "I'm sorry. I should've checked the weather." He shakes his head as he opens the trunk.

"Hey," I say grabbing the side of his shirt. "I like the rain."

He slams the trunk closed and turns to me. It's raining hard now, soaking my hair and running down my face. "I had this all planned out. We didn't even have dessert." He blows out a frustrated breath, sending a mist off his lips. All I can think about is how the rain will feel on his mouth. Against my mouth.

"Shut up," I say as I pull him against me. "You can be my dessert."

One of the things I love about Mason, he just goes with it. He embraces me, lifting me onto the top of the trunk and stepping in between my legs as our mouths come together once again. He moves to my neck and I let my head fall back. The rain cools my face and my hair clings to my arms. I push my knees into either side of his waist. His warm hands slide over my wet body and he moans loudly.

"Jesus, Hope. You have ruined me. I love you so much."

I find his lips again, desperate for his kiss. His closeness.

Our eyes meet, gazes locking as the water plasters our clothes to us. Lightening illuminates the sky as more thunder shakes the ground, ending our moment. He takes my hand and we stumble into the car, drenched from head to toe. His white shirt sticks to him like an extra skin, revealing every defined muscle in his arms and abdomen. His dark hair lies across his forehead, dripping over his eyes. He's never looked more gorgeous.

Mason grins widely. "All right. I can officially say I love the rain."

31

Mason

God, Hope looks amazing wet. And that little white dress—yeah, I'm having a hard time keeping my eyes on the road. She smells so good too. Her raspberry scent mixed with the rain fills the car. I can't tell if I'm in Heaven or Hell. I'm fighting the urge to pull over and find out.

Hope turns the heat on. Her teeth are chattering and that helps sober my desire some. But she looks damn good shivering too, so not by much. I take her cool hand in mine. "I'll get you home," I assure her.

"I don't want to go home."

I glance at her. "You're freezing. You're soaking wet. You need to get something warm and dry on."

"Take me to your house. I can throw my dress in the dryer."

I suck on my lip for a moment while I try to think. "Yeah, okay. Mom probably has something you can wear," I agree.

Hope looks down at herself and laughs. "I'm going to make a great first impression."

"My mom is going to love you. You could be wearing a garbage bag and she wouldn't care." My eyes linger on her wet form and I bite down on the inside of my cheek. *I have to take her home. I cannot pull over. Hands to yourself, Patel.*

"What's she like?" Hope doesn't look at me; instead she keeps her focus on the tress outside the window.

I scratch my head and sigh lightly. "She's cool. I mean, I hate the way she can't deal with shit and keeps moving us around. Like running from state to state will keep her from feeling the loss of Dad. But I get why she does it. She's easy to talk to, and works her ass off to make sure we have a roof and food." I smile and glance at Hope. She's watching me carefully as I continue. "She loves music. Just as much as Dad did. We've had the cops called on us for noise disturbance. They come out thinking it's kids having a party and it's my thirty-nine year old mother blasting the radio."

"Does she play an instrument?"

I shake my head. "Nah. Mom's a listener."

"What's her favorite band?"

I chuckle. "Why do you always ask that?"

"It's a good question. You can learn a lot about someone by the music they listen to."

"Like what?" I ask curiously.

"Well, like, if someone listens to only one kind of music that says to me they're probably a black and white person. You know, everything is either one way or the other. No in between. They're most likely someone that's set in their ways and I probably wouldn't get along with them. Someone who listens to a broad assortment of music is more open to different things. Sees there's more than one way to look at things. Therefore, a person I could possibly relate to. A person who likes music focusing on the lyrics is most likely deeper than someone who wants to dance to techno. Again, my kind of people."

I smile. Leave it to Hope to sum up personalities based on their taste in music. "So, what about people that like, I don't know...jazz?"

"They're a musical people, which mean they're sensitive and creative. They like a variety of sound, so they're probably harder to satisfy."

"Hmm. What did it say to you when Kellin told you his favorite band is Green Day?"

She looks at me for a moment before turning back to the window. "It wasn't that he liked Green Day that said something, although Green Day is a good band, even though they're overplayed, so I knew he had good taste. It was the admiration on his face when he said you're teaching him to play the guitar. But that said more about you, I guess."

That throws me off. I gaze at her profile, feeling my brows pull together. "What did it say about me?"

She clears her throat, still not looking at me. "Playing an instrument says you have passion. Taking the time to teach someone else, especially someone younger, says you're not only sweet, but patient. It told me you obviously like music. Musicians typically appreciate all music, so it told me you were more open. The fact that your little brother thought you were good meant you're dedicated. And the way he looked at you, like you hung the moon, spoke loudest of all. It told me that someone loved you. That you had to be a good person to have so much respect from your brother when most brothers can't seem to get along. It told me you were special."

I don't have a response to that. I'm torn between arguing with her that that's not who I am at all and hugging her for saying those things. I don't think anyone's ever said anything so nice about me before.

"Then I got to know you and now I know my theories were right." She finally lets her eyes settle on mine. "You're fucking awesome, Mason Patel and I'm grateful you're mine."

I pull in the driveway and practically pull her out of the car. I just want to touch her. My mind's reeling. I love the way she called me hers. But at the same time I'm starting to get scared. Like something is going to happen because the universe can't allow one person to have this much happiness. Like it'll decide it has to set things right by taking it away.

The wind picks up, making it rain sideways. I drag Hope through the side door and straight down to the basement. "I'll get us some towels." I run back upstairs, checking each room for Mom and Kellin. I fish my phone out of my pocket hoping it's not waterlogged. It's damp, the screen fogged, but it works and I call Mom's cell.

"What's wrong?" she asks panicked.

"Nothing. Calm down. I came home because we got caught in the rain. Where are you?"

"Zack is taking us to dinner," she says.

"Who the hell's Zack?"

Her voice is quiet, her tone irritated. "Our neighbor. Kellin is at his house all the time playing with his son. You should know this, Mace. He asked us to have dinner with them. Do you need me to come home?"

"No," I say slowly. "Is this a date? I don't even know this guy."

"Mason Xavier, your *brother* and I are on our way to share a meal with friends. I'm trying to enjoy our evening. I suggest you go do the same."

"When will you be home?"

She sighs. "I'm not sure. A couple hours maybe."

I grunt and she sighs again. "We'll talk when I get there," she says. "I love you."

"Love you too."

I throw my phone on the table and grab two towels. I stop at the bottom of the stairs, my breath hitching in my throat. Hope's back is to me, her dress a soggy pile at her bare feet. She's twisted her hair to one shoulder as it drips down her arm, her bare back smooth. Round, purple bruises dot her spine. I move tentatively, opening the towel and wrapping it around her, in no hurry to cover her up, but wanting to hide the reminder that flashes like a neon sign across her back. She leans into me and I press my lips to her neck.

"Your mom's not here?"

"Hm-mm. Just us."

She turns around, letting the towel fall to the cement floor. I move to kiss her, but she puts her hands on my chest, unbuttoning my shirt. She slips it over my shoulders, her fingers sliding over my arms. I go in for a kiss just to be stopped again. I groan and she strokes her hands down my stomach, stopping on the button of my jeans. I stare, fixated on her fingers as she works the button loose. My jeans stick to me as I help her maneuver them off my legs. And then she picks up our clothes. I rub my face as I watch her bend over to put them in the dryer.

"I'm cold, Mason." She bites her lip, looking anything but cold. She takes deliberately slow steps toward me and I'm a second away from dropping at her feet. This girl is a goddess and I am her slave. "Keep me warm?"

I take two quick steps and drag her against me. This time she doesn't stop me from colliding with her mouth. I grip her ass and lift her. She wraps her legs around my hips. Walking backward, I collapse onto the old loveseat. "You feel... plenty warm," I gasp.

"Oh, good. It's working then." She smiles and nips my neck. She presses into me as her tongue massages my skin and I forget my reply. With expert movements, Hope unhooks her bra, tossing it to the floor. "Mason," she breathes against my ear.

"Yeah?" I choke out.

"I'm having a great time on our date." I laugh, grabbing her tightly. This hasn't gone according to plan, but it's been the best night of my life.

"What are you doing tomorrow? Because I wouldn't mind doing this every night."

She kisses me, softly at first, but the longer it goes on, the rougher her mouth becomes. Her hand glides into my boxers and as she grabs me I nearly lose it from one touch. "Every night," she repeats my words.

"I love you, Hope." I can't stop saying it. I want to shout it. I want everyone to know it.

"Show me," she whispers.

And so I do.

32
Hope

"I forgot about these last night," Mason says, sliding a square container across the lunch table. I feel my cheeks warm, remembering why he forgot. "Your chocolate."

I pop the lid off and stare at the chocolate covered strawberries. Damn him and his mission to get me to eat fruits and vegetables. He smirks knowingly as I pick one up. Cheese and rice. Chocolate covered strawberries are the absolute best things ever. "Mmm," I moan. He kisses me, his tongue searching for chocolate on my lips.

"I want one," Chase whines. I reluctantly pull away from Mason and offer the container around the table.

"So, about tonight," Guy says slowly. "I told Warren we'd play his party." I glare at him and he hurries on. "I assumed that was okay since Park renounced his condition and we could all use the money. We need to be there by eight. Park's stopping by so we can run through a quick practice after school." He shifts to face Mason. "I told him you would most likely be there and he said he'd be cool as long as you keep your distance from him."

Mason's jaw tightens, a fine vein on his neck standing out. "Yeah, man. I won't be striking up a conversation with him."

Chase laughs around a bite of strawberry. "I love a good fight."

"Nobody's gonna fight, Chase," I say quickly. "Shut up."

Chase shakes his head, smirking. "Park's been lit all week. You know he'll be wasted at the party. Alcohol tends to loosen one's inhibitions. The minute he sees Mason touch you, he'll be all over his ass." He nods at Mason and rubs his hands together. "I'm just saying, shit's about to get interesting."

Mason massages his forehead and stares at me for a moment. "He starts shit with me, I'm going to defend myself. If he starts shit with you, I'm going to defend you. I just want that out there now."

"Then I'm not going," I say.

"You have to go," Guy replies. I give him a hard look and he rolls his eyes. "I'll talk to Park again. Nothing will happen. This afternoon can be, like, a dress rehearsal. If anything goes down at practice, then we won't go to the party."

Mason squeezes my hand and smiles. "I'll be on my best behavior."

"I'm not worried about you," I mumble. My phone vibrates on the table and Mason's eyes scrunch as he reads the name.

"Who's Princess Bitch?" he asks, chuckling.

"Annie," Guy and Chase say at the same time.

I read her text and close my eyes. Inhaling deeply, I send back a reply. "She's going to the party with us," I announce.

"Oh, joy," Guy states flatly.

"Hell yeah," Chase says. "Fights and cheerleaders. It's gonna be an epic night."

Guy backhands his arm. "Dude, would you shut up already?"

Chase rubs his arm, laughing quietly. "What?"

"What's his name in your phone?" Mason asks me, not so subtly changing the subject. He nods at Chase and I smile.

"Escalator."

He lifts one brow. "Escalator?"

Guy and I laugh. Chase glares at us and crosses his arms. I wipe a tear from the corner of my eye. "Dumbass got his shoe lace caught in an escalator at the mall," I say. "What was it? Like a year ago? Anyway, his lace gets caught and he falls flat on his face. Guy had to take the shoe off to get him free. Then Park cuts the laces to free the shoe. Funniest thing I've ever witnessed." I laugh again.

"He cried like a little baby, thinking he was going to get sucked into the escalator," Guy adds. "We had to take him straight home so he could change his pants."

Mason chuckles and Chase smacks the table. "I did not piss myself! Somebody spilled a drink on the floor and it got on me when I landed. Shut the fuck up."

We laugh harder and Chase shakes his head, fighting his own laughter. "You guys are dicks. I could've died."

I can barely breathe now. I lean into Mason and wipe at my eyes once again. It's been awhile since I laughed this hard.

"That's all right, man," Mason says. "Same thing happened to me once."

Chase sits forward. "Really?"

Mason shakes his head, grinning. "Hell no. I tie my freaking shoes."

Guy bangs his fist on the table and points at Mason, unable to talk. He tries to throw his hand over his mouth, but it's too late. Orange drink spews across the table and we all wail with obnoxious laughter. I jump up to grab napkins. I make it only a few feet before I catch Park watching me. His expression is amused, but he also seems kind of sad. I offer him a smile. I don't know if he returns it because I drop my gaze and grab the much needed napkins.

~***~

Mason is perched on Guy's amp and I sit on the floor between his legs, my head resting on his thigh. It's weird how this is normal already. The way we connect ourselves has become second nature. There's no awkwardness in the way we reach for each other. If we're close enough to touch then we do. His fingers brush through my hair in a hypnotic way that has my eyes fluttering. It's one of those really great moments where the silence isn't awkward. Instead, it's soothing and completely comfortable.

It doesn't last. Guy clomps down the stairs, followed by Chase. "Get your lazy ass up," Guy shouts. "We've got preparations to…*prepare*."

I smile, but stay right where I am. I'm not ready to move away from Mason yet. "Park's not here."

"Yes, he is," Park says as his legs appear on the steps. He runs down the remaining stairs, his footfalls light. His eyes find me immediately, take in my position, and flick away quickly. Rubbing his hands together and staring at the wall, he adds, "Let's get this over with."

I use Mason's knees to push myself up and he places his hands over mine. He kisses my forehead and I press into his lips. "No fighting," I whisper. He nods, his expression innocent, and I wonder how sincere he is. I squint at him and he chuckles, releasing my hands.

"I'll be good. Promise." I can't help it, I shiver at those words. His little reminder that I asked him not to be good. Even though it's totally different, he gets the desired effect. All I can think about now is his lips, his hands, his body, and the way they press against me.

"Can we maybe do this sometime today?" Park sighs. "I've got shit to do." I blink out of my desire-hazed thoughts and reluctantly turn away from Mason.

Chase gasps. "What? You have other friends? I feel so…so *betrayed*." He wipes away a pretend tear.

Park's face is stoic. He shakes his head and picks up a mic. "Yeah? Join the club. I ordered jackets."

I bite my lip to hold in my retort. Snatching my drumsticks off the snare, I plop down behind the drum set and slam my foot down on the base peddle. Mason catches my eye and I'm surprised to see something like regret tracing his features. His gaze slides to Park and I realize it's more like pity. Mason feels bad for Park. My stomach pulls tight, twisting, and I feel nauseous suddenly. If Mason feels bad for Park then what does that say about me? It's not like I didn't feel bad already knowing I hurt him, but to have Mason thinking it—hurts. Too much.

My eyes burn. My stomach churns. I hate feeling like this. I want to scream. I need to cut. My fingers squeeze the drum sticks until my knuckles whiten. I bang them down hard enough to knock the snare over, but I don't care. I just kick it out of the way and shove past Guy. He reaches for me and I flinch away. I just want out of this basement. Away from Park. Away from Mason.

"Hope," Park calls, an apology in his voice.

"Fuck off," I murmur.

I pound up the stairs and straight out the back door. I don't even know where I'm going.

"Hope?" I freeze at the sound of Park's voice and tuck my hands into my sides. "What?" I don't turn around. I don't want to look at him. Mason is the first dude I have ever felt this way about, the first I've ever wanted to let in, and I will always pay for it.

"Hey, I'm sorry," he says quietly. "I shouldn't have said that. I didn't mean it."

I laugh in a way that's supposed to sound cold, but comes out strangled and pathetic. "Yes, you did."

He's quiet for so long, I finally glance back at him. "Okay, maybe a little. I just feel that way sometimes. It's hard, ya know? I don't think you understand how things were for me. How things are for me now. I didn't believe you. When you said we weren't together, I thought you were just talking shit. I thought you were afraid I'd hurt you or something. I thought it was your way of feeling secure. I had no idea you really meant it." He shifts the hair out of his eyes and crosses his arms. His boots scrape at the cement step. I don't know how to respond. All I know is there is so much guilt inside and I loathe myself so completely.

"I was in love with you." I flinch away from his words or his tone. They both strike at me. "That's not easy to turn off. I'm hurt and I'm pissed. I'm trying to deal because I want you in my life, but I see how you look at him." He peers at me, that same expression on his face from lunch. “He makes you happy and I will always want that for you, but—shit—it hurts like hell that it isn’t me making you smile.” He gestures at me, frowning. “I do *this* to you. I know we can’t go back, but I’m going to work on being your friend.”

“Park—I loved you. I did. I do. It just wasn’t…”

“Yeah. I know.” He unhooks his arms and shoves his hands in his pockets, shrugging. “I get it now.”

“I didn’t mean to hurt you. I never meant for this to happen.”

He smiles sadly. “I know that too. You can’t help how you feel.”

“I don’t deserve you.” My voice is shaky. I take a step in his direction and he knows what I want without me having to say it. Park pulls me into a hug, his arms wrapping securely around my back. He makes a noise and sighs. “We shouldn’t make a habit of this.” He’s right. I don’t own the dating rule book, but I’m pretty sure hugging your kind of ex-boyfriend is a pretty big no-no. “I don’t want to let you go,” he whispers. I don’t know if he means the hug or something more. Either way, I pull back.

Park sighs. "I may make more shitty comments in the near future, but I don't mean any of them. Just ignore them, or punch me, or something."

I laugh weakly. "All right. Deal."

"I'm gonna go back inside. I think your boyfriend wants to either kick my ass or talk to you." He smiles ruefully. "Probably both."

I look up at the door where Mason paces in and out of view, hands on hips. I can't help the way my body relaxes at the sight of him even when he's obviously aggravated with me.

Park opens the door and he and Mason slide past one another as if the other doesn't exist. I lean against the house, the siding flexing with the pressure from my back.

"You all right?" Mason asks. He stops in front of me, his shoes on either side of mine, and he smoothes his palms across my hips.

"I'm confused. You act like you can't stand Park, but you feel bad for him. You want details when I talk to him, but it bothers you the way he's hurting. The way I hurt him."

Mason blinks slowly and steps back. "I do feel bad for him. It's apparent he's in pain. That doesn't mean I can't still dislike him."

"And it's my fault."

He tilts his head, eyes grazing slowly over my features. His voice is soft, careful. "You're the reason he's in pain, but it's not your fault. I don't think blame can be assigned in a situation like this."

I look away. "I knew it. I don't know why I fooled myself into thinking it could be different."

Mason's grip tightens on my waist. "What does that mean?"

I can't look at him. I won't. "You see it. The real me. The fuck up." I huff out a small laugh. "I knew it wouldn't last."

"What the hell are you talking about?" His voice is angry now and I don't know why it surprises me.

"This is what I do. I hurt people." I take a breath, but I can't *breathe*. "It's in my blood. My mom, she turned Guy's uncle, Donnie, into an alcoholic. She ruined him. He wanted to help her, and she killed him. All he wanted was to help her change, but she changed him. She was good at one thing, Mason, hurting people. That's what she always did. It's what I'll always do."

He shakes his head, disgusted. "Why are you letting someone else's past decide your future?" His words rake over me like gravel. "First off, I'm pretty damn sure it's not possible to turn someone into an alcoholic. Donnie had to do that to himself. And your mom didn't kill him. He was driving."

I look up quickly at that. "Guy told me," he says. "His uncle made his own decisions, Hope. Your mom didn't force him. And yes, Park is hurt over you. He loves you and wants to be with you, but you didn't try to cause him pain. I can relate to him because I love you and I can imagine what it would feel like if I lost you. You're not a fuck up. I hate to break it to you, but you are completely normal. And you're beautiful. The problem isn't who you are. It's who you *think* you are."

"Ugh." I push him away from me because that speech felt too good. I want to lean into him and allow his words to consume me. "Don't call me that."

"What? Beautiful? I don't want to be afraid to tell you how I feel. I think you're beautiful. I can't help that. *I love you.* You will always be beautiful to me. I know that word means something awful and ugly for you, but fuck that. Fuck *him*. Don't let a pedophile ruin who you are. Don't let him have that kind of power over you. Be your own kind of beautiful. Give it your own meaning. I'm going to tell you every day until you see you how I see you. Until you know who you really are."

There's a denial on the tip of my tongue, but Mason swallows it with a kiss. "Shh. Stop pushing me away. I don't want to keep fighting you. Just accept that I care about you too much to go anywhere."

"I don't know how," I whisper into his skin.

"Then I'll show you. Every single day."

"That's a long time."

He nods, his head moving against mine. "Forever."

"Why Mason?" I plead. "Why me? I need to know."

"I don't know, Hope. Life is funny that way, I guess. I mean, I walked through the world, passing this person, and that person. And nothing meant anything to me. Everything, everyone was just a blur in my peripheral. And then I saw you. *I saw you.* I don't know why you. And I'm not going to question it because I'm afraid that maybe if I gnaw at it too much, I'll mess with whatever happy fate made this happen. If that's not enough, there's always this." He tilts my head back and brings his mouth to mine softly.

"I don't want to be like this. All…" I shake my head, searching for the right words. "Scared and insecure all the time."

"Then don't be." His thumb glides across my lip and I look up, meeting his green eyes. "Trust me."

"It's not that I don't trust you," I say very slowly. My mind is racing. "I don't trust me. There is only so much of me you're going to be able to take. At some point, you are going to hit your limit. I'm going to keep having these insane freak outs and pushing you and you are going to get sick of me."

He laughs loudly, his eyes crinkling, the dimple winking at me. "Never gonna happen. I kind of like your freak outs. Or the part where I calm you down."

I open my mouth to argue, because it's what I do, but he shakes his head and smothers my words with another kiss. "Just shut up."

33
Mason

The band finally got their practice in after I talked Hope back into the basement. Park and I were on our best behavior, which means we ignored each other really well. I figure at some point we're probably going to have to acknowledge the other's existence, but for now, our arrangement works.

Hope's been writing lyrics across my arms since everyone took off to get ready. Her writing is small and stick like and I have to squint to read it. I keep going back to the lines on the back of my hand. ***I'm done counting days. Now because of you I'm making the days count***.

I wonder if it's part of a song already or if she's composing on my skin. The idea makes me smile and my heart beat faster. I'm also curious if I'm the inspiration behind those words. If so, it's awfully ironic because the same is true for me. Since I've met Hope, my life actually counts for something. I'm not just filling the hours. Now I'm enjoying them. I'm making plans. I'm thinking about the future and liking what I'm imagining. Life is good.

I kiss the top of her hair, inhaling her shampoo. Mangos. Funny how someone who doesn't like fruit always smells like it.

I pull my wrist up to see her newest addition. ***Sometimes when I'm kissing you, I forget***. She wraps her fingers around my wrist, shielding the line, and brings her mouth to mine. Her fingers comb my hair back from my forehead. "Don't read them right now. When you go home tonight to change, read them then."

I nod. "Okay. Are these from songs?"

She bites her lip and I nuzzle her neck, urging her to talk to me. "Guy has this music he's been holding onto for awhile. It's meant to be the big love ballad. He's pushed me to put lyrics to it since he got it finished, but I couldn't." She ducks her head into my shoulder. I feel her teeth graze against my tee shirt.

"This is them," she whispers. "It's your song."

I pull back, trying to look at her, but she comes with me, keeping her face hidden. "My song? You wrote me a love ballad?" My stomach pulls tight and my throat feels raw. Everything feels raw. I don't think I've ever felt so cut open. How can she be mine? I don't deserve her. She wrote me a song. *She wrote me a freaking song.* I want to read every word on my body right this very second.

"Hope, look at me." I push her back as gently as I can, detangling her fingers from my shirt.

"I'm embarrassed."

"Why? I love it. I don't even have to know what it says or how it sounds. I love it. I can't believe you did this for me."

"It's me. It's everything I am. Everything I feel. Things I've never felt before. I'm putting it out there. It's scary." She tries to hide again, but I grab her face and make her look at me.

"This is the nicest thing anyone has ever done for me. I don't care what anyone else thinks about it and neither should you." I kiss her and sigh. "I cannot believe you seriously wrote a song for me."

She smiles. "You're great motivation."

"When will I get to hear it?"

Hope glares at her hands, fisted in her lap. "I don't know. I don't want to ask Park to sing it."

"You can sing it," I suggest carefully. I love when she sings.

"I hate singing. I don't like everyone looking at me." She shakes her head, her hair flaring around her. "I should have Guy sing it since it's his music."

"Can Guy sing?"

"Not to save his life," she says with a grin. "Dogs can't even listen to him."

"So I'll never get to hear it?" The thought is so depressing I can't help the frown from forming.

With her first finger, she softly smoothes the crease between my brows. "I'll sing it for you. I promise. I'm just not ready yet. I wrote it, and that was hard and... I love you. Can't that be enough for now?"

"It's more than enough. I want to hear it, but I can wait." I kiss her again. I can't stop kissing her. "You're the best girlfriend," I murmur between kisses.

"That reminds me," she says standing up. "I have something for you. I'll be right back. Don't...go anywhere."

I chuckle and lean back against the wall, my hands behind my head. "I'll be here." I grin and wink at her. Her cheeks turn a soft shade of pink before she runs up the stairs.

As soon as she's gone, I obviously look at my arms. I don't read everything because she asked me to wait, but it's torture to have it right here and not at least take a peek. My breath catches as I read the words. ***You've turned my wounds into wisdom, teaching me to learn from my mistakes. Which ones are mine, and which were out of my control***.

I hear her footsteps overhead, so I lean back in the position I was in when she left. "All right, it's nothing big, but I saw it at the store with Annie the other day and it made me think of you. So—here." She holds out a plastic shopping bag and I take it. My movements are slow because I wasn't expecting her to buy me something. Even when she said she had something for me I just thought it was candy or something, because, well, it's Hope.

Inside the bag is a small box. I look from it to Hope and back again. My hand is shaking as I reach inside and if I could, I'd kick my own ass for acting so ridiculous. With a deep breath, that I hope she doesn't notice, I take the lid off the box.

A shiny silver pick catches the overhead light, blinking at me. A cursive M is printed in a metallic blue in the center. I take it out and run my thumb over it. "This is awesome, Hope. Thank you."

"Flip it over," she says quietly and instantly I know that whatever is on the back is important just from the level of her voice. I turn it over and smile. The words *take these broken wings* are gently engraved into the back. *Blackbird*. Her song. My song. Our song.

"Marry me," I say and I'm only half joking. "You are seriously the coolest person ever."

She laughs and I stand up, pulling her in for a hug. I have a beautiful girlfriend who writes me a song and gives me this awesome gift for no other reason than she saw it and thought of me. I love that she thought of me.

"I'm glad you like it."

I tuck her hair behind her ears. "I love it. I love you. This doesn't even feel real. I have to be in some long, elaborate dream because there's no way I'm this lucky." I twist my fingers into her hair. I can't explain how I feel at this moment, but it's almost like I could run to the top of a mountain, jump off, and land on my feet. I feel—powerful. Invincible.

She digs her nails into my hip, twisting painfully. "Ouch," I yell. "What was that for?"

"So you know you're not dreaming," she sings.

"You could have just kissed me."

"Mm, I didn't think of that."

"You can still kiss me," I whisper as I bring my face close to hers. She closes the last inch of space, pushing her lips hard against mine. She licks at my bottom lip and I suck her tongue into my mouth, kissing her back with equal force.

She pulls back, breathless. "You have to use it. The pick, I mean. Play for me."

I reach behind me and grab Guy's acoustic. "What do you want to hear?"

34
Hope

"I really don't want to go to this party tonight," I insist. "If you loved me at all you wouldn't make me."

Guy sighs loudly. "Then I guess I don't love you 'cause you're going," he says flatly. "It's two hours for two hundred bucks. Shut the hell up and suck it up. This will be good for us."

I cross my arms over my chest and stare out the windshield. "You do understand that the entire football team will be there. Right? You know, the dudes that make your life a living hell? The same dudes that harass you every single day at school?" I eye him in the rearview mirror, wanting to point out that one of those people did something to Annie, but unable to state it with her sitting right beside him. "Everybody we hate."

"I don't give a shit about them."

"You will when they mess with us," I mumble. This is seriously not how I want to be spending the night. I'd rather be alone with Mason, snuggled up on the couch watching a bad scary movie and munching on candy.

"What's taking so long?" Guy asks changing the subject.

"Mason had to take Kellin over to the neighbor's house. His text said he'd be out in a minute. Keep your panties on."

"I don't wanna be late. How will that look?"

"Like I don't give a shit, which I do not," I say and Annie laughs. Guy shoots her a dark look. She tucks her lips and raises her eyebrows, but doesn't comment.

"I want to at least appear professional seeing as how we are getting paid," he states.

"Well, we're not professionals," I counter. "And if you don't stop bitching I will turn around and take us back home." He leans back and runs a hand through his hair.

Mason opens the door and plops heavily onto the seat beside me. He places a kiss on my cheek and a candy bracelet in my hand. I smile, pushing it onto my wrist. Could he be any more perfect for me? I think not.

"Awe. That's sweet, Mason," Annie squeals. "Is there more of you? I want one."

"Kellin's taken," I say.

"Yeah, I'm not a cradle robber anyway," she replies. "Have they perfected that whole cloning thing yet?"

Mason chuckles and shakes his head. Guy rolls his eyes. "Can we go?"

"What did I say about your bitchiness?" I hiss. "This car is only big enough for one of us and with Annie filling that spot you need to knock it off."

"Hey!" Annie protests. "I am not being a bitch!"

"Yet," Guy and I say at the same time. I smirk at him in the mirror and he smiles back, his body noticeably relaxing.

"I don't know why I hang out with you guys. You're always so mean to me." She frowns and turns her body toward the window.

"Yeah, I don't know why you insist on hanging out with us either," I say as I back out of Mason's driveway. He and Guy laugh and Annie glares at me. I blow her a kiss and she flips me off.

"I can feel the love in this car," Mason laughs.

"Guy already made it clear he no longer loves me," I explain matter-of-factly. "And as you know, Annie's a bitch. But I love *you*."

"I love you too," he says. He grabs my hand and squeezes it.

"Oh. My. GOD!" Annie's eyes are wide as she sits forward, grabbing the back of the bench seat. "Did you…did you just say you *love* him?"

My eyes flick back and forth, from the mirror to the road. "Uh…yeah. I did." I know I've had this thing about love and relationships and commitment, but is it necessary for her to freak out like this?

She peers suspiciously at Mason. "What kind of black magic have you performed?"

He grins at her and Guy coughs to cover his laugh. His lips twitch ridiculously as he fights the smile that wants to form. "Well, I am a warlock," Mason agrees, eying me conspiratorially. "But I just used my natural charisma on her. She fell for it hook, line, and sinker."

I shrug. "Actually, it's the candy." I hold up my arm, shaking the bracelet as proof.

"Jesus, Hope," Guy says, his voice exasperated. "I'm gonna have to break out those kindergarten videos again. You never, *ever*, take candy from strangers!"

"I believe you introduced us before I gave her candy," Mason corrects.

"Yeah, by like, five minutes," Guy replies.

"You're kinda like a candy slut," Annie says to me, winking into the mirror.

I smile widely. "I regret nothing."

Mason squeezes my hand again. I glance at him and he brings my fingers to his mouth, skimming his lips across the knuckles. "Me neither."

Guy presses a fist against his mouth and makes a gagging noise. "Shut up," Annie scolds him. "I think it's adorable now that I know it's more than a booty call." She brings her head up over the seat between me and Mason. "Have you done the whole booty part?"

"Ugh. Ew, Annie. None of your business." I smack at her until she sits back. Mason just smirks, completely amused.

"You did! Ohmygod! You really are a slut. You lost your V card for candy."

My mouth falls open. "I did not lose my V card *for candy*! I love him."

"What?" Guy chokes. My eyes meet his in the mirror and I flinch at the betrayal I find there. "You didn't tell me." His head turns slowly to regard Mason. "You promised me you would take care of her. That was not the way I thought you meant." He shakes his head at Mason's raised brow. "She's like my sister. You couldn't manage to keep it in your pants longer than a few weeks?"

"Hey! Stop it," I nearly shout. "Don't be an ass. I didn't freak out when you lost your virginity. Or when you sleep with anything that has a penis. It was my choice. He didn't even want—" I pause because this is none of their business. "I love him, Guy. I'm happy. That's all that should matter."

His expression softens and he presses two fingers into each temple. "I know. You're right. It does matter. I love that you're happy and I know it's because of him. I was just surprised. I can't believe you didn't tell me something that big. You said you wouldn't keep things from me anymore."

"This is different," I murmur. It really is different. The cutting was mine alone. Mason... It's like all these years I spent so desensitized to love and men, I was just waiting for him. I don't want to share this feeling with anyone but him. It's special. It's ours. "I'm sorry I didn't tell you."

Guy stares at me for several seconds before rolling his eyes. "I do not sleep with anything that has a penis." He points at Mason. "Case in point." I smile at his easy acceptance and obvious subject change.

Mason laughs and grins at me. He brushes the hair off my shoulder and leans close to my ear. "Just so you know—I don't do anything I don't want to. I wanted to make love to you that night. Badly. Every day, from the moment I first saw you in that Beatles shirt, and every day since."

I glance at him, biting my lip. "But you said—"

"I said I wanted it to be special," he whispers, his breath tickling my neck. "I never said I didn't want to. I just want to clear that up. Don't ever think I haven't wanted you desperately every second I've known you." He bites my shoulder gently and I shiver. Stifling a moan. I really, really, *really* do not want to go to this party.

~***~

Warren Grant lives in a large two story house. There are two other cars parked in the driveway and a pink bike lies on its side in the freshly mowed lawn. Brightly colored, helium filled balloons are tied to the mailbox and Guy beams as he flicks one. "Nice."

"You've gotta love these kick ass middle school parties," Annie says with an irritated roll of her eyes.

"Maybe if we're lucky there'll be a thrilling game of spin the bottle."

Park pulls in behind Neko and I drag Mason back as Guy rings the doorbell. "No fighting tonight."

He kisses me, a quick peck that makes my stomach clench, wanting more. "I know."

"Promise," I add.

One side of his mouth lifts slightly. "I promise." He puts his hand over his heart and pecks me again. "I'll be expecting a reward for my good behavior, though."

My brows shoot up. "What did you have in mind?"

He shoves his hands into his pockets and turns on his heels. "I'm sure we can agree on a mutually beneficial arrangement."

Oh, I know we can. *Damn this party.*

"Hey, come on in," Warren says, opening the screen door wide. "My mom's still here, so be cool."

"I like your balloons," Guy mocks. "Festive. Please tell me there's crate paper and pointy hats."

Warren replies by scratching his nose with his middle finger.

"I like the hats," I say. "Oh, will there be cake?"

Warren smiles and puts his arm around my shoulder. “My mom made cupcakes. I think there’s some frosting left over. We can go upstairs later—”

Mason tugs me away from Warren, sending him a warning glare. “What the hell, man?”

“Oh.” Warren holds his hands up. “You two,” he points his finger from me to Mason, “got a thing?”

“She’s my girlfriend,” Mason says clearly.

“S’cool, dude. I didn’t know.” He looks over my head at Annie and nods. “What’s up, Beautiful?”

“Ug.” Annie swallows and looks away. She wiggles her fingers in a quick hello and mouths, “Help.”

I let my hair fall over my face as I suppress a snort. “Park, dude, how’s it going?” Warren calls and leans between Annie and I to do the whole fist-bump-guy-thing.

“Hey, man. Where do we set up?” Park’s bloodshot eyes bounce to me then away.

“I was thinking living room,” Warren tells him. “I cleared a whole wall. You should have plenty of room.”

“Lead the way,” Park says nodding. His gaze flips back to me and he gives me a goofy smile as his eyebrows jump.

Warren introduces us to his mom, stepdad, and a younger sister. The stepdad forks over four fifties before they leave and Guy is humming with excited energy.

"Let's get this party started," Chase sings, dancing into the room with a bottle in each hand.

"That's what I'm talking about," Annie says. She relieves him of one bottle and pulls me into the kitchen to search out shot glasses while the boys set the equipment up. "Tonight I am getting frat girl drunk. It's the only way I'll be able to deal with my awesome friends."

I quirk a brow at her. "Why are you here if you don't want to be? Better yet, why are you friends with these people if you don't like them?"

She swallows back the drink and hands me the glass. "Honestly?"

I nod as I pour the shot. "Yeah. They're a bunch of assholes. I don't get it. Especially when you know someone as amazing as me." I grin and tilt my head back, hissing out a breath trying to relieve the burn.

Annie follows suit, downing another drink. "I don't know. I hate my friends."

"Then don't be friends with them anymore." I slam the glass on the counter and inhale quickly trying not to gag on that last shot.

"It's not that simple," Annie protest. "You don't understand."

"Actually, I think it would be extremely simple."

"Everything's easy for you," she says quietly.

"Uh, no. It's not." I squint at her, taking in the blonde locks curled into perfection. The overly shadowed eyes. The pristine outfit bordering on slutty, but covering just enough to pass as girl next door cute. How hard is it for Annie? How hard does she try to fit in with her friends? "Why would you say that?"

She laughs and I don't miss the bitter undercurrent. "You can sing. You play all these instruments. Guys trip over themselves when you're around. Alec likes you more than me. He can't even be bothered to talk to me, but he rebuilt a car with you. I'm Guy's stepsister, but he claims *you* as his sister. Even Dylan and Misty prefer you to me." She holds her hand up when I open my mouth. "Don't even get me started on the twins. And my baby sister would rather hunt you down then ask me to fill her stupid juice cup." She shakes her head and throws back another shot. "You have real friends. And you don't even try. You make no effort to have everything you have. I work my ass off. Cheer practice, studying, volunteering. I try to be a good person, but it's like I'm never enough."

"Alec doesn't like me more," I say. "Dylan hates me. Yes, I play a couple of instruments. So what? You find the only thing I have going for me and hold it against me. Your mom is always trying to turn me into a carbon copy of *you*. My grades suck. I don't have a *single* female friend." I take another drink and shove the glass away from me, angry now. "You still have both your parents and Jenny may be a slightly overbearing perfectionist, but she has always been there for you. You have led a princess' life compared to mine. When you have to wonder where your mom is, or where your next meal is coming from, or if your mom's newest boyfriend is going to lay his hands on you, then you can cry about your life. Until then…just *shut up*." I push off the counter. "You want real friends, Annie, then stop playing pretend and grow up."

35

Mason

Drunk Hope is pretty entertaining. Even though I feel like her bodyguard as opposed to her boyfriend right now, I think she's the funniest thing I've ever seen. At school, she's quiet and usually keeps to herself, but here, with alcohol flowing through her veins, she's chatting everybody up like they're old friends.

"Hey Zack. I like your shirt," she calls to some guy. I'm not sure what's so great about his shirt. It's a plain black tee. Probably from a pack that came with two more just like it.

"Shirt," she says again and snorts. "Shi-rt. *Shirt*. That's a funny word."

It's really not.

"I wonder who named it. Who was that first dude that was all like: I will call this a shirt?" She laughs again and I chuckle at her. "Noggin. That's another funny word. Nog-gin. Oh, and blubber." Now she doubles over, shaking with quiet laughter. "Blubber."

"Shenanigan," I offer, because how can I not? She's hilarious right now.

"YES," she exclaims, slapping my chest. "See, you get it. Oh, look, Mason. They have a pool." She turns to face me straight on and smiles widely. "Do you think you'll manage to keep your pants on?"

"Oh, haha. You're a freaking comedian now?"

Hope blinks her eyes slowly, trying to look innocent, but her lips do this twitch and she presses them together to keep from laughing. I lean into her and bring my mouth close to her ear.

"You going to manage not to puke all over your drums?" I tease.

She shrugs, unaffected. "Hopefully." Her eyes go big and she bounces on her toes. "If I get sick I won't have to play. We could leave."

"I think Guy would be pretty pissed off. Plus, you guys got paid." I don't really give a shit about either of those things, but I know Hope does. Well, maybe not right now, but she will when she's sober.

"Yeah," she sighs, defeated.

"Hope," Guy calls. "Come on, it's time."

I squeeze her waist as she pouts her lip. I kiss it back into place. "The sooner you get through your set the sooner we can leave."

Her lips turn up under mine and she beams at me. "True." She places a quick kiss on my cheek and lets Guy pull her away. "I'll be back. Don't leave." Uh, where would I go? There is no way in hell I'd leave her here, especially all sweet and tipsy.

"I'll be up front watching," I promise. She grins and does this weird finger flutter wave as Guy drags her farther from me.

I grab a Coke off the bar and squeeze my way through the crowd. I want to get as close to Hope as possible so she can see I'm there. Also, I want her in my sight at all times. I find a spot on the wall with a perfect view. Damn she's sexy behind those drums. She twirls her sticks and I'm impressed she's still able to do that without dropping them.

"Hey, Mason," Bailey purrs. I glance sideways at her. Her strawberry blonde hair is a mass of curls. Her red lipstick is smeared onto her chin like she's been making out with someone and she smells like tequila. I don't like the way she's looking at me, like I'm her next victim.

"Hey," I say, tipping my head to acknowledge her.

Her hand sweeps up my arm, wrapping around my inner elbow. It's clammy and I raise an eyebrow at her. "Do you want to dance?"

"Uh, no thanks." I step away from her, detangling her arm from mine. "I don't really dance. And I'm just watching the band right now." I flick my gaze to Hope and wink at her. She wrinkles her nose and shakes her head, but she's got this cute little grin and I laugh.

Bailey looks over like she's seeing the whole set up for the first time. Her nose crinkles. It's not adorable like Hope's. "Why?"

I huff out an exasperated breath. "Because they're my friends and they're really good." I focus my attention back on Hope, trying to ignore Bailey. After our exchange in school, I can't believe she's still trying to talk to me.

"We could do something more interesting than this." Her hand slides down my arm and I swing my head to look at her. She's got fuck me eyes and I realize I could have this chick right now. If I wanted to, I could lead her upstairs to an empty bedroom and probably do whatever my dirty mind could conjure up. The key phrase here being: If I wanted to. I take a step away, trying to put some distance between us, but it's difficult with so many people.

"I have a girlfriend, Bailey." I explain slowly, carefully, so there's no misunderstanding.

She laughs without humor. "Who? Hope Love?"

I just stare at her, challenging her to say something negative about my girl again. I wish she would take a hint and back the hell off me. Even if I wasn't with Hope, I wouldn't be into this girl. Not since she's shown me how bitchy she's capable of being. And not in the fun way Hope is bitchy, but in that smug, holier-than-thou way that makes my skin crawl. I don't want to be a dick 'cause she is a girl and all, but I will if I need to.

"Look Bailey, if this was a month ago, I'd have been all over your ass, but..." I trail off, finding Hope again. She's concentrating on her drums, but I can see the tension in her shoulders. She's not relaxed like she usually is when she loses herself in the music. It's like she's only halfway paying attention and I know it's because of me. Because of Bailey being all up on me.

"I'm with Hope now," I finish. The first song ends and I'm irritated that I missed the entire thing.

"You don't want to mess with her," Bailey continues. She leans in conspiratorially, but doesn't bother to lower her voice. "Her mom was some crack whore psycho or something. Mental illness is, like, hereditary or whatever. Plus, I heard they *shared boyfriends*." Her eyebrows lift and she shakes her head, disgusted. "You'll probably catch a disease."

There are so many things wrong with those five sentences; I don't even know where to start. I'm too pissed to speak right now anyway. Before I get a chance, Hope is there, her hand on Bailey's shoulder as she pushes her back against the wall. It's surprising gentle for a girl who kicked a football player into submission.

"My mom didn't smoke crack," Hope says. "She was an alcoholic who liked pills." Bailey rolls her eyes and crosses her arms. "She did have mental issues, though," Hope continues in a soft, matter-of-fact voice. "And yeah, she also had problems closing her legs, but no more than you do."

Bailey pushes back at Hope who barely moves. She's always got herself braced for an attack. Knowing her history, it makes this weight settle in the pit of my stomach. I hate that she's always ready for someone to hurt her.

Now Bailey raises her hand to strike. Hope smiles at her, inviting her to swing. It's almost like she wants her to do it. Of course, with Hope, I'm sure she does. She probably will welcome the pain.

"Chick fight," someone yells.

Hope swats Bailey's hand away, causing her back to thud against the wall. "Don't ever talk about me or my mom again," she says in that eerily calm voice. "You never know what a mentally ill person, like me, might do."

"Hope," Guy breathes. "Honey, come on. Let's finish our set." He reaches for her and she nods, following after him.

"Awe, come on! Kick her ass," someone shouts.

"It doesn't matter," Guy says quietly. "She doesn't matter. Let's just play."

"It doesn't matter," Hope agrees. Her voice cracks and I can't stand it. I want to go with her as Guy leads her away from Bailey who is now surrounded by several of her shocked friends.

“Wait,” Hope says, stopping in the middle of the living room. She pivots around and the crowd, anticipating another altercation, parts as she makes her way back toward Bailey. “Where did you hear about my mom?” She barely whispers the words, making my head jerk toward her.

Bailey glowers at Hope, braver now that her friends flank her. “Why don’t you ask Annie,” she hisses. A cruel smirk twists her mouth when she notices the hurt expression masking Hope’s face.

“Ooh,” some guy coos. “Shit just got real.”

Hope turns around and makes a straight line for her drums.

Park moves up behind her, arms crossed over his chest, hands in tight fists. “Come on, Hope. You don’t have to play if you don’t want to. Let’s just go. Fuck these people.”

“From what I hear she already has.” I blink in surprise and search the crowd to find who the voice belongs to. Christian Dunkin. And he’s smirking at Hope in that same smug way he did the first time I saw him. I immediately push my way through the bodies, trying to get up close to Hope. “I’m just waiting for my turn.” He takes a step toward her, his eyes scaling her body like he's picturing her naked. I flex my fingers, struggling to restrain the urge to tackle him. "Too bad you and Annie aren't really related. I've never had sisters before."

I step into his personal space, cutting him off. He's talked way too long. "You have no idea how lucky you are that I promised Hope I wouldn't fight tonight," I sneer.

"Fuck that," Chase scoffs, pushing past me. "I didn't promise shit." He pops his arm back and lets his fist fly into Christian's jaw. The room goes quiet as Christian's head snaps back. The only sound is Chase hissing as he shakes his fist.

"Fight!" people cheer in unison.

In the moment it takes me to register what happened, Christian's friends are blocking our path. Drunken arms start swinging. I glance at Park who shrugs, a sly smile turning up his mouth like he's been waiting all his life to scrap with these people. I raise a brow and smirk back. This is my element. I am always down for a fight and now it's in my girl's honor. I nod at Park, declaring a temporary alliance between the two of us before jumping into the mayhem. I catch sight of Hope being shuffled backwards as I land my first blow.

I get knocked in the head twice by a guy I've never even seen before tonight. I don't know when Guy got into the mix, but I see him punch that kid, Zack, that Hope complimented on his stupid-ass shirt. Chase takes a hit to the eye that doesn't look like it had enough force to do much damage, and then I lose sight of everyone else because Christian is right in front of me. I'm pretty sure someone kicks me in the shin. I don't fully feel it. All I can concentrate on is the sound of my knuckles pounding against Christian's flesh. God, I love this feeling. I have so much rage and it feels so damn good to release it on an asshole like him. All I see is red. Blood trickles from his lip, pours quickly from his nose. There is something satisfying about someone else's blood on your knuckles. That's twisted, right? Yeah. Yeah it is. I don't even give a shit right now.

Someone hits me in the stomach, knocking the air out of me. I grunt and swing, catching the guy in the side of his face. He stumbles back, falling into Christian and they both go down. I'm pretty sure they're getting trampled. Hope takes the opportunity to grab a hold of my arm and yanks me away. And now I notice the sirens. The fight wasn't going long enough for cops to be here already. The neighbors must have called in a noise complaint. Though I don't think that qualifies sirens.

"Come on," she huffs. "We have to get out of here."

"Cops," Chase pants. His cheeks are bright red, the collar of his shirt is ripped, and his eye is swollen. A few guys give up and make a run for the door, wanting out before they get busted.

"Where's everyone else?" Hope asks. Her eyes dart around the room as she pulls us to the back door, which is genius since everyone else is heading for the front. I don't see Guy or Park anywhere.

"Man, my bass," Chase sighs.

"Leave it," I say. I'm not getting arrested over a guitar.

"I have to find the others." Hope stops at the door. "Park's wasted and Guy can't drive."

"They went out the front," Chase says.

"What about Annie?"

Chase shrugs. “I didn’t see her.” I can’t remember the last time I saw her. I was too occupied with Hope, as usual.

Hope closes her eyes for a second. She shoves her keys into my hand. “Go, find them, and get them home. I’ll find Annie and get a ride.”

I pull my hands back, refusing her keys. “I’m not leaving without you.” What the fuck? I am not going anywhere if she isn’t beside me.

“You have to. You’re the only sober one.”

“No,” I insist. I would do just about anything for her, but I’m not leaving her.

Hope rolls her eyes. The sirens sound like they’re close. Maybe a few houses away if we’re lucky. She turns quickly and heads back through the house. The living room is empty, except for some guy that had his ass handed to him. He’s lying in a heap on the floor. I follow Hope and she shakes her head. “At least go outside, Mason. Don’t let Park drive.”

The sirens stop. Red and blue lights flash through the windows. I ignore her, staying close. If she’s getting busted, then I’m going down with her.

36
Hope

I find Annie perched on the stairs. Black mascara runs down her cheeks, mixed with fresh tears. She jumps up when she sees me. I grip her wrist tighter than is necessary, but I'm still pissed at her for telling Bailey about my mom. Plus I'm irritated I had to come back and look for her.

"Come the hell on. Cops are here."

"Hope, I'm sorry. I said that stuff before I knew you." She won't stop crying and she's being too loud as we make our way out the back door. I hear shouting from inside as the screen door closes behind us. Chase and Mason are pressing into us as we sneak around the back of the house. Neko's parked in the driveway right beside two police cruisers. Seriously?

"You've got to be shitting me," Chase hisses. "We are so screwed."

"No," Mason murmurs. "They're empty. They must be inside."

I shove my keys at him. "I don't see Park's car," I say.

Mason takes my hand. "You guys ready? Run like hell." We do, sliding into the car and gently closing the doors as quietly as we can. Mason turns the key and shoves it into gear. We roll out of the driveway and he takes off down the street. He sails through the stop sign and rounds the corner. I let out a breath I hadn't realized I was holding.

"Wooh!" Chase shouts.

I laugh, relieved and glance at Mason. He grins at me as I let my head fall back against the seat.

"You know they're probably going to smash our instruments," I say to Chase. He moans and rubs his face.

"Yeah, probably." He groans again. "And Warren's probably going to want his money back since we only played one song."

"Yep," I agree. I'm not giving my share back if my drums get tore up.

I fish my phone out to call Guy just as Annie makes a strangled sound in the back seat. "Pull over," she demands. Her voice is muffled by her hand.

"Oh, shit," Chase says, panicked. "She's going to blow. Pull the hell over, now." He squirms away from her. "Don't puke on me, Annie. I swear to God."

Mason swings the car to the side of the road and I jump out, pulling the seat forward and Annie stumbles out. She makes it two steps before she falls to her knees, emptying her stomach. I push her hair out of her face. I'd hold it back for her, but I'm not ready to be that nice yet. She sold me out to her friends and that's not something I'm going to easily forgive.

"I'm sorry," she cries.

I'm getting sick of her saying that.

Annie wipes her mouth with the back of her hand. "Please don't be mad at me."

I shiver from the amount of anger consuming me. "They called me a whore, Annie! You told them about my *mom*. You told them I shared my mom's boyfriends. If you understood how fucked up that is, you wouldn't be asking for forgiveness." I turn away. The stench of alcohol and vomit only making me more disgusted with her.

"I said that stuff before I knew you," she cries.

I just shake my head. As if that makes it better. I don't want to hear her anymore. My phone is still in my hand and it startles me when it rings, playing the imperial march. Jenny's ringtone. I take a deep breath, hoping I sound completely sober even though the whole fight and police thing was a pretty good buzz kill. “Hello?”

“Hope. Thank God you answered. I can’t get a hold of Annie.”

“She’s with me. Her phone must’ve died,” I say, the lie rolling off my tongue automatically. I glance at her on the ground and roll my eyes.

“I need you girls to get home right away,” Jenny says before I’ve fully finished my sentence. Her voice is shaky, thick.

“What’s wrong?” My head spins and my gut twists. Something bad happened. I can feel it. I know this feeling well.

“Honey, Guy was in an accident. Alec and I are on the way to the hospital. Listen to me. I need you to get home. Misty’s with the kids, but she’s scared. She needs you girls.”

The tears are instant. I can’t help it. They stream down my face, dripping onto the front of my shirt. I cry for Guy like I should have cried for my mom. I feel like I might be sick. Mason’s warm hands grip my waist, but I can’t look at him yet. “Is he okay?”

Jenny sobs into the phone and my knees go weak. If Mason wasn't holding onto me, I think I'd be on the ground.

"Jenny?" I plead the one word. Please, please don't let this be happening again.

"We don't know, Hope. We'll call as soon as we know something." She sniffles and I hear her swallow.

"Was Park with him?" I whisper into the phone and my voice hitches.

"I don't know. They didn't give us details. Just get home. All right? I'll let you know what I find out."

I nod before I realize she can't see. "Okay." The line goes dead and I pull my phone back and stare at it. "We have to go home," I say numbly.

"What's going on?" Mason asks. I hear the concern in his voice clearly and I pull away from him.

"Annie!" I scream. "We have to go NOW!"

"Hope? What the hell's happening?" Mason grabs my arm, pulling me into him. I push him back gently even though what I really want to do is hit him. I want to yell at him. Why? Why didn't he stop them like I asked?

"We have to go. Guy was in an accident." I stomp over to Annie, still on her knees in the grass. I jerk her up, squeezing her until she whimpers. "Get your worthless ass in the car," I demand.

I fall onto the seat and call Park. It rings. And rings. And rings.

"Is he all right?" Chase asks.

I shake my head. "Don't know yet."

"What about Park?" he asks.

New tears spill. "*I don't know.* He isn't answering."

Chase yanks his phone out of his back pocket and places a call. "Shit." He closes his eyes. "Park, man. Call me when you get this. We're freaking out." He rubs his eyes, trying to hide the moisture there as he disconnects. "They were together. They would've stayed together. Shit." He presses the heels of his hands into his eyes hard.

Mason pulls into the driveway and I'm out of the car before he shuts it off. Misty opens the door, meeting me on the porch. She flings herself into me. I hug her, brushing my fingers through her hair. "Have you heard anything?" I ask.

She shakes her head.

"It'll be all right. It'll be all right." I don't know if I'm trying to comfort her or convince myself.

Mason puts his hand on my shoulder as Misty releases me. I flinch, but I don't pull away. He guides me inside.

"The kids in bed?" I ask Misty. She nods, wiping her face.

"Can you go get Kellin?" she asks Mason. "I was on the computer with him when Dad got the call. He said to have you pick him up."

Mason glances at me and I nod. She needs someone that can make her feel better. "Yeah, sure." He kisses my forehead. "They'll be okay," he assures me. "I'll be right back."

My hand shoots out, grabbing his fingers. "Be careful."

He smiles sadly. "I will."

I leave Chase in the living room with Misty and Annie and go up to check on the kids. The twins are sleeping soundly, so I peek in on Addie. Her blanket's slipped off and she's curled into a small ball in the middle of her bed. I cover her up and brush the hair off her face before I tip toe out of the room.

I stand in the hall outside my room. The need to cut is suffocating. Mason took my razors. I have to keep reminding myself of that. I step inside and look around, searching for something that might work. The curling iron is sitting on the desk. I run my fingers over it. It's cold, smooth. I flip the button. My eyes blur as I stare at the orange light indicating it's on.

Another accident. I can't wrap my mind around it. This can't really be happening.

There are some papers scattered across the desk and I straighten them slowly, making sure each sheet is aligned perfectly with the one below it. It's lyrics. Stupid lyrics.

They have to be all right. They can't die on me. Life cannot be that incredibly cruel.

I can't lose them.

I can't lose them.

I can't lose them.

I don't know how much time has passed, but when I pick up the curling iron I can feel the heat coming off of it. A calm comes over me as I bring it to my wrist. There's a split second where I hesitate, where I actually try to think past the fear shaking my body. I try, but I can't. At some point, hurting myself has gone past the need to be in control. It's routine now. An addiction. I cannot cope without it, and when things get bad, the need to feed the habit flares.

I press the iron into my skin. I cry out, hissing through my teeth. A gasp makes me jump, pulling it back sharply. My gaze flicks up. His green eyes are wide, his brow's furrowed. There's a mix of horrified revulsion and pure shock on his face.

I'm just as horrified with myself, with being caught. This is extremely personal. People may know I do it, but nobody has ever witnessed it. It's worse than if he'd seen me naked.

"Kellin," I breathe.

37

Mason

I take the steps two at a time in my rush to get upstairs. Kellin's standing in Hope's doorway, his skin shockingly pale. The panic I felt when he screamed my name somehow doubles.

I don't need to see the curling iron gripped tightly in Hope's hand to figure out what happened. I don't even need to see the red stripe across her wrist or the sickened expression on my brother's face. I can smell the stench of burnt hair and flesh filling the air in her room. I heave the cord from the wall and pry it from her fingers.

"God, Hope." I push Kellin out and close the door. Without another word, I drag her into the bathroom and turn on the cold water. As soon as it hits her arm she gasps for breath. Her chest rises and falls as if she's fighting to get air.

I push her into the wall, trying to bring her back. I don't know where she goes when she gets like this, but it's not here with me.

Hope's head bangs against a shelf and it's like she doesn't even feel it. My fingers dig into her arms with just enough pressure to get her attention. I want to scream at her, but I know that will only make it worse. "It will be okay," I say fiercely. She looks at me, but I can tell she doesn't believe it. "You have people that need you. You need to get your shit together."

I slide my hands down her arms, grasping her wrists, holding up the one with the burn. "Look! Look what you did to yourself. You have to stop."

She blinks, focusing on the blister already forming, white and puffy. "Did it make it better? Are you any less scared? Is *anything* better?"

"No," she chokes. Her mouth opens like she wants to say more, but can't manage to find the words.

I pull the first aid kit out, fighting the urge to punch the wall.

My little brother saw this. This is hard enough for me to deal with, let alone a kid. I quickly smear first aid cream onto the wound before wrapping it in gauze. "I know you're worried, but you can't do this anymore." I pull her into my chest, choosing to hug her instead of shaking her like I really want to.

****

I get home from Hope's around noon. I'm only coming home long enough to shower and change my clothes. It's been a long night, but as much as my body wants to crash, Hope needs me.

We didn't get an update until close to four in the morning. Park was with Guy, just as Hope suspected. He scathed the accident with minor scrapes and only a broken nose, thanks to his seat belt and the airbag. After he was checked out, he was arrested for DWI. Guy wasn't as lucky. Head injury. I didn't understand most of it, swelling and bleeding on the brain, but he just came out of what the doctors insist was a successful surgery before I left. I refused to budge from Hope's side until we knew he was in the recovery room. Alec promised she could go up to the hospital in a few hours. I talked her into a shower and hurried home. I don't want to leave her alone for too long. It's not that I don't trust her, but—I don't trust her to not hurt herself right now.

This is so messed up.

I am in way over my head. How do you make someone stop self-harming? I'm not sure you can. I want to, though. I want to force her to quit. She tried to explain it to me last night.

The house was quiet with everyone sprawled across the couch falling in and out of sleep. We snuck to the kitchen where Hope mixed dough for chocolate chip cookies. Apparently she needs to be doing something with her hands. It was too late for her to play the cello, and she couldn't hurt herself with me right there, so she baked. I personally think it's a much healthier stress reliever.

She bumped her bandaged wrist on the cabinet and tried to hide the tears that filled her eyes.

"Tell me what I can do," I said. "I can't stand to see you in pain. Tell me how to help you."

"You are helping. I just need you here with me."

"It's not enough, obviously," I hissed at her, eyeing her arm. "And I can't always be here. Shit, Hope, I left for ten minutes and look what you did." I jabbed my finger toward the bandage.

"I've gotten better. You don't understand what it's like. What goes on inside of me," she whispered.

"Then explain it to me. Please."

Shaking her head, she turned back to the bowl and mixed it furiously. Flour sifted over the side and onto her shirt. She closed her eyes and dropped the spoon. “It’s like telling an anorexic person to eat or an alcoholic not to drink. It’s an addiction and it’s a process to stop. Before tonight, I hadn’t done it since that night at your house. I’m so much better than I was.”

My stomach twisted painfully. *This is better?* “Alcoholics go to AA. How do we get you where you don’t do it at all?”

Hope turned quickly and placed her hands on her hips. “Don’t judge me, Mason. You’ve told me what you did to help deal with your dad’s death. Just because you do things in a different screwed up way doesn’t mean they’re any less screwed up.”

I recoiled at that. She’s right. I know she is. But it was still a low blow. She might as well have slapped me in the face. I don’t throw her mom in her face. And yes, I did try to fuck the pain away. It never worked. “I’m not judging you,” I sighed. “I’m worrying about you.”

Dropping her hands, she stepped into me, pressing her body against mine in apology. “This is a lot. Guy is…” She squeezed her eyes closed tightly, moisture forming on her lashes. “If he dies, I don’t know what I’ll do.”

I grabbed her hard, hugging her to me. I wanted to promise her he wouldn’t die, but I couldn’t go there. We’ve both seen how easy someone can be taken. So I just held onto her, skimming my fingers through her hair over and over.

I rub my eyes and open the front door. Kellin yawns as he moves past me. He drops to the couch and is out in seconds. Besides the long night, the conversation on the car ride home was emotionally draining. But in the end, I think Kellin understood about Hope. It freaked him out and I know he’s far from comfortable about it, but he agreed to keep quiet. I know it’s as fucked up as a situation can get and I hate to ask that of him, but Hope’s got enough shit to deal with at the moment. I promised him I was taking care of it, and I think out of everything I’ve ever done, that could be the lie that sends me to hell. Because I don’t know how to help her. But I will find a way. I have to.

Mom's in the kitchen and the sight of her in front of the stove doesn't match the delicious smell wafting through the air. "Hey," I say.

She comes around the bar and hugs me. "How are they?" She leans back and touches my cheeks for a moment. "You look like shit."

"Don't say shit, Mom."

She smiles weakly and backs up. "Any news?"

I sit on the stool and let my head thud onto the counter. "Guy's out of surgery. We can go up when he wakes up and gets moved to his own room."

"How's Hope?"

I raise my head and rest it on a fist. "She's a mess. She expects everyone she cares about to leave her on a good day, so this is... She's not taking it well."

Mom nods. "Mm. Glass half empty girl."

"It's more like she assumes someone emptied half her glass just to mess with her."

She moves back to the stove. "She has good reason to feel jilted, Mace. The poor girl's had a shit life." All her attention is focused on the pan in front of her. "You know better than anyone how hard the loss of a parent can be."

Yeah. I do.

"It's my fault they were in the accident," I say. Mom looks at me, brows raised. "I waited all night for her to call me on it. I just waited, thinking he was going to die and she would realize I could've prevented it, she'd hate me, and I'd lose a friend and the only girl I've ever cared about. Then he gets out of surgery and I think it'll only be half as bad. I figure it's coming, any moment she'll say it. Break things off with me. Now that he's in the clear, ya know? But nothing. I'm terrified to go back."

"How is any of this your fault?"

I rub my forehead, trying to smooth away the stress induced pain there. "She asked me to stop Park from driving, but I stayed with her. It would've taken me a minute to run outside and tell them to give me the keys."

"Did you give them the alcohol? Make them drink?"

"You know I didn't," I say. I know what she's doing. She's always been big on taking responsibility for your actions. But that's exactly what I'm trying to do.

"They knew they shouldn't drink and drive. They made a choice." She touches my shoulder and I look up at her. "It's not your fault. That's why Hope isn't blaming you."

I don't say anything. There's no point arguing with Mom, whether she's wrong or not. I let it go and change the subject. "What are you making?"

She spins around and peeks into the pan. "Vegetable soup. I'll bring it by later. I figure it will be easy to heat up and should feed all those kids."

"Don't you think they've suffered enough?" I say with a smirk.

She glances over her shoulder and gives me the Mom Glare. "I got the recipe off the internet. It was really easy. I don't think I can screw this up. Plus," she adds, stirring the soup gently, "I'm cooking it on a low heat so I can't burn it."

I grin. She can burn anything. It took her nearly a year to get grilled cheese down. "Just test it out before you make the trip over to Hope's. Maybe wait an hour after you eat it, too."

"Why?" She sips broth from the spoon and shrugs.

"If you can keep it down that long we'll know you won't accidentally poison everyone." I chuckle and she throws the spoon at me.

"Go away. Don't you need a shower?"

I stand up and lean over the counter, kissing her on the cheek. "Thanks, Mom. They'll appreciate it, I'm sure."

She smiles and shoos me off. "Get out of here." I'm halfway down the hall when she calls my name.

"Yeah?"

"I love you."

"Love you too."

She never misses an opportunity to say it. You never know when you can run out of chances.

****

Everyone's sitting on the floor in the living room, a plate full of cookies in front of them. Cartoons play loudly on the TV. Dylan and Chase are playing a game of Go Fish. Archer's glued to Hope, his fingers buried in her wet hair. I lower myself beside her and Addie crawls onto my lap. I'm surprised because she's always seemed scared of me, but she acts like this is an everyday occurrence. She offers me a cookie, the chocolate is slightly melted from her hand, but I eat it anyway. It's really good and I wink at Hope, letting her know.

"Where's Annie?" I ask, just noticing she's not here.

"Staying as far away from Hope as she can," Chase says.

My gaze flicks to hers quickly. "What happened?"

Her lips form a thin line and she sighs. "Nothing."

Chase squints. "That's bull sh—poop." He glances at Addie then back to me. "She was talking a bunch of poop. Saying Hope shouldn't have started a fight last night."

"Wait. What?" I look at Hope, my brows furrowed. "She's blaming you?"

"It's fine," she says quietly.

No it's not. Not at all. It's messed up and seriously pisses me off.

"Technically," Chase says, "I started the fight. But if she hadn't been such a B.I.T.C.H. and spread your business to all her friends, none of that shit—poop would've happened in the first place."

"Christian started the fight," I correct. "You threw the first punch and Bailey talked crap, but he went too far."

"Regardless of who started the fight, it didn't cause the accident," Chase says. "Park's a dumb butt for driving drunk and when he gets out of lock up, I'm going to kick his butt."

I look over at Hope. She's been quiet through our back and forth. I bump her shoulder with mine. She closes her eyes and I get nervous. Right here would be a good time for her to accuse me. To blame me. I scoot Addie onto the floor and take Asher from Hope, handing him off to Chase.

Hope looks up at me confused when I stand and grab her hands. "Come with me," I say quietly.

She lets me help her up and follows me into the kitchen, but I can tell she doesn't want to talk right now. I could hold off, but it's like waiting for the executioner. I'd rather have my heart ripped out quickly.

I take a deep breath and just say it. "I know I'm responsible for the accident. I know I should have listened to you and stopped them. I know I fucked up and it's a huge fuck up. What I don't know—what I need to know—is what you're going to do about it."

Hope blinks slowly, her mouth opening, but she doesn't say anything. She just stares at me. For way too long.

"Say something," I whisper.

"I did," she says so softly I almost miss it.

"What?"

"I did blame you. For a split second, that exact thought ran through my head. I'm human. It happens." She pulls her fingers through her hair, tugging on the ends. "Then I blamed Chase because he did hit Christian first. And then I blamed Annie because she couldn't keep her stupid mouth shut. Hell, Mason, I even blamed my mom for giving Annie something to tell. I blamed Park for being the freaking idiot to get behind the wheel when he was drunk, especially knowing it's how my mom died. After Guy made it through his surgery, I decided it was his fault. He was the one that insisted on playing that dumbass party and Donnie was his uncle. He should never have let Park drive or even got in the car with him in the first place knowing he had been drinking.

But after Annie freaked out on me, I realized everything that happened was because of me."

I feel my eyebrows crinkle. And I know I'm squinting at her, but I wasn't expecting that. My brain's trying to switch gears because what I had anticipated was her breaking up with me. I'm stuck between relief that she doesn't hate me, feeling like an asshole that I was worried about myself, and a sick, nauseated feeling that she thinks she caused this. Above all that, I'm silently thanking God that nobody died because I don't know what she would have done to herself thinking it was her fault.

"Bailey was talking about me. About my mom. I was jealous that she was touching you. I was embarrassed of the things she said to you. In front of everybody. Embarrassed they were true. I shouldn't have let it bother me. I should've let it go. Christian said that stuff about me because I humiliated him in front of his friends at school. It all comes back to me. So I don't blame you for anything."

I should have seen this coming. In hindsight, I can't believe I didn't. Hope always tries to find herself guilty. I guess then it helps all that shit that happened to her as a kid make sense in her mind. But she didn't deserve it no matter how much she tries to convince herself she did.

I want to hit something so bad because I don't know how to make her see she's wrong. I don't know anything when it comes to Hope. I can't make her quit hurting herself. I can't take her pain away. I can't make her stop blaming herself.

I'm completely useless.

I press her into the counter with my chest and place my hands on each side of her, locking her in place. "You didn't cause this." My forehead touches hers and I gaze into her eyes, refusing to let her look away. "You didn't cause any of this."

She tries to shake her head, but I press against her harder. "This wasn't your fault," I whisper. My hands snake up into her hair and I massage my fingertips into her scalp. "So much happened and we all have a piece in it."

"It was because of me, though. Maybe Park wouldn't have been drinking if I hadn't hurt him."

Now I shake my head. "It's not your fault," I say firmly. My mouth moves over hers as she opens it to protest again. I let my tongue find hers. My hips are flush with hers and I conform to her body. My hands rake down her sides and I lift her onto the counter. I pull her legs around my waist and take her face in between my palms. She leans in and kisses me this time, biting at my lip. My grip tightens as she works her fingers into my jeans and grasps me.

I look around quickly and pick her up, my hands cupping her thighs. I walk us toward the pantry.

"No. Laundry room," she gasps before bringing her mouth back to mine.

I turn and kick at that door. She reaches behind her and turns the handle and we're in. Leaning her into the washer, I jerk her shirt over her head. She pries my belt open and I help her with the button. I tear at her shorts, trying to get them out of the way.

"Condom," I say as my bare flesh caresses hers.

"I don't have any," she breathes. A whimper escapes her lips and she wiggles closer, fighting to feel me against her. "Mason." My arms are locked, holding us less than an inch apart, but I can feel her heat and I want it so badly. "Please. I need you."

A shiver runs through me. I'd like to say I think it over, weigh my options, but I don't even hesitate. I slide inside her and find a way to take some of the hurting away for both of us.

38
Hope

I open the door to a woman, bright red oven mitts on her hands, holding a large, steaming pot. Even if Kellin wasn't beside her, I'd know exactly who she was. It only takes her wide smile, complete with dimple, for me to know she's Mason's mom. I see where his dark hair and skin tone comes from. Although, Mason's dad must have been tall because she is smaller than me.

"Hope?"

"Yes, hi," I say, pushing the screen door open for her.

"I'm Mason's mom. Gabbie." She raises the pot. "I made soup." I step out of the way to let her in and lead her into the kitchen. Kellin avoids eye contact with me and goes straight to the living room where Misty is.

My face flushes as Gabbie sets the soup on the stovetop right next to the counter where her son and I made out just hours ago.

"Hey Mom," Mason says coming around the corner. I watch as he kisses her cheek like it's something he does all the time. It's so sweet and even though it's totally a Mason thing to do, I still find myself surprised by the gesture. "You tried it first, right?"

She gives him a sharp look. "Kellin ate two bowls and he's still walking, so shut up." She takes the lid off and turns her attention to me. "Bowls?"

"Oh, uh, that cupboard," I say, pointing behind her.

She starts filling the right number of bowls without asking how many are needed and places three of them in the freezer to cool. Kellin and Misty bring the kids in and Chase follows behind Dylan. Mason handles introductions as I help get everyone situated. The only one missing is Annie. She's been hiding all day.

Gabbie hands me a bowl and nods at my arm. "What happened there?" she asks.

Instinctively I tuck my arm into my side and glance at Kellin. He looks down at the floor and I feel horrible all over again. "Curling iron mishap," I say. Her eyes bore into me for several seconds and I feel frozen under her gaze.

She nods slowly. "Make sure you keep it clean. You don't want it to get infected."

"We're on top of it," Mason offers as he leans into me. "Any excuse to play doctor." He makes his brows jump and my cheeks ignite in embarrassment. Who says stuff like that to their mom?

"Mason Xavier," she sighs, but she's fighting a smile at the same time. She shakes her head and hands him his own bowl of soup.

I sit down, looking into the bowl for the first time and cringe. Vegetable soup. I look up, wondering how I can get around eating this crap and Mason chuckles. He takes a large bite and winks at me. Jerk.

"All right," Gabbie announces. "I'm out of here."

"Thank you for the soup," I say, trying to sound sincere, because I am grateful. I just don't plan on eating it.

"No problem." She pulls a Snickers bar from her back pocket and slides it across the table to me with a knowing smile. "It was nice to meet you, Hope."

I stare at the candy, dumbfounded. "It was nice to meet you too," I murmur absently. She and Mason both laugh. She kisses the top of his head then does the same to Kellin before she goes.

I tear into the Snickers and push my bowl to Mason.

~***~

I hate hospitals. I hate their smell, what's meant to be sterile, but really seems like they're trying to mask the stench of death and sickness. I hate their neutral décor that borders on boring and ugly. Mostly, I hate that people come here to die.

I press the number for Guy's floor three times. It doesn't make the elevator go any faster, but I do it anyway. Mason laces his fingers in between mine and squeezes. It's a silent reminder that he's here for me. I take in a slow breath and blow it out through my mouth.

"Better?"

I manage a smile. "Yeah."

The doors open and I follow Mason to Guy's room. He's propped up in the bed. My heart skips an actual beat as I move to his side. I had this image in my mind. His head bald and wrapped in gauze like a mummy. Tubes inserted in all sorts of orifices. Looking pale and frail. But there's only a small bandage on the back corner of his head. His blonde locks are still in his face and he looks good. Tired, maybe, but no paler than usual. The only tube is an IV in his arm. He lifts the opposite one inviting me onto the bed with him and I climb in quickly. It's a tight fit, these beds aren't made for more than one person, but I snuggle against him and we make it work.

Guy strokes the ends of my hair and rests his head on top of mine. "I'm sorry," he says and his voice is thick, scratchy.

Jenny moves to the other side of the bed and fills a cup with water. He sips it and clears his throat as if he wants to say more.

I shake my head. "It's all right. You're all right. That's all that matters. Just…don't do that again. Okay?"

His lips press together until they turn white and he nods slowly. His gaze lowers to my arm, to the dressing covering my wrist. "You too." I swallow, returning his nod tightly. "No more," he whispers against my temple. "Please, Hope. No more."

"We're going down to the cafeteria to get something to eat while you visit," Alec says. He stretches and yawns loudly. "Don't get crazy in here. He needs to rest."

"We'll try," Guy jokes, but he sounds worn, tired. Mason takes Alec's vacated seat and looks around.

"You know, if you wanted to lie in bed and be waited on hand and foot, I'm pretty sure there are easier ways. Maybe just play sick next time."

Guy smirks. "I'll keep that in mind."

"So, what do you do here for fun?" I ask, trying to keep the light mood in the room. He hands me a weird looking contraption and it takes me a second to figure out it's a remote then a few seconds more to figure out how to use it. We settle on an old episode of SpongeBob. Guy closes his eyes and his breathing turns deep with sleep. My eyes grow too heavy to fight and I finally give in, nestling closer to him with the reassurance that's he's going to be okay.

"My turn," Chase announces loudly. I jump, disoriented. It takes me a moment to remember where I am through my grogginess.

"Uhh," I moan.

Chase leans over the bed, his face inches from mine. "You had your turn sleepy head. Now it's mine."

"What time is it?"

"Almost eight."

I sit up, trying to not jostle a still sleeping Guy. I don't know how Chase didn't wake him up. Then I see Mason. His legs stretched out in front of him, hands folded over his stomach, chin resting on his chest. Asleep. And completely adorable.

"I tried to wait," Chase says in a low voice. "She was pretty persistent." I look around him to see Annie hovering by the door.

"It's fine. I didn't mean to stay so long. Where are Jenny and Alec?"

"They went home for a little bit to see the kids. Said they'd come back after you got home."

I nod and maneuver my way off the bed. Guy stirs and I lean down, placing a kiss on his cheek. I have the strangest sensation in my chest. My heart is beating way too fast, making me feel like I'm scared, but I know I'm not. For the first time in my life, I'm not afraid at all. I'm relieved.

So I don't understand where the tears burning my eyes come from, but I blink them back and smile at Guy's worried expression. "What's wrong?"

"No, nothing. I'm good." I lick my lips and smile wider. "I've been kicked out, so I'm gonna go." I hug him awkwardly. "I'm so glad you're all right. Don't ever do that to me again."

He clasps his hand over my arm and tugs me closer. "I know. I swear." He doesn't need full sentences. I get it. I wake Mason up and he says his goodbyes in the sexiest, deep, just-woke-up voice.

I take his hand in the hallway and let myself enjoy the way his skin is warm against mine. Appreciate this small thing that means so much to me. I stop abruptly and he cocks a brow at me in quiet question.

"Kiss me," I say.

With a wicked smile, he pulls me into an alcove and happily obliges. I want this. For the rest of my life. I want this. Happiness, and kisses, and Mason.

39

Mason

Mom's up before me when I wake up Sunday morning. That's weird, but the fact she's packing away her DVD collection into one of our mangled, taped up boxes is enough to stop me in my tracks.

"What are you doing?" I demand. My gut clenches. What the hell is going on?

"Packing," she says in that tone that makes it clear I shouldn't push, but I'm in full panic mode. There is no fucking way I am moving again. It's my senior year and she swore she would let me finish in the same school. And now I have Hope. Kel has Misty.

She can't pull this shit. Not now.

I stomp over to her and tip the box upside down, spilling the movies across the floor. She sits back on her heels, shocked. I grab a handful and shove them back onto the shelf. "No. You're not. I'm not moving. Not this time."

I reach for more and she takes hold of my hand. I jerk away. My head is hot and I'm pissed. I'm seconds away from putting my fist through something. The wall's looking pretty damn good right now. Why is she doing this to me?

"I've been up all night thinking about this. We're on a month to month lease. I can get the security deposit back—"

"No."

"I found a couple places online—"

"No." Another handful of chick flicks back on the shelf.

"You and Kellin can pick where we live—"

"No."

"I was thinking we could go back to Illinois."

That stops me cold. Home? She wants to go home? Why? Why now? I've begged to go back. I've threatened to go on my own. She's always refused. "What?"

"There's a two bedroom house, so you'd have to share a room, but it's close to our old house. Kellin could go to your old school. Or there's a three bedroom duplex. It's bigger, but it's not as nice of an area. Different school district."

She starts placing the DVD's back into the box. I'm just staring at her. I can feel my entire body shaking. My head and my heart are at war. And I can't. I can't do this.

"Why?" I choke out.

Mom lifts her gaze to meet mine and she sighs. "I knew she was lying," she begins, shaking her head like she doesn't want to do this with me, but knows she has no other option. "A big part of my job is reading people. I'm good at it. And I'm a mom, it's ingrained." She stands up and picks up the box, moving it to the shelf on the other side of the TV and starts on the CD's.

"My first thought was that she was involved in the accident. Maybe she was the one driving drunk and you didn't want to tell me..." She trails off and I'm fighting to catch up. She's talking about Hope, I'm fairly certain, but I don't know where she's going with this.

"Then after I thought about it, I figured that would be too big of a secret to hide and that other boy was arrested. It seemed too unlikely he would be willing to go to jail for her."

She finishes the CD's and dusts her hands off on her jeans as she pivots to face me. "So then I thought maybe she tried to kill herself. Let's be honest, the girl has been through a lot." Mom shakes her head sadly. "You always want to save people. Just like your dad."

My eyes burn and I close them so tightly I see white. "Mom…"

Clearing her throat, she continues. "I asked Kellin."

My eyes pop open and I swallow hard. *Don't do this. Don't do this to me. Please don't do this.*

"My twelve year old watched his big brother's girlfriend purposely take a curling iron to her flesh and burn her arm." Her voice drops and she looks sick. "He said he could smell it, Mason. I will not let my children be subjected to that."

Fucking Kellin. Fucking big mouth Kellin. I might puke. I might actually puke right here on the carpet of our shitty, month to month leased house.

"You knew. Didn't you?"

I don't answer. I can't.

It's all clicking quickly, piecing itself together in my mind. That's why Illinois. She knew I wouldn't go. She knew I would choose Hope. So she's tempting me with home. Using Dad and our memories to get me to do what she wants.

"I cannot believe you would take your brother over there around that."

"Around that?" I ask, my voice rising.

"That girl is sick, Mace. She needs help. Kellin should never have seen something like that. Ever. I have done everything in my power to protect you kids. To shield you from things like this—"

I huff out a dry laugh. "Protect us? Shield us? How? By moving us every five minutes? Not letting us have friends? Stability? That's such bullshit and you know it."

"You have friends."

"Now! Now I have friends. And you're taking me away from them, Mom."

"I'm doing what is best for you both. He's too young to have to deal with something so big and scary."

"He's dealt with worse." She knows I'm referring to Dad dying. To our father being beaten to death down the street from his home while we sat on the couch watching TV.

"I had no control over that. But I do over this. I can put a stop to *this*."

"By moving him again?"

"Last time. I promise you. You can graduate from the same school as your dad." Her voice hitches up an octave sounding hopeful.

That is all I ever wanted. And she knows it. It's so low that she would dangle this in front of my face. I put my hands on the top of my head and try to breathe. Fuck. I'm going to cry.

"Kellin can grow up where Dad grew up. Go to the same schools. Visit the same places. You can pass on all the stories Dad told you."

That's how it should have been all along. Can I take that away from him?

"What do you say?" Mom moves toward me hesitantly. "You and Kel can check out the two places I found and choose where we live." Her eyes are flicking over my face quickly.

"I love her."

Her face doesn't change. "I know you do."

"I don't want to leave her." I am definitely going to be sick. I run to the bathroom and dry heave with my head in the toilet. Mom's there, placing her hand on my back.

"Everyone leaves her," I rasp, struggling to get the words out. "I can't do that to her. I can't be like everyone else. She needs me."

Mom pulls my face up to look at her. "We need you. I need you. Kellin needs you. This is what you wanted. I'm giving it to you. And maybe Hope will get the help she needs. If you aren't there making her think all she needs is you. Because you aren't enough, Mace. She needs professional help. Please tell me you understand that."

I do. I know I'm not enough. If I were, she wouldn't keep hurting herself. But if I leave and she hurts herself again, or worse...

Fuck.

I dry heave again. When I can catch my breath I slam my fists down on the toilet seat. I shouldn't be this torn. I should be stronger. I should be able to tell Mom no. I don't need to go back to Illinois. I don't need to go home. I need Hope.

So why the hell can't I say it?

Why do I want this so bad?

My eyes fill and there's nothing I can do as the tears slide down my cheeks and splash onto my shirt.

"It's for the best," Mom says. "I can talk to her foster parents. Make sure she gets the help she needs."

"No. You *can't do that* to her."

"They need to know. You aren't a parent, so you don't understand. If it were you, I would want to know. I'd need to know. They can take care of her."

No they can't. That's my job. I'm supposed to take care of her. I'm supposed to calm her when she freaks out. I'm the one that's supposed to always be there. Hugging her. Kissing her. Protecting her. *Loving her.*

"Please," I whisper. "Please don't make me do this. Don't make me choose."

She brushes the hair out of my eyes and caresses my cheek, wiping away the moisture. "It will be okay."

I shake my head. It will never be okay. Hope is going to hate me. I'm going to hate me. I hate myself already.

I slump back against the wall and bring my knees up in front of me. My hands fall to the floor at my sides and I stare at the sink. I'll make this work. We won't be that far apart. We can switch off and see each other a couple weekends a month. It doesn't have to be permanent. I could go just long enough to finish school. Hope and I could do the long distance thing for eight months. Then I could come back and we could go to college together. We could move back there after we graduate. Together. She could see where I came from. She'll love Chicago.

It's not forever.

Hope won't really be alone. She has Guy and Chase. And she and Annie will make up. There's the twins and Addie. Dylan will keep her busy. Misty. And Park.

I thud my head against the wall a few times. If she ends up back with Park... I don't know what the fuck I will do.

But I can't be pissed about it if I'm leaving.

No. She's mine. She told me that herself. She won't run to Park just because I'm a couple states away.

A couple states away.

States away.

I close my eyes and Mom backs out of the room, giving me space. I can hear her moving around, packing. I stay where I am. Too weak to make her stop. Too weak to help her.

I give in to the rage boiling inside and slam my fist into the wall.

I'm such a bastard.

40
Hope

It's weird not having Mason with me. Not that Chase isn't good company. It just feels weird. Not even a full day since I've seen him and I miss him like crazy. I pull into Park's driveway and kill the engine. But I don't get out yet. I need a minute. I hadn't realized I was angry with him until we got to his house.

I have a startled realization. I'm so mad at Park because he purposely did something that hurt him. Just like I do—all the time.

This helpless, betrayed feeling is what Mason feels every time I do something to myself. I mean, I knew this already, but I didn't *understand* it until this moment.

"Are we going in or…are we staying in the car all day?" Chase's hand hovers by the handle, waiting.

I nod. "Let's go."

Park opens the door before we knock. His eyes are both blackened. I don't know if it's from his broken nose or the fight prior to the accident. He looks terrible. I glance down at his fingers, expecting to see them dark with fingerprinting ink. They aren't. I think they do that with a computer now.

He moves past us and sits on the top step of the porch and lights up a cigarette. My hand itches to pluck it from his lips and throw it in the yard. But I don't have that right anymore. As his friend, however, I still scowl and make a spectacle of waving the smoke away.

One side of his mouth turns up in smile. "Let's get it over with," he says.

"Get what over with?" I ask.

"You came here to either berate my ass or beat it. I'm tired. Didn't sleep well in jail. So get on with it. I wanna go back to bed."

"I am mad at you for being stupid, but I didn't come here to yell at you."

"I did," Chase huffs. "I'm here to smack some sense into you."

I grin at him. Chase thinks he's such a badass since he "single handedly served Christian Dunkin his ass to him on a platter." I'm pretty sure that first surprise hit he got on Christian was the only one.

Park smiles too as he blows a puff of smoke out. "You forgot your army."

"I don't need one," Chase says, insulted. He gestures at me. "Hope's all the backup I need."

"Hope can kick my ass by herself. You aren't as gifted in that department."

"We'll ask Christian about that." Chase lowers himself beside Park and plucks the cigarette from in between his fingers and tosses it down, stepping on it.

"What the fuck?"

"You need to get your shit together man. Quit being dumb. Quit smoking. Quit drinking so much. Quit driving drunk."

"I got it," Park says, his voice sharp. "I know what I did. I don't need you to tell me." His jaw works as he looks out at the driveway where his car should be, but isn't. "How's Guy?"

"He's doing really well," I offer. "He'll be in the hospital for a week or so. Hopefully less."

"You should go see him," Chase says dryly. "Apologize for almost killing him."

With a tight nod, Park stands up. "I'm going to bed."

"That's it?" Chase cuts him off before he can open the door. I stay where I am, not sure what I want to say or do yet.

"That's all I got," he says with a shrug.

"That's pretty weak," I counter softly.

Park turns his glare on me. "Add that to my list of faults. I'll review it later."

I don't know who I'm disappointed in. Me for not pursuing the issue? Park for acting like he doesn't care? Both of us for being cowards? All I know is it consumes me as I watch him walk inside, swinging the door closed behind him.

~***~

My day drags without Guy and Mason. Chase takes off after Park's house. Annie and I still can't be around one another without murder plots being formed in our minds. Now I'm lying on the couch, dreading going upstairs where I have to share a room with her.

I pull my phone out and text Mason.

Me: I MISS U.

Him: MISS YOU TOO.

Me: WHAT WAS IT U TOLD UR MOM ABOUT PLAYING DR?

Me: I COULD COME OVER & SEE IF I COULD MAKE U FEEL BETTER.

Him: NO. DON'T WANT YOU GETTING SICK TOO.

I sigh. He must really feel horrible if he's turning down sex. That makes me miss him more. I want to make him feel better. He's always trying to take care of me.

Me: I DON'T CARE ABOUT GETTING SICK.

Him: I'M TIRED ANYWAY. JUST GOING TO GO TO BED.

I frown at my phone. Even his texts are off. I don't like the nervous sensation that runs through me, raising the hair on my arms. Too much has happened lately and it must be making me paranoid because I feel like he's lying to me.

But this is Mason. He pushed this relationship. He's been several committed steps ahead of me at all times.

Me: K. FEEL BEETER. LUV U. NIGHT.

Him: LOVE YOU TOO. GOODNIGHT.

I stare at the screen rereading the message a few times. Yeah. I'm paranoid. He just doesn't feel good and this weekend sucked for sleep. He's probably exhausted. I roll off the couch and make my way up to bed.

~***~

As much as I'm dreading school after all the ridiculousness of the Friday night rumble, I can't wait to see Mason. I know it was just a day, but it was long and excruciating. I miss his face. I need his always-there smile. His adorable dimple. Those gorgeous green eyes that look back at me like I'm something special.

I park Neko and lean back against the seat with my iPod as I wait for Mason to find me until it's clear he isn't coming.

Me: R U COMING 2 SCHOOL?

Him: NO. STILL NOT FEELING VERY WELL.

Me: THAT SUCKS. WANT ME TO COME TAKE CARE OF U?

Him: GO TO SCHOOL. I'LL SEE YOU TOMORROW.

My stomach twists and my eyes prickle. He's asked me to trust him, and I do, I want to. But something feels so off and it's driving me crazy. My fingers move to the ignition, hesitating on the keys. Part of me wants to ignore him and turn the key, go to his house, and see for myself what's going on. A huge part. But then that's me not trusting him. I yank the keys out and tuck them into my book bag instead, making an active choice to believe in him.

Me: GET LOTS OF REST CUZ TOMORROW UR ALL MINE. SICK OR NOT! <3

I don't get a response right away, so I pocket my phone and head inside. I don't know exactly what I was expecting, but it definitely isn't this. People I have never spoken to stop me to ask about Guy or to wish him better. It happens in the halls. In every class. At my locker. Even in the bathroom and that is just so…past my comfort zone. Can't a girl pee in peace? It's weird. I don't like people as it is. I'm feeling claustrophobic by the time I get to lunch.

Our table is sad with only me and Chase there. He drops an oatmeal cream pie down in front of me with a pointed look. Guess he isn't letting that go.

"Where's Park?" I ask.

Chase shrugs. "Home in bed, feeling sorry for himself?" He rips the plastic off his pie and takes a huge bite. "Where's Mason?"

"Still sick." I hate this day. Seriously.

The chair beside me slides out noisily and Adam Harris sits down. As in Christian Dunkin's evil boy wonder, Adam Harris. Have I mentioned this day sucks?

"What do you want, Adam?"

He stares at me for several extremely annoying seconds. “How’s your friend doing?”

I raise an eyebrow and he grins. “My friend?” Chase makes a noise across from me. My eyes flick to him and he’s watching Adam so closely it’s like he’s trying to set him on fire with his eyes. I almost explain to him that he doesn’t have laser vision, but I skip the smartass comment and turn back to the dumbass beside me.

“The little gay one. Heard he was in the hospital.”

Guy is gay, it’s well known, but the way Adam says it, he makes it sound like a big joke, which irritates me even more.

“He’s doing good,” I say, my words clipped.

He nods, leaning closer to me. “Good. Good. And Park? He got arrested, right?”

I’m suspicious about where he’s going with this. My eyes narrow into a warning glare. His smile widens at the look I’m giving him and it throws me off enough to answer.

“Yes. But he’s out.”

“Really? Isn’t it a hate crime? Trying to kill a homo?”

I know my mouth is hanging open and my face must be bright red because it's burning. *Did he just say that?*

"Dude, get the hell outta here," Chase demands, his voice scary low. He stands up, hands balled into fists at his side.

"Hey," Adam says defensively. "I'm just concerned. This is my school and it seems like they'll let anybody in. Fags, attempted murderers," he nods at Annie sitting at the next table. "Whores." And then he looks at me. "Psychopaths." He shrugs his broad shoulders and splays his hands out in front of him. "I'm thinking it's time something is done about it."

The smart thing is to get Chase and walk away. Go talk to a guidance counselor or something. I, however, am the first person to admit I am not smart.

I know I'm getting suspended again today as I push my chair back and stand. Not much else runs through my mind though. I reach back quickly and pick up somebody's book. Who's? I don't know. Gripping it with both hands, I pull it above my right shoulder and swing it sideways, right into Adam's face. His chair tips back with him still in it. As he's lying on the floor in shock, holding his mouth, I toss the book and move in so I can kick him.

Bad thing about fighting during lunch, there are too many people packed too closely. I have no idea whose hands are on me, but I'm being wrenched away, my feet still trying to reach Adam.

"Get the fuck off her," Chase shouts. I'm able to turn my head enough to see Christian's profile. A nauseated shiver runs through me. I hate that he's touching me. I squirm and wiggle, trying desperately to get out of his grasp.

"Calm down and I'll let you go," he grunts. I do. I stop immediately and he drops me in a heap onto the sticky cafeteria floor. "You need to take your crazy ass outta here before I forget you're a girl."

I don't get a chance to respond. Mr. Andrews takes me by the arm and it's like déjà vu as he leads me away from Christian.

41

Mason

Today sucks almost as badly as yesterday.

I know I'm making the right decision. I just wish I felt a little better about it.

42

Hope

I get suspended. Obviously I don't mind. My only regret is that I didn't leave Adam bleeding like I had with Christian. Is it right? Nope. I'm thoroughly aware of this. I'm also aware that I'm having yet another realization about how terrible I am. I gave Mason shit for always using his fists when he freaks out. And guess what? Yep, I do the exact same thing. I hurt myself or I hurt other people. Not necessarily with fists, my method usually involves anything other than my actual hands, but the idea's the same.

I don't want to be like this.

I'm staring at my laptop, my hands shaking. I can't remember the name of the site Guy told me about, so I Google self-harm help. 79,500,000 results. Not kidding. Guess Mason was right when he said I was normal. And that is so messed up that I close my screen and shove it away. Not the normal thing. I know he meant the way I deal with things is normal and that doesn't bother me. But that so many people hurt themselves 79,500,000 results pop up in seconds.

Feeling alone isn't new to me. I spent most of my childhood alone. Loneliness and I go way back. I just haven't felt it much since meeting Mason. With 79,500,000 search results for self-harmers, I shouldn't be feeling alone at all right now.

But I've never felt more alone.

How fucked up is it that I want to cut?

Not enough to stop me.

I start for my bathroom before I have to remind myself for the 79,500,000th time that Mason took my razors. I do an about face and head for the kitchen. A knife will work. I stare at the knife block, deciding on a small paring blade. I take several paper towels and head to my room.

I sit on my bed and put the blade to my skin.

I'm still sitting here when I hear the bus pull up in front of the house. I'm still sitting here when I hear the front door open and close. I'm still sitting here when I hear Misty and Dylan thudding around in the kitchen.

I don't want to do this. I don't want to *be* this. Not anymore.

I suck in a breath sharply and release it with a sob.

I only allow myself to cry for a few moments then I wipe my face with the paper towels and I take a deep breath.

If there was ever a time I needed a candy fix, it would be now. I'm talking heavy duty candy fix. Like Cow Tales and Sugar Daddy pops. Maybe even Pixie Stix.

Slipping the knife into my back pocket, I go down to the kitchen. "Hey," I say to Dylan. "Where's Misty?" I slide the knife back into its place, putting myself in the way of his view.

He shrugs. "Don't know. I'm hungry."

"She rode the bus home, right?" I ask as I take a sleeve of crackers from the box and open them.

"Yeah. She was crying."

"What?" I freeze, nearly dropping the glass I pulled out of the dishwasher. "What do you mean she was crying?"

"She was crying." He looks at me like I'm an idiot.

"Dylan, did she get hurt?" He shrugs again and I put the empty glass on the counter and go to find Misty.

Sniffling makes me pause in the hallway. I step into the living room. It takes me a second to find her, sitting on the floor, her back pressed to the back of the recliner. I lower myself to sit with her.

"What's up? Why are you crying?"

She rolls her eyes and wipes a tear off her chin. "Why were you crying?"

That throws me off and I turn my head. "Just had a bad day. I got suspended again."

Her brows crinkle and she wipes at her face. Her confusion pauses her tears and she shakes her head. "Why?"

I fold my legs in front of me and run my hands across my knees. "This dude was being a huge ass. I hit him with a book." She laughs lightly and sniffles. "So, what's up with the tears?"

Misty looks at me funny again and something in her expression causes my stomach to knot. "Didn't Mason tell you?"

"Tell me what?"

No. No. No. No. No.

She pushes her blonde hair out of her face. "That they're leaving?"

"Leaving?" My voice barely comes out.

No. No. No.

“They’re moving back to Illinois…” she trails off as new tears run down her pink cheeks. “He didn’t tell you?”

“When?” I choke.

She shakes her head slightly. “They leave by this weekend.” *No. No. No*. “Their mom already has a job and house lined up.” *No. No. No.* “She starts Monday. They have to be there by then—”

“Are you sure?” I’m screaming inside.

Misty huffs out a harsh laugh. “Positive. Kellin told me today. He said everything’s packed.” She cries harder and I know I should hug her, comfort her in some way, but I’m selfishly counting the pieces of my heart that lie on the floor around me.

One for every touch.

One for every kiss.

One for every time I told him I loved him.

Five for every time he told me.

“I have to go. Watch Dylan.” I don’t wait for her to reply. I’m out the door before I can think about what I’m doing.

I vaguely remember putting the car in park, but I have no recollection of the ten minute drive over to

Mason's. I stare at the door, summoning the strength to knock. But I know once I do, he'll confirm he's leaving.

Why didn't he tell me? I knew something wasn't right. I knew it and there is no consolation in being right this time.

I finally rap my knuckles against the peeling wood. I do it hard enough to feel a burn and scold myself for it.

There are certain things people remember better than others. Something that impacts them deep enough to ingrain itself into their memory forever. The look on Mason's face when he opens the door is something I will never be able to forget as long as I live, no matter how long I try. It's this mix of sadness, indecision, anger, shock, and guilt.

It's all the confirmation I need. I take a startled step back and force myself to look past him. To see the piled boxes. The empty shelves built into the living room walls. I take another step back. Then another. I think I'm shaking my head because I don't want to hear him say it. I can't hear him tell me he's leaving me just like I always knew he would.

I stumble to Neko and throw the door open. My head is dizzy and I can't get a decent breath. This is where Mason usually comes in. He helps calm me. But he can't this time.

Those days are done.

Oh shit.

Those days are done. Gone.

Mason blocks the door before I can close it. The sun reflects off the side mirror, momentarily blinding me. And all I can think is: *how is the sun shining when my heart is breaking?*

"Wait. Hope, wait."

"No," I whisper. "I have to go."

"Please." He grabs my arm and I can't stand him touching me, but I want to melt into his hold at the same time. I am two people at war with each other. I want him so much, but I want to hurt him. I want him to feel the pain I'm feeling.

This. Is. Why.

The people you love most are the ones who hold the power to hurt you so completely.

This is why I told myself every day that I hated my mom. This is why I tried to stay away from relationships. This. Right now. I don't want to feel this.

I yank my arm away from him and pull on the door. *I need to go. I just need to go.*

"Let me explain."

"Explain what? That you lied to me? That you've been avoiding me? That you're leaving and you had no intentions of telling me?"

"I was going to tell you about this. I just had to be sure first." His eyes are pleading with me, crumbling what is left of my heart.

"Let. Go. Of. My. Door." My voice is cold, emotionless, and he hears it. He drops to his knees in between me and the open door.

"I love you, Hope. I want us to work. I need us to work."

"Move now or I will make you move."

Mason lowers his head, shaking it quickly. "You need to listen to me."

I slap him. I cannot believe I slap him and from the shocked, hurt in his eyes, he can't either. A red outline of my hand glows across his cheek and he stands up, moving away from Neko.

"You know where I am when you're ready to listen."

"For now. Who knows where you'll be tomorrow," I murmur as I pull the door closed. He locks his fingers on top of his head, watching me as I drive away.

43

Mason

I'm not certain how long I stand in the driveway waiting for Hope to come back, but it's starting to get dark before I figure out that she isn't going to. She wouldn't listen. She wouldn't give me the chance to explain.

I should have made her listen. I should have told her yesterday.

I stare down at the ground with my hands on my hips. Doesn't she understand this has been the hardest decision I have ever had to make in my life?

I'm not going to let her end it just because she feels abandoned and betrayed. Everything I've worked out has been for us. To make sure I don't lose her.

I can't leave until she understands.

44
Hope

Annie breezes into the room like she doesn't have a care in the world. I look up from my pillow and watch her flip through the hangers in the closet. I kind of hate her right now. She thinks my life is so easy. Yeah. It's great.

She turns around and meets my gaze. "What?"

I blink slowly and bury my face back into the comfort of my pillow. It smells like Mason and I'm not too proud to admit that I'm trying to soak up every bit of his scent.

"I'm sorry, Hope. I don't know how many times I have to say it. I'm sorry I told people about your mom. I'm sorry I said Guy's accident was your fault. I mean, it was an accident. Right? It just happened." I hear her feet brushing against the carpet as she moves closer. The bed dips as she perches beside me. "I was scared. I said things I didn't mean. And that stuff I said about you… When you first came to live with us, it was weird. Mom just married Alec. I had three step siblings and another dad. Things had already changed so much and then you were there. I had to share my room and everyone was tiptoeing around you like you were this fragile little thing. But I could see you were stronger than they were giving you credit for. I could barely breathe in this new life, but you came here like it was just any other day to you. I hated you for that. I was so jealous."

I roll over so I can see her. I don't know what to think yet. That was a horrible time. What she just said, about not being able to breathe in her new life, that was exactly how I felt. It's how I feel all the time. She could be describing me.

"You know, Annie, we're not so different."

She cocks a perfectly plucked brow. "We couldn't be more different if we tried."

I sit up and look at her. Really look at her. "What did Christian do to you?"

Annie diverts her eyes. Her hands open and close several times in her lap. "It's not like you think," she says finally. "I wanted to. He asked and I was more than willing. I've liked him forever and I thought he liked me." She pauses and rests her eyes on me. "He didn't rape me. We had sex in the back of his car. I thought we were together. Ya know? I thought he was my boyfriend.

"Did you know he has a girlfriend?" She goes on before I can answer. "Because I didn't. She's away at college. I don't know what I was thinking. Like what? He would be mine because I gave him my virginity? God, he made it crystal clear I was nothing more than a "*pump*". I didn't even know what it meant. He had to explain it to me."

I don't know what to say. I'm partially pissed that she let me think he raped her. Part of me feels bad her.

"I was so embarrassed and hurt. He used me, but then it occurred to me that I used me too. I had sex to get a guy to like me. It's so stupid now that I look back on it." She straightens up and shakes off the memory. "Anyway, that's what happened."

"He still deserved the nut kicking," I say.

She smiles and nods. "Yes. He did." She sobers suddenly. "I know I can't take back what I did, all those things I said, but I'm sorry. We've never been all that close…and now we're miles apart, but I hope you can forgive me because I think of you as a sister."

With a sigh I pull my knees to my chest. "I'm sorry too. I've said some shitty things to you. But I'm still pissed."

She acknowledges that with a jerky nod. "We'll work on it."

~***~

"I thought you forgot about me," Guy says when I push his door open. I dump the bag of goodies I got him on his bed and drop into the chair.

"Never."

"What's all this?" He pokes through the pile of books, magazines, candy (because it's me), a notepad, and pens. "Are you moving in?"

"No. It's provisions."

"Staying awhile?"

"Yep."

Guy tilts his head, studying me. "What's going on?"

"Nothing is going on. I miss you. I want to visit you."

"You're missing your better half," he says and I can almost see the little light bulb flip on above his head. He narrows his eyes. "Where's Mason?"

I shrug and pick imaginary lint off my shirt until I can actually look at him without crying like a baby. I haven't allowed myself to cry over this yet, and I don't want to start now.

"Park came by earlier," Guy says and I'm grateful for the subject change. "He didn't wanna come when Dad would be here. He's afraid to see him."

"I would be too. What'd he have to say?"

"Not much. He apologized, which I told him he didn't have to do. I knew what I was doing. We were both stupid. Now we move on with a little bit of wisdom."

I snort. "You're a miracle worker now?"

"Ha. Ha. Ha."

"Everybody was asking about you today. And most of them seemed legitimately concerned. It was really annoying. This girl actually asked me to tell you to get better soon. While I was peeing."

Guy laughs. "Who?"

"I don't know. I got outta there as soon as I could. It was awkward enough without me getting her name."

"At least you didn't hit her with a book," he says smirking.

I cringe. "You heard about that?"

"Chase," we say at the same time.

"He's such an old church lady gossiper," I mumble.

"Thanks for defending my honor."

I grin at him. "Anytime, sweetheart."

"All right. You've avoided it long enough. You need to start talking. Where is Mason? Why isn't he glued to your hip like usual? And why do you look like a kitten that's lost her ball of yarn?"

I take a deep breath, staring at the white sheet covering his legs. "Mason is at his house, I think. Packing. Because he is moving. Back to Illinois. With his mom and brother." Saying it out loud like this makes it all sink in. Mason's leaving and I will probably never see him again.

"Why? What happened?"

"I don't know. He didn't love me enough, I guess."

"You didn't talk to him?" He rolls his eyes. "Of course you didn't. You can be fruitier than me sometimes, honey."

"I don't even know what you mean by that."

"Bitch, you know exactly what I mean. You didn't bother to find out why he's going. You just freaked out. And probably haven't talked to him since."

"Guy, he told me he wanted to go home. The look on his face when he talked about Illinois… He loves it there. It's where he grew up. Where all his memories of his dad are. That's why he's going back. And even though it hurts, I want him to be where he's happy."

His lips pucker to the side in thought. "I know Mason loves you, Hope. There's more to this. I'd bet my left nut on it."

"The left one?" I say, raising my eyebrows. "Nobody cares about the left one."

"I care about both my testicles, thank you very much."

"What about testicles?" A familiar looking dude stands in the doorway with a single red rose in his hand and it takes me a second to place him. I look from him to Guy's broad smile then back again.

"Samuel." Guy and I say at the same time, only mine is a question and Guy's is all day dreamy.

As much as I don't want to sit home thinking about Mason, I know this is my cue to leave.

I stand up, gesturing to my chair. "Here," I was just leaving. I lean in and kiss Guy's forehead. "No hospital sex."

He pouts his lip.

"Okay. Okay. Maybe a sensual sponge bath," I suggest. I turn back to Samuel. "You look different with clothes on."

His lips turn up on and his cheeks turn a bright shade of red. Guy snorts with laughter as I walk out the door.

45

Mason

I have to stop myself from throwing my phone. Hope still won't answer my calls. I'm going to school tomorrow and making her listen to me.

46
Hope

Mason called me all night until I turned my phone off. When I turned it back on this morning I had four voicemails. I haven't listened to them yet, but I haven't deleted them, either, so I know I will. Just not yet.

I didn't tell Jenny and Alec that I was suspended again. I don't want to put any more on them right now. Maybe I'll get out and job hunt. My birthday is around the corner and they'll lose the money the state gives them for fostering me. With the added expense of Guy's hospital bills, I really need to make sure I'm contributing instead of being a burden.

After my shower I dress in my blue sundress and try to pretend I don't remember this was what I was wearing when Mason and I kissed for the first time.

I get hired at the first place I apply. A pizza parlor five minutes from home. I'm surprised, and happy, and annoyed I didn't do this sooner. I guess it was my open schedule that sold them. I have no social life. No drums. So I told them I could work after school and any time on weekends. The fact I'll be eighteen in less than two months means I'll be able to close soon, as well. Another positive I had going for me.

A perk for me, all the free pineapple pizza I can eat during scheduled hours. Plus, they have candy machines in the front. I already know where my loose change tips will be going.

I'm so excited I practically run into Guy's room. He's watching TV and picking at his hospital provided lunch. It looks disgusting and from his less than thrilled appearance I assume it tastes that way as well.

"Oh, thank God. I'm bored outta my mind."

"Guess what." I bounce on my toes, unable to stay still.

"You talked to Mason?"

I feel like a shriveled up balloon, deflating onto the floor. "No," I hiss. "I got a job." All my enthusiasm gone, I plop heavily into the chair beside his bed.

"That's awesome. Where at?"

"Nope. Nu-huh. You've already squashed my joy. Just forget it." I prop my head on my fist and glare at him.

"Stop sulking and tell me." He pushes the table on wheels away, ignoring his lunch, and picks up his can of Sprite.

"Newton's Pizza. I start next week," I tell him with not even half of my earlier elation. "Their uniforms aren't bad. Black tee shirts, black pants, black baseball cap."

"Because nothing says pizza like emo dress."

"That's right," I agree. "Emotional people often eat their feelings away. It makes sense. Speaking of which—" I eye his discarded lunch. "Want me to go get us some food? Something *not* from the hospital?"

"God yes. Please."

"All right. Any requests?"

"A cheeseburger from anywhere that isn't here. And a strawberry milkshake." Guy's eyes take on that same dreamy look they did when he looked at Samuel. I stifle a laugh.

~***~

After lunch with Guy, where he found ways to bring up Mason in every other sentence, I decide to go home. I almost pull right back out of the driveway when I see Mason's car. He's sitting on the porch steps, his head in his hands. I don't want my heart to beat faster or my breath to come quicker. I don't want to want to rush into his arms.

I get out and he looks up when I shut the door. He stands quickly and meets me in the yard, holding out the biggest bag of Skittles I have ever seen.

I don't want them.

I look away, but I don't walk away. What does that say about me?

"I let you go last night because you were too raw. I didn't want either of us to say or do anything we might regret." By which he means me. And by me, I mean when I slapped him. "But I need you to listen to me now."

"No. Don't say anything. I don't want to hear this right now. *I can't* hear this. I get it, all right? Your Mom's moving. You have to go. It's perfectly logical. But it doesn't make it hurt any less. It doesn't change the fact that you're *leaving me*."

"Stop being mad and listen to me."

"I'm not *mad*, Mason. I am *crushed*. Acting mad makes it easier to deal with than letting it rip me apart."

"Have you cut? Done anything to hurt yourself?"

I scoff, but I know it's a legitimate question. I'm still wearing the sundress, so I do a slow spin, lifting my arms. "No. I'm trying really hard not to do that anymore." I take a step away. "I have to go."

"You don't have to go—"

I whirl on him. "No. *You* don't *have* to go. You're choosing to follow your mom like you always do. I get she's your mom and if your mom moves, you follow, but you're eighteen. You don't *have* to leave. I mean, when will you stop trying to fill a hole that is impossible to fill? You're not her husband. You're not Kellin's dad." I cover my mouth. I cannot believe I just said that. I didn't mean any of it.

It's his home. I can't blame him for wanting to go just because it hurts to lose him. I shouldn't blame his mom. And I most definitely should never have said that about his dad.

"No, I'm not. Because he's dead. Don't worry, I didn't forget that." He jerks his fingers through his hair.

I hate that I could etch so much pain into his features with just a few sentences. "I'm sorry. I didn't mean that."

He nods tightly. "I know you didn't." He closes his eyes and inhales sharply. "I'm leaving tomorrow."

My body goes cold. Tomorrow? I thought I had another day or two. Three if I was lucky.

"We'll talk this out when I get back."

What? "When you get back?" I want to move closer, but my legs aren't responding, anchoring me to this spot in the yard.

"I'm driving the U-Haul so I can have the time with Kellin. I'll spend the weekend with them, helping them get settled. Then I'll be back. Kel's taking it hard. Losing me and Misty both is shitty, but they're young, and he can stay with me during school breaks and see her then. He'll get used to me being here eventually."

"Being here? To stay?" I whisper.

Mason takes a step toward me. "I couldn't leave you. I used some of the money from Dad's insurance. Put a deposit down on an apartment. Bought a car. I need to pick it up this evening. I signed up for counseling. I thought we could both go."

"Counseling?"

"I didn't think it was fair to ask you to get help for your cutting without me getting help for my anger."

I take a step now. The distance between us just inches. "I need you to spell this out for me, Mason. Slowly."

"Mom thought she could bribe me with Illinois. Still does, actually. I'm sure it won't take her long to understand I'm serious." He shakes his head and takes the final step. "When she first told me, I didn't know what to do. I thought maybe I could go and we could try to make it work. But I was suffocating just thinking about it. I spent the last two days getting everything taken care of. As much I as I wanna go back there, I realized it isn't my home anymore. You are."

"You should've told me."

"I needed to be sure I was making the right decision for the right reason."

"You chose me over Illinois?"

He pushes his hands into my hair and smiles. "I chose us." He brings his lips to mine and I swing my arms around him, clinging to him as I return the kiss.

I pull back and gaze up at him. "Can I have my Skittles now?"

"Depends," he says quietly.

"On?"

"You owe me a song," he reminds me.

"Skittles for a love song?" He nods, grinning wide enough to show off the dimple. "Deal."

Epilogue

Mason

"Tell me what you can do instead," I say. This is part of our therapy: think of a healthier way to relieve stress other than harming yourself or others. I thought it was pretty stupid at first, but we've turned it into a game, trying to outdo each other. It works surprisingly well—taking my mind off whatever I'm struggling over.

Right now Hope's the one struggling. She's having a mini panic attack about having to go out on stage. It's been over three years since she's hurt herself, but it's something she still struggles with on occasion.

"I could go home and have wild sex with my gorgeous fiancé." She bats her lashes, grinning, and I'm tempted for half a second.

"No," I say more to myself. "Nice try." I slip a Jolly Rancher into her hand, hoping it will last until her name's called. "You've worked too hard for this. You need to get out there with your class and get that diploma."

She crinkles her nose and I still think it's the cutest thing. "They could mail it to me."

"They could, but then I couldn't take pictures of you."

She bounces on her toes and beams at me. "What if we go home and I let you take pictures of me. You can have full creative control. You can dress me, or not." She winks. "You can pose me. I'll even sing while you do it."

Wow. She's pulling out the big guns. I clear my throat. "That's evil," I say, but I can't seem to put the right amount of heat in my voice. It comes out sounding like she almost has me where she wants me, which she does, but I can't let her know that. "Your whole family's here for you. Now come on, give me something real."

Hope sighs, defeated. "I could hug you."

I open my arms. "Sounds good to me."

She wraps her arms around my waist and buries her head in my chest, taking a deep breath. I run my fingers through her hair until she pulls away.

"Better?"

"Better," she agrees. "Thanks." I kiss her forehead softly.

"I'm going to watch you until you get to your seat, and then I'm going to go back to my seat in the audience. Okay?"

"I'm going. You don't have to watch me." She turns and I smile.

"I like watching you," I call. "You've got an amazing ass."

"You can't see my ass in this gown, pervert," she sighs without looking back.

I chuckle. She's right, I can't see it right now, but I have a good memory. Once she's seated, I head up to the balcony where Guy's saving me a spot.

"She good?" he asks, his face etched with concern. He knows as well as I do that she's gotten better, especially when it comes to dealing with what happened to her as a kid, but her panic attacks will always be something she battles.

"Yep, she just needed a hug." He nods and sits back.

Kellin leans into my shoulder. "How long's this going to take. I hate these things." He adjusts his tie for the hundredth time since we've been here.

"You just sat through my graduation last week. You know how long it takes. And if you don't want the tie on then take it off."

"Mom will kick my ass," he hisses.

"Don't say ass."

"Dude, I'll be eighteen in three months." He glances behind us at Misty, checking to see if she's paying attention. She is, even though she's pretending not to. "Back off me. I hear that shit enough from Mom."

"So she scares you enough to keep the tie, but not enough to make you watch your mouth at my fiancé's college graduation?"

"She didn't hear me, but she'll notice the damn tie in a heartbeat."

"I do hear you, Kellin Montgomery Patel," Mom says leaning around Guy. "Don't make me come over there."

I point at Kel and laugh. "Ohhh."

"Shut the hell up," he whisper yells as he shoves my arm. I nearly fall off the chair because I'm too busy laughing at him.

"Knock it off," Mom scolds. "I don't want to miss anything." Nothing is even happening yet, but I settle back and look down to find Hope. As if she feels my gaze on her, she turns around and looks up. Our eyes lock and she smiles widely. Mom waves at her excitedly.

Mom and I went through a rough patch for awhile. She wasn't happy that I stayed in Ohio. That's putting it mildly. It got really ugly when Mom got Jenny and Alec involved, but in the end, it was for the best. After they got over the hurt and shock, they've been nothing but supportive. But things with Mom got worse when she found out Hope moved in with me after turning eighteen. She almost didn't let Kellin come visit anymore. It took a huge blow out, a major heart to heart between Mom and Hope, and a few family-counseling sessions for her to agree to a weekend visit.

Over the last four years, Mom and Hope have become close. I don't know if it was the realization that I wasn't giving Hope up, or it might have been the counseling, or possibly that Hope decided to go to college at Vandercook, here in Chicago, majoring in music education. I guess it was the combination of it all. I know the main reason she chose to attend here was for me. For me, for Kellin, for Mom.

I followed her, obviously. Did the community thing and got my degree in fine arts with an emphasis in photography and a secondary degree in business. Hope wants to open a center that specializes in art therapy for children. Knowing how much music helped Hope, at some point, this became my dream as well. It's a while off, but we are well on our way.

First we have to get through this ceremony. Then there's the wedding next month. Same church Mom and Dad got married in. I don't know who's more excited about it, me or Hope, but I can't wait for her to become Mrs. Hope Love-Patel. Isn't that the greatest damn name?

When they call Hope up to accept her diploma, I whistle as I click pictures. She looks up at me and grins beautifully as she opens her gown. She's wearing her *Beatles* tee shirt over the dress she's supposed to be wearing. The same shirt she was wearing when I fell in love with her. She throws her hand up in the "rock on" symbol as she holds her diploma high above her head.

I never thought I could love someone so much, but sometimes never is a distorted perception, because I continuously find myself falling deeper in love with her every day.

Hope and Mason's playlist:

Wondering by: Good Charlotte

Dark Side by: Kelly Clarkson

Animal by: Neon Trees

Amazing by: Aerosmith

How to Love by: Lil Wayne

Crash into Me by: The Dave Mathews Band

More than Words by: Extreme

Looks like Love by: Needtobreathe

When She Begins by: Social Distortion

The Only Exception by: Paramore

Love Like Woe by: The Ready Set

Lost In You by: Three Days Grace

Down by: Blink 182

Truly Madly Deeply by: Savage Garden

After Midnight by: Blink 182

You Make Me Smile by: Uncle Kracker

Say When by: The Fray

I Wanna by: The All-American Rejects

Blackbird by: The Beatles

And Then He Kissed Me by: The Crystals

Paradise by: Craig Owens

Demons by: Imagine Dragons

Marry Me by: Train

Lovesong by: Adele

Kissing Wounds (Mason's song):

I must have been sleeping
Before I met you.
My heart was unbeating. My eyes unseeing.
I didn't want to feel. Didn't care to.
I was deaf, and I was blind.
I passed each day.
Each day passed me.
Just colors and sounds, time and amounts.
I'm done counting days.
Now, because of you, I'm making days count.

You've turned wounds into wisdom.
Teaching me to learn from my mistakes.
Which ones are mine and which were out, out of my control.
I was a shadow.
Cold and dark.
Angry and alone.
Until your lips found mine. Now I have a goal.
You woke me from the nightmare.
Made me feel more than pain and loneliness.
I love the way you frighten me.

I want your kind of scary. Every minute of every day.

Bliss.

I only count minutes now, until your lips find mine once again. Until your lips find mine.

Sometimes when I'm kissing you I forget.
I forget there's a world out there.
I forget that I'm a part of it.
I forget that I've been hurt.
All I know is you.
The pressure of your hands.
The softness of your tongue.
The scent of your skin stuck on my shirt.
You hold the pieces of me together and I don't want that to end.
I don't want to fall apart again. Not again.

You've turned wounds into wisdom.
Teaching me to learn from my mistakes.
Which ones are mine and which were out of my control.
I was a shadow.
Cold and dark.
Angry and alone.
Until your lips found mine. Reaching my soul.

You woke me from the nightmare.
You made me feel more than pain and loneliness.
I love the way I'm not scared.
I want you. Every minute of every day for forever.
I only count minutes now, until your lips find mine once again. Again.

You don't need to talk.
There's no need for words to show me how you feel.
Your body does that for you.
It's the way you look at me
Like I'm the real deal.
It's in your touch
Warm and gentle against my skin. Against my skin.
It's in the way your mouth smiles
When your eyes find me across the room.
Your silence screams for me. For me. Again.

You've turned wounds into wisdom.
Teaching me to learn from my mistakes. Mistakes.
Which ones are mine and which were out of my control.
I was a shadow.
Cold and dark.
Angry and alone.

Until your lips found mine. Mine. My soul.
You woke me from the nightmare.
You made me feel more than pain and loneliness.
I love the way you frighten me. Frighten me.
I want your kind of scary. Every minute I confess.
I only count minutes now, until your lips find mine once again. And again.

Find me. Find me.
Wake me. See me.
Keep me. Touch me.
Until you lips find mine.
Again.
And again.
And again.

Reachout.com is a confidential, safe, and supportive site where teens and young adults can share stories and find resources to help them get through tough times. You are not alone. There is help.

REACHOUT.COM or call 800-448-3000.

I want to say a quick thank you to Sean for being a great father to our three children. (And for taking them to the library, or store, or anywhere you could come up with just to give me a couple hours of quiet in which I could write.)

Thank you to my mom for believing I had more stories in me. I think I got that gene from you.

To my big sister, Dawn, I thank you for being my first reader, first fan, and my much needed editor. I couldn't have done this without your support.

Theresa, thank you for taking the time to give me some much needed professional insight into self-injury. It changed the tone of the book from hopeless to encouraging.

My dear niece, Becca, thank you so very much for inspiring the snarky side of Hope.

A special thanks to my awesome nephew, Charlie, for allowing me to turn you into my model, and for creating an amazing book cover.

And last, but certainly not least, thank you so much to my readers. I appreciate each and every one of you more than you could ever know.

About the Author

Cheryl McIntyre is a mother of three. When she isn't chasing kids, she enjoys reading and listening to music. If there isn't a book or an iPod in her hand, she must be writing or sleeping. She is also the author of the paranormal romance, Dark Calling.

Let me know what you thought about Sometimes Never. Follow my author fan page on Facebook.
http://www.facebook.com/CherylMcIntyreauthor

Or follow me on Good**reads**.
http://www.goodreads.com/author/show/6431156.Cheryl_McIntyre

And please leave a review on Amazon and/or Good**reads**.

19729420R00285

Printed in Great Britain
by Amazon